To Cha[...]
Hope you enjoy!!,

E. Wade

ISBN: paperback-978-1-79-885493-8

ISBN: ebook- 978-1-38-636729-1

Prologue
THE ECHO CHAMBER

Timothy Smithers had a resting heart rate of 71 beats per minute. It was even lower with the use of Gamma-Hydroxybutyrate, commonly referred to as the date rape drug. Stripped of his clothes and fashioned to a chair, duct tape restrained his wrists and ankles to the four corners of his Lazy-Boy recliner. His head sloped downward as he lay comatose, courtesy of his new friend, which he thought would be a one-night stand at best. But this encounter would prove to be a rude awakening, that would more than double his current heart rate.

"Is everything in order?" A disembodied, female's voice echoed from inside the remnants of an old compact mirror.

"Yes," was the one-word response from a sultry voice. The only difference, this voice was not disembodied.

She opened the compact mirror to a set of probing eyes. They were hazel with grey surrounding the left pupil. The eyes dawned black eyeliner.

"What are you planning?" the Sultry voice asked.

"Something for the taste buds," the disembodied voice echoed.

"Taste Buds," the sultry voice repeated, as if making a statement and asking a question.

She peered into the compact mirror to see black lipstick being applied to a full set of savory lips. But it wasn't her reflection, and she wasn't wearing black lipstick. Nor did she have hazel eyes.

"A taste of wrath and retribution. It's time to make history," she said.

"Make history, how?" the sultry voice mused.

"By alleviating society's false sense of security," the voice in the compact mirror declared.

"By giving them what they've been begging for."

"Really, all of society," Sultry voice mused again.

"Patience! Cold, calculating, patience," the echo commanded. Those words lingered in the air like smoke waiting to dissipate after a long drag.

"Patience isn't my thing!" Sultry voice crowed.

She stood in Timothy Smithers' basement in a daze, gazing into the small compact. There weren't many houses in Central Florida with basements. On paper, the basement didn't exist. It was the perfect bonus room. The perfect in-home getaway for Timothy Smithers, or so he thought.

The reflection glared back with deliberate eyes as the echoes died down.

A muffled cough snapped her out of her trance. Her eyes shifted and focused to the lower right side of the full-length mirror. Timothy Smithers was coming out of his drug-induced state. A shiny strip of gray duct tape was placed over his mouth for obvious reasons. He wobbled his head while squinting his eyes in an effort to regain his focus. Groggily, he rolled his eyes, left then right, to a sudden stop. An IV bag caught his attention. His eyes followed the line from the bag to the needle in his arm.

An attractive figure sporting a tight black dress stepped into the light. She was tall, slightly thick, yet athletically built, with defined facial features.

"How's the date so far?" she asked.

He gave her an evil squint. In an attempt to free himself, he jerked his right arm. But instead of movement, there was a flesh-ripping sound. He unknowingly ripped the skin from his right bicep.

"Not wise," She told him, as she massaged the morphine drip.

He squinted at her black latex gloves. His eyes followed her with a vengeance as he shook his arm again.

"No, no, no," She calmly said, waving her index finger. "Don't ruin my study. I need solid benchmarks, with genuine reactions," she added while stepping out of the path of the full-length mirror.

He glared at her with a hateful fury. She nodded her head towards the mirror.

He was in disbelief from what the mirror displayed. A shortness of breath forced him to hyperventilate. Streams of tears exploded from his angry eyes. Vomit careened up his throat, filled his mouth and propelled through his nose as he tried to cry out. The mirror revealed him in his underwear. Sewn into his recliner with fishing line, the stitching on his arms and legs left no wiggle room. He bled profusely from jerking his right arm. Aside from massaging the morphine drip, his mysterious date put a coat of Elmer's glue over the fresh wound on his arm. The glue was good for subsiding open wounds at the source. She added a heavier coat than what was used on the rest of his stitching.

Unable to move his head much, he studied the mirror. On the verge of shock, he rolled his eyes at her, clenching his fists in an angry protest. From the neck down, his body was riddled with slits and lacerations, also coated with Elmer's glue. He heaved again, and vomit scuttled down his left nostril. With no seepage from the duct tape and needing to breathe, he involuntarily swallowed the underflow.

"That's disgusting," his capturer called out. "But I guess you gotta do what you gotta do."

He began to mumble and tried to slide the duct tape from his mouth, by chafing it to his shoulder. Unable to feel the full effect from stretching the polyethylene stitches, he yanked his arms and legs back and forth, until a loud whack walloped across his face.

"Consider saving your strength. The morphine will wear off soon," The mysterious lady remarked before unfolding a straight razor and moving in towards him.

Part One
A CURE FOR MENTAL ILLNESS

Chapter 1

I was up earlier than my usual 6 a.m., going over my daily reading material before the kids came down for breakfast. Today it was the Thompson murder files. Over the last week, a couple of high schoolers wound up dead. Actually, they were murdered. So far, we had a partial suspect. Julius Walker also known as J. Walker, an Anderson Rains High School student that transferred to Edgewater High. I was hoping the judge would okay a no-knock search warrant for his parent's house. If this kid was hiding something, we needed to find it before he got wind of being a suspect.

A conversation at a crime scene with Kamille Ashland, undercover vice, revealed a young man fitting Julius's description bought a .38 last week from one of the locals. Her facade was a baller with a pipeline of 'anything you want' between Atlanta and Orlando.

I'd have to say from what I saw, she played her part well. A little too well I thought. I'd seen her around from time to time. Most recently in Dr. Kennedy Julian's office, the OPD psychologist.

It's mandatory for cops in various departments to see a shrink every six months. In my case, I had to pay Dr. Julian a visit after a downtown shooting a couple of months ago. I have prescribed Xanax for my level of anxiety. Every time I look at the bottle, I hear her saying, "Detective Jackson, Xanax can become habit forming and addicting."

The kids came down and gathered around the island while Uncle Elton made breakfast. Eggs sunny side up and sausage with a side of wheat toast. That was the end of my morning quiet time.

"Where are the Cheerios?" Andre asked.

Cheerios in a bowl without milk has been his breakfast of choice ever since he was two years old.

"The dog ate them," Uncle Elton said in a serious tone.

Andre tilted his head and squinted his eyes, "we don't have a dog."

"Oh, well I guess you ate them," Uncle Elton snickered as he slid a breakfast plate towards him.

Andre examined the plate and asked, "Where's the real toast?"

Andre, like his sister Renee, has never been fans of anything not wired for teenage taste buds. He was thirteen and Renee was 14 going on 30.

"That is real toast," Uncle Elton declared, "It won't raise your blood sugar, give you diabetes or make you fat."

Andre stood, raised his arms and turned a full circle. "Do I look like I'm in danger of being fat?"

"No, but two out of three ain't bad," Uncle Elton joked.

"It looks like French toast," Renee said.

She pressed down on the center of it to see if it would rise back into shape.

Uncle Elton took a bite of her toast and slid it back onto her plate. "Nope, it's genuine wheat toast." He muffled with a mouth full. "Would you like me to sample your eggs and sausage?"

Renee gave an incredulous look, shifting her eyes between the toast and Uncle Elton. "We need a new cook."

Uncle Elton imitated her look, "I happen to be the family chef," he proudly announced.

"What's the difference?"

"The cook does the dishes," he chuckled.

"I see you got jokes this morning,"

Andre asked, "Does that mean Renee and me are cooks?"

"It's Renee and I," I corrected him, not moving my eyes from the Walker file.

"If that means being able to make ramen noodles," Uncle Elton snickered again.

Renee, the older of my two was on the verge of running late for a cheerleading meeting that started before school. It's funny how her and my partner, Bernard have running late in common.

"Guys, take it easy on your Uncle. He's becoming less stable with age," I joked, to which Uncle Elton shot me a look over the rims of his glasses.

"I'm just evolving," he crowed.

Uncle Elton, a retired Special Forces leatherneck, was kind enough to live with us while my husband, Wayne, also special forces was away in Afghanistan. He and Uncle Elton had a little too much in common if you ask me. Always talking in code and using lots of acronyms.

I've always teased Uncle Elton, asking if he's sure he wasn't a cook in the military. Aside from being a once certified nightmare, he can really burn.

"Mom, Mr. Bernard just pulled up," Andre roared with excitement.

Bernard, who goes by Davis, rode a metallic red and grey Suzuki 1000. Most of the time we'd take my squad car to work. He was my fourth partner and the youngest, at twenty-five.

"Good morning fam, what's going on?" Davis greeted, walking in and taking notice of Uncle Elton's handy work. "Looks like the cornerstone of a nutritious breakfast," he added while picking up a slice of toast and taking a bite, not knowing it was from Uncle Elton's plate.

"Are you feeling okay?" Uncle Elton mused. "That was my toast."

"My bad, Uncle Elton, I thought this was the community plate," Davis snickered and winked an eye at the kids. "Old people will set it off over their wheat toast," he whispered.

"And young people lose their train of thought when they get hit in the head with frying pans," Uncle Elton remarked. "I don't want you to have an accident today," he added, while wiping down the cast-iron skillet he used for the eggs and sausage.

"How so?" Davis asked.

Davis and Uncle Elton have always given each other grief. They've always had that funny bond with each other. Must be a guy thing.

"This skillet can make you see Jesus," Uncle Elton murmured. "And who you calling old?" he said, giving Bernard a hug and handing him a breakfast plate. "This might be the best thing you guys eat all day."

Immediately, Bernard went to work grubbing and was done in under two minutes.

"Dammit man, you hungry as a hostage."

"You know I'm a connoisseur of the eggs and swine," Davis muffled while motioning at Andre and Renee's plates. "Are you guys going to eat that?" to which they both covered their plates and began eating.

"You sho ain't no Muslim, chomping on that sausage like that. That's southern Baptist eating. Are you even chewing?" Uncle Elton quipped.

"Okay, we gotta run," I said. "Bad guys ain't gonna catch themselves!"

I put the Walker files back into the manila folder and kissed the kids and Uncle Elton on my way out.

Davis gave Uncle Elton a handshake, Andre some dap and snapped his fingers sideways at Renee.

"You two make good decisions," he told Andre and Renee. "And you," He pointed at Uncle Elton with two fingers. "Do something I would do. But, make sure you use protection," He snickered to which Uncle Elton giggled.

Chapter 2

For once the timing was perfect. As soon as I fired up the cruiser we got a call from dispatch. The judge okayed our no-knock warrant for the Walker residence.

A part of me didn't want to find anything. On paper, Julius Walker seemed like a well-rounded kid. He came from good stock. His parents were longtime employees of Orange County Public Schools. He was a Magnet student at Edgewater High school who participated in baseball, debate, and chess, aside from being an A- B student to boot.

"What makes a kid like that pick up a gun?" Davis questioned.

"Peer pressure or protection," I commented. "There's nothing in the reports about him being affiliated with gangs."

"As the story goes, Walker and Michael Thompson were longtime friends. Witnesses say they got into an argument last Wednesday and Michael was dead the next day," Davis said while thumbing through the report. "That chick, Ashland, from vice squad said he bought a .38 revolver last week," he added.

"Yes, but ballistics says Thompson was shot by a 10 mm and the Tanner kid was shot with a .45," I said.

"Witnesses on both accounts say the victims keeled over and started bleeding. No one heard a gunshot." Davis said.

"The velocity of the guns used may not have been that strong. Maybe that's why they were shot multiple times."

"So maybe Walker is our guy. Who knows, maybe he's getting crappy guns from the same low life peddler."

"That doesn't add up though. Why go back to the same guy who sold you a crappy gun? Unless he's doing away with the guns for the sake of having bodies on them. Maybe he's alternating guns."

Another summary page was stuck to the back of the Tanner file, and after reading it...

"So much for our theory. The Irving kid was also shot with a 10 mm. In broad daylight and no one saw or heard anything. 10 mm rounds are mostly used for hunting, which means he may have been at a distance with a scope."

"We know he's a smart kid," Davis said.

"Maybe he came up with something creative. We just need to find one of those guns." I keyed the radio. "This is 6062 requesting back up for a no-knock at 5212 Meadow Green Lane. ETA is approximately fifteen minutes."

"This is unit 712, we can be 10-51 in ten minutes." A patrol unit responded.

We arrived at a beautiful two-story red cobblestone colonial house on the outskirts of Wekiva and Apopka, just off Hiawassee Road. The house had a manicured lawn, four off-white pillars that stood out front and an Oakwood wrap-around porch. Two patrol units, O'Malley and Sims were on opposing sides near the rear of the house. Davis and I took positions on each side of the front door. An across the street neighbor stood out front as an onlooker while I gave a courtesy knock.

KNOCK, KNOCK, KNOCK! "Police warrant, open up!" I yelled above the echo of a barking dog. "Damnit, the last thing I wanted was to deal with a freaking dog!" I commented, holstering my service weapon.

"Correction, the last thing you wanted was to be FILMED, dealing with a freaking dog," Davis whispered, nodding his head to the neighbor standing in her driveway, queuing her phone to record us.

The Walker's family dog was a 60-pound pecan Cur that went berserk to the sound of the knocking on a door.

"It's never a dull moment," Davis remarked. "Last week it was a homeless man trying to bite us and the other day a crackhead chased us with a syringe."

"Until I tasered him."

"Do you think he had to fart before or after you tasered him?" Davis spewed a burst of laughter.

"I don't know. He was probably holding it. Can we continue this conversation later? I need you to focus." I added, pointing two fingers at my eyes and then back at the front door. "And that syringe was missing a needle." I chirped, slowly shaking my head.

I believe that was Davis's way of easing the tension before something potentially big went down.

I had Officer O'Malley pull his cruiser onto the front lawn and open the back-passenger side door closest to the house. I motioned for Davis, O'Malley and Sims to keep their distance while I stood in front of the glass door and the family pet.

"This shit only works on television," Davis whispered.

"I can shoot and taser people but not animals," I said while getting into position to kick the door in.

There was a loud crumpling noise from my boot to the bottom of the doorknob. The door flew open. Before the dog could lunge, I made an about face and ran into the back seat of the squad car. My plan was to go out through the other side, trapping the dog inside the cruiser. The family pet followed me as planned but Officer O'Malley failed to disengage the safety lock on the back driver's side door. Davis shut the back door, expecting me to climb out through the other side. But when the back driver's side door didn't open, that was cause for concern. There was struggling and tussling. Davis unholstered and took aim at the dog through the window. A red dot dawned the back of the family pet's head as he slowly added pressure to the trigger of his 9 mm.

"WAIT, WAIT!" Officer O'Malley yelled, placing a hand on Davis's shoulder.

The dog had me pinned to the floor of the cruiser and was licking me in the face.

"I don't fucking believe it!" Davis said as he eased off the trigger.

O'Malley carefully opened the driver's side back door, and I climbed out, careful not to let the family pet out.

"I don't believe it, that dog doesn't like anyone!" The neighbor across the street shouted as she lowered her phone in awe of what just happened.

"Ma'am, what's his name?" I called out.

"His name's Bama and he's possessed."

Officer O'Malley kept the cruiser running with the air conditioner on so that Bama would be comfortable. I conducted a full sweep of the Walker residence. In the downstairs office, a veterinary bill lay face up.

"Looks like Bama got into something that wasn't good for him," Davis said. "This was dated a few days ago." He took out his phone and snapped a picture of the invoice.

***

Jarred Huggins woke up to the sound of a 520-cubic inch engine. That sound alone meant he would already be late for school. He sat up, rubbed his eyes and peered through the blinds to see an Orlando Waste Management truck dumping trash cans with a mechanical arm. Jarred, had long been waiting for this day. He dressed in blue jeans, black boots, and a white T-shirt under his favorite army jacket.

Today he would take his black backpack that was slightly bigger than his normal book bag. It contained a 10 mm and a .45 magnum handgun. Both with silencers and scopes. He had five fully loaded ten round clips, which would be more than enough for what he wanted to do. The 10 mm was his father's favorite handgun. His father mentioned, he hadn't seen it in over two weeks. He dismissed it as being misplaced or lost at the hunting grounds in Ocala. But it was buried deep in Jarred's nap sack.

Just last year Jarred was diagnosed with a disruptive disorder. However, his parents refused to believe there was anything wrong with him. Getting into arguments and throwing tantrums every day didn't seem to be a big enough clue. To hear them tell it, it was just a phase he would soon grow out of. But, it only got worse. He would scheme and carry out plots to torture and kill unsuspecting animals. As time went on, he undertook more cowardly deeds. Giving homeless people food containing rat poison.

His specialty was grinding up broken glass, putting it in meatballs and dropping it where the neighborhood dogs would run and play. He had since graduated from killing animals when he murdered a homeless man. He stood on a milk crate behind a wooden fence. Laced the homeless man's head through the crosshairs of his scope. Took a deep breath and squeezed the trigger. A near perfect bulls-eye to the temple caused the homeless man to collapse and die.

Jarred arrived at school just after the second period began. He walked into Ms. Jolson's Art class and took a seat in the rear of the room. Today was a free day, meaning they could draw anything they wanted. He drew a minuscule stick figure ant smashing people with a colossal sledgehammer. The people were bloodied and dismembered. He wrote "IVXX" in bold numerals on the head of the sledgehammer. Ms. Jolson gave it a second glance and figured he was just expressing himself. After all, a big part of art is being creative she thought to herself.

A few classmates rubbernecked and ogled his drawing before whispering amongst themselves.

"Is there a problem?" he remarked in a loud voice, to which there was no response.

***

The room upstairs across from the bathroom appeared to be Julius's. His walls displayed honor roll plaques and varsity achievements letters along with newspaper clippings to go with all the trophies on his dressers. The things you see from promising young athletes. I slipped on a pair of latex gloves and took pictures of his room, felt around the perimeter of the dressers, floorboards and closet walls. I found a 9mm Ruger and a full ten round clip under his mattress. In the corner of the closet, a miniature Stuff the Magic dragon doll fell over, making a knocking sound against the floorboards. I moved the sports doll back in place but noticed that it was lopsided with a strange distribution of weight. I eased the doll away from the inside corner of the closet and squeezed it. The left side was firm and heavy. I moved it into the light to get a better look. There were signs of it being re-stitched and as far as I knew Stuff the Magic Dragons were regular stuffed animals. There was a sealed envelope attached to a buck knife inside. I opened the letter that read:

Julius,

The deaths of some classmates have not been mysterious. Looney has been plotting and planning this for two years now. He thinks I'm in on it with him. At first, I humored him because I thought it was amusing and he was being silly. Who in their right mind would want to kill people who don't agree with their crazy rantings? But when Tanner turned up dead, the same way Looney predicted, I knew he was crazy. And he's double crazy if he thinks I'm joining him on Thursday in the fifth wing bathroom to load up and go on a shooting spree after lunch. I think I'll disappear for a while. At least until this thing blows over. If, it blows over. I'll be at our hideaway by the railroad tracks if you need me. I suggest you do the same. My knife is inside this doll. Just in case you come in contact with Looney. Whatever you do, don't trust him. He's out for blood. IVXX is what he's been writing on some walls at the school.

M.T.

It was Thursday and a quarter till ten. I rushed downstairs and got Davis.

"We have to run, lives are in danger. O'Malley and Sims, call a CSI team, rope this house off and catalog everything upstairs in the second room to the left. And keep an eye on Bama." I said.

"Where to partner?" Davis asked.

"Edgewater High School. I'll explain on the way."

"Isn't this area zoned for Anderson Rains or Apopka High?"

"Yes, but he's a magnet student. The gun found under his bed is registered to his father, Syrus Walker, so no harm there. But we still need to follow up at his school and have a word with him."

I lit the rack lights, put the Charger in sports mode and smoked the tires fishtailing out of the Wekiva subdivision onto Hiawassee Road.

"This is 6062, I need 10-10, 10-20, and 10-30 to Edgewater High School. Possible hostage situation. We understand the perp to be someone named Looney. And keep it quiet." I called into the radio.

"What's your twenty?" Dispatch asked.

"Clarcona Ocoee Road and Edgewater Drive."

"Detective, I need you to stand down," A husky, abrasive voice boomed through the radio. It was Kirkland Hodges, the lead DIC.

"I've uncovered time-sensitive information that leads me to believe something bad is about to go down at Edgewater high school."

"My team will be assembled in twenty minutes. Stand down."

"10-9 sir you're breaking up."

"In case you missed it, detective, that was a direct order!" Hodges barked.

"10-1 can you repeat?" I said before turning my radio off.

I slapped the steering wheel in frustration. "This is our collar. Let him do his own work."

"He pulled rank on Stevens and Winowski a month ago without a plan of attack." Davis griped. "And now he wants to do it to us," he added.

We set our phones to silent. Davis made a quick change before we pulled in to the High School. He turned his shirt inside out. He went to the dumpster and put eyes on the fifth wing building with his wino appearance. I went to the fifth wing bathrooms.

"Hey buddy, you can't come on school property," a security guard with a name tag that read Bob, said as he stopped his golf cart to escort Davis away. Davis got in the golf cart, flashed his badge, and explained that we were looking for a perp, and that he needed to be a combination of a distracter and a blender.

"I need you to act like I stink to high heaven and drive around building five, like your trying to figure out where to drop me off," Davis said.

He swayed from side to side and made big arm movements.

He fell off the moving golf cart and stumbled towards a trash can near the back of the five hundred building. He took the lid off a waste bin and dug in the trash.

"Are you sure you're the police?" Bob asked. "Because this is some suspect shit."

"Goes with the territory," Davis said. He blindly grazed his hand across what looked like orange vomit. "YUK!" He wiped it on his shirt.

Bob's radio chirped a code 10-87.

"I got a notice to meet the police," Bob said, while looking down at his radio.

"You go do that, I'll keep wandering around." Davis bent over to adjust his ankle holster.

I arrived at the fifth wing restroom just after the first lunch period started. We held our positions for twenty minutes, and no one saw anything out of the ordinary, suspicious or eye-catching. "Starting to look like nothing's going down," I whispered into my mic.

"You just cost us lots of man hours with this half-baked stunt," Hodges roared through on the channel. "All clear, all teams to exit," He boomed.

"How about keeping all teams in place for ten more minutes or doing a thorough sweep?"

"You're on your own and see me when you get back at the station. We're going to have a lot to talk about. Starting with a write-up and possible suspension. By the way Nancy Drew, there is no one name Looney that attends this school."

One by one the police cruisers and SWAT funneled out of the parking lot onto Edgewater Drive. I had just cost the department a few thousand dollars from what Hodges was saying. I unhooked my earbud, walked out of the fifth wing building and sat next to Davis by a garbage can.

"This is going to be a fun thing to explain," Davis said.

"I don't mind so much as explaining it. We're losing at both ends. If something here would have panned out, Hodges would have gotten the credit and another pat on the back from the top brass because of work we did. Since it went south, we're the ones holding the shit end of the stick. And speaking of the shit end, what's that on your shirt?"

"Probably somebody's vomit."

"Disgusting."

"Maybe this M.T. is a figment of the imagination."

"That's it!" I boasted.

Chapter 3

Davis and I rushed to the administration office for Julius Walker. After a few minutes, he came down. He was a tall, dark-skinned, lanky kid with glasses.

"I'm Detective Jackson and this is my partner Detective Davis. Who is M.T.?"

"Is she in trouble or something?" Julius asked.

"That all depends. I have a feeling you know more than you're letting on. We need answers and we need them fast," I said.

"M.T. is Megan Tyler, she's been warning me to steer clear of Looney."

Julius began fiddling with his hands and biting his lip.

"I'm sensing that you and this Looney character have a beef of some sort. Why?" I asked.

"It's not that we have a beef, he's evil and very vindictive. If you don't agree with what he talks about, then you're on his blacklist."

"How long has this blacklist thing been going on and why are kids you're supposed to be friends with turning up dead?" I asked.

"I don't know when it started, but it's been getting worse every year since the eighth grade. He needs to be locked-up away from people," he said in a breathy voice.

"About three months ago a girl named Sandy called the police on him. She said he poisoned her dog but couldn't prove it. She died a couple of weeks after that."

Julius began to breathe heavily.

"What does her dying have to do with him?" I asked.

"She was pushed into oncoming traffic on the way home from school."

"And you know this because?"

"My friend Tanner saw the whole thing. Immediately after that, he transferred to Apopka High School. They must give him a lot of homework because his phone has been going to voicemail over the last couple of days?"

My heart dropped. Right then, I knew he hadn't read the letter from Megan. We walked him into the hallway to continue our talk.

"Julius, I'm sorry but Tanner is dead," I murmured.

He broke down crying.

"Tanner's dead, how?"

"We can't tell you specifics, but his death fits a pattern. What can you tell me about Michael Irving?"

"I tried to help Michael. I spent all my money on a gun for him, so he could protect himself. We argued because he didn't want anything to do with having a gun," Julian cried. "So I gave it back."

"Is that why you keep your father's gun under your bed? To protect your family?" I asked.

"Yes ma'am," he sobbed.

"What does this Looney look like?" Davis chirped.

"He's a pale creepy looking gothic kid with cropped jet-black hair."

"Is Looney his first or last name?" I asked.

"We call him Looney because he's crazy. His real name is Jarred Huggins." Julius wiped his eyes and in a solemn voice asked, "How long will I go to jail if I kill Jarred?"

Davis and I glared at each other with a serious notion.

I thought about my own kids. What would I tell them? I didn't know Julius from Adam, but he was somebody's child. And I could hear it in his voice he had an innocent heart.

"Killing Jarred Huggins won't bring your friends back, son. It will do more bad than good. I know how you feel. Killing him will not only destroy your life. It will ruin the lives of the ones you love. Your innocence is what's at stake."

"Promise me you won't do anything senseless, youngster," Davis said. "We know this is a tough time, don't throw your life away."

Julius eyed Davis, "Yes sir."

"Where do you think Jarred Huggins is most likely to be right now?" I asked.

"He goes to Anderson Rains, so maybe there and plotting another murder."

The last time I saw Megan she said he was plotting to join the ranks of legends, IVXX, whatever that means. She said he's been writing it on some walls out there. He's sick," Julius said.

I gave Julius my card and told him I would be in touch.

A buzzer sounded school-wide.

"It's lunchtime!" I said before Davis and I sprinted back to our cruiser on the far side of the parking lot. I hit the rack lights, blared the siren and sped on to Edgewater drive.

"The note said, IVXX. Those kids go to different schools now," I remarked, trying to rationalize the reasoning.

"So, his work should be done. Why would he want to kill anyone else?" Davis asked.

"Because most of the kids in that eighth-grade class go to Anderson Rains now," I said. I made a hard left, accelerating onto Clarcona Ocoee, "What does 'IVXX' mean?" I said out loud.

I had Davis pull up the date of the Columbine shooting on his phone.

"WOE! Dick fucking Traycee, that's today! April twentieth, Columbine shooting," Davis said.

"This will be Columbine all over again unless we can stop it," I said as I maneuvered the Charger out of a hard skid, accelerating onto Hiawassee Road. Davis had dispatch patch him through to the Anderson Rains principal as he maintained his death grip on the sidebar. He explained the situation and asked for the lunch times. And first lunch began five minutes ago.

"We have reason to believe Jarred Huggins is a threat to your school. I need you to quietly exit as many students as you can without letting the first or second lunch periods know, including teachers. My partner and I should be there in a few minutes. Don't say anything over the intercom. And keep the same lunch schedules." Davis told Principal Stein.

I killed the rack lights and sirens before pulling into the parking lot.

"Go to channel two," I told Davis and did a mic check into our earbuds.

"Are we calling the watch commander?" Davis questioned.

"Procedure says we should, and if this goes sideways, at least we won't have another Rose Parade and speech about resources and manpower hanging over our heads." I parked in front of the school. "It's showtime," I said as we exited the cruiser going different directions.

Davis still had his shirt inside out because he didn't want the orange stuff touching his skin. Once he got to Principal Stein's office he disconnected the call from his earbud. The cafeteria was near the front, which made it easier to quietly evacuate a portion of the school. Instead of a full lockdown, Davis had Principal Stein make an announcement to teachers to check their email about a change in meeting time. All teachers, with the exception of Ms. Abbot, were put on a quiet lockdown through email. That way Jarred would not be the wiser if his plan was to harm other students.

Ms. Valdez looked into the system and assured he was in Ms. Abbot's Algebra class. She pulled up the picture of his student ID. He was a pasty complexion kid with an oval-shaped face and dyed jet-black hair.

I checked the hallways and the bathrooms on the lower level of the 500 building, which were clear. Upstairs, was a different story. The hallway was clear, but when I creaked open the door to the girl's restroom I spotted a .45 bullet on the floor. I un-holstered and proceeded with caution. Sniffling sounds caused me to train my Sig toward the stalls.

"Who's there?" I crooned, training my 9mm on the first stall.

I eased them open one at a time, until I came to a locked one where I heard a muffled whimpering.

"I'm a policeman, I need you to open the door," I said.

"I don't want to die," a young girl's whimpering voice murmured.

"Shhh, it's okay, you're not going to die, sweet-heart," I said as I steadied my aim and slid my creds under the stall door. The door creaked open, reveal-ing a young girl, not more than fourteen years old, hunched down with both feet on top of the toilet lid. I extended my hand to help her out. "I'm officer Jackson, What's your name?"

"Amanda," She sobbed as tears streamed down her face.

"Where is he?" I whispered.

"Ms. Abbott's room near the end of the hall. I heard him say he was going to kill everyone."

I escorted Amanda to the opposite end of the hall and told her to go to the office when I heard the heart-wrenching sound of a muffled gunshot and screams. "Go!" I told Amanda.

I scurried down the hall training my Sig at each door as I peeped through the windows. Three rooms were empty and in two rooms the kids had taken cover behind desks and lab tables.

Cries and whimpers were coming from the last door on the left. I glanced through the window to see Jarred holding a student hostage and pointing a gun at the rest of the class. He had a gun in his right hand and one in his waistband.

"WHO'S LAUGHING NOW!" Jarred yelled. And then he shot another student.

I switched channels on the radio, "Shots fired, I repeat shots fired in the 500 building at Anderson Rains High School. Send paramedics, EMTs and back-ups with first responders!" I squawked into my radio.

Davis ran down the hallway in a low combat crouch, training his weapon on every door he passed. I signaled him to the opposite side of the door across from me.

"Did you make the call?" he whispered in an out of breath low voice, to which I nodded.

"Go to channel six."

"YOU'RE NOT SO FUCKING TOUGH NOW, ARE YOU!" Jarred shouted, and shot another student causing him to cry out in pain.

"FUCK YOU MR. FOOTBALL PLAYER!" He said and then he shot him again. The student's yell went from a loud cry to a slight groan.

"What's the play partner?" Davis asked in between bouts of trying to catch his breath.

Hodges came through on our radios, barking orders, which prompted us to remove our earbuds.

"Hodges?" Davis asked.

I nodded. "I'll go in and distract him or see if I can reason with him," I said, motioning to Jarred Huggins.

"There's no reasoning with that! This kid, by definition, is committing an act of terror, and his body count is rising," Davis whispered.

There were two more shots causing multiple students to cry out in pain.

I opened the door and yelled, "Jarred, I'm Detective Jackson, can we talk?"

"WHAT DO YOU WANT!" he shouted. And then he turned his attention back to the class. "WHICH ONE OF YOU FUCKERS CALLED THE COPS?" he added before firing two more rounds, hitting another student.

"I'm here to help."

Davis whispered, "We can't reason with that. We have to put him down."

Before he could get the last syllable out I was through the door and in the classroom full of terrified students.

"Wait, Jarred!" I yelled. I trained my gun in his direction leaving one hand free even though he was using a student as a shield. "We can talk this out. No one else needs to get hurt here today." I looked around and took inventory of the dead and wounded.

The teacher who I assumed was Ms. Abbot was lying on the floor, covered in blood and slowly fading. A female student knelt over her on both knees, holding her hand, sobbing and snuggled tight around her neck. Aside from one hand covering her wound, Ms. Abbot's other arm lay draped around the young girl's neck, offering what little protection and comfort she could summon. I recognized the girl from the hand-me-downs she wore. She was one of the homeless kids that wore the same outfit at a feed the homeless function held by the city a week ago.

"Please don't die, Ms. Abbot, you're my only friend." The girl sobbed.

All the other students had taken cover behind desks and tables. I couldn't help but to admire the courage and love the young girl had towards her teacher.

On the other side of the room, multiple students lay in puddles of blood. Three were moaning and crying and another three were laying unresponsive. Jarred looked different from the picture I had. Aside from his black eyeliner and black fingernail polish he couldn't have been more than fifteen years old or sixteen tops. And he was already a murderer. Sadly, I wasn't surprised to see an aura of hatred and evil in his eyes.

Knowing what I know about the "so-called" system. This kid could kill all of us, and still live better than most of our vets. They'd Put him in a nice room and study him for the rest of his life because he has alleged 'mental illness.'

"THEY ALL NEED TO DIE!" he boasted.

"Help me understand why?" I asked, as I took small steps to my left, turning Jarred in a half circle and drawing his fire away from the students.

"So, they'll finally know I'm not to be fucked with!" he said. He had a strange look in his eyes. Glossy and high.

"I'm sure they get it," I empathized. "You're a young kid. You haven't even begun to live. You have a whole life ahead of you. We all get teased at one point or another and it's usually in high school, which is the hardest part of life for a lot of kids. Be better than this. Please, put down the gun." I begged.

He extended his gun arm towards Ms. Abbot, aimed and shot a round into her upper torso. She growled out a crying moan before her arm relaxed from the young girl's neck, slowly coming to rest in a growing puddle of blood.

"No, no, wake up Ms. Abbot!" The girl cried.

"NO! YOU DIDN'T HAVE TO DO THAT!" I shouted.

Jarred sensed my movement and shifted to his right, training his gun at me. The girl he had clutched around the neck had a growing stream of urine running down her leg. She pleaded for him to let her go. Davis was at Jarred's direct six shining a red beam to the back of his head.

"If you don't drop that gun, I'm going to kill you and then kill this bitch!" Jarred said, with his gun arm extended towards me, anticipating the recoil and adding steady pressure to his trigger.

Before he could fully squeeze the trigger, a burst of blood and brain fragments splattered over myself and the student he held. His body went limp, dropping the gun as he collapsed to the floor.

Part Two
RETALIATION, BELOW BOARD

Chapter 4

The phones were busy at SC&D short for (Snook Cellular and Data). The providers of internet and cellular service to just over one million customers in Central Florida. But something else was going on aside from taking calls and customer service. A new culture was taking shape. A dark culture.

Beep-

"Thank you for calling SC&D, this is Joshua, how can I help you?" Joshua said in a dull voice.

"Yes, my router has been on the blink all week, and I want someone here to fix it." An angry customer squawked into Joshua's headset.

"I'd be happy to help you with that, who do I have the pleasure of speaking to?" *It's anything but a pleasure.*

"Margaret Croucher, and it's not a pleasure. I spend a ton of money every month on your crap service and I need to be reimbursed," she barked.

"I apologize for the inconvenience let me—"

"—It's more than an inconvenience, this shit happens every other week."

Joshua let a few beats of silence go by, in case she had something else to add. It was times like this that the pulsating thought of working for his father seemed more attractive and definitely more lucrative than his call center gig. However, he was determined to be his own man. Which wasn't hard to do with the number of zeros in his active trust fund.

"I see you have our Snook modem but a different router. This is what happens when they go out of sync. I'm going to reset your modem and check a few things," Joshua said.

"So why is this thing going out of sync damn near every other day?"

"It could be several things like a power outage, having it on a bad surge protector or being plugged into a light switch."

"Oh, my Gosh! I'm so sorry I snapped at you, all that stuff is hooked up in the kids' room and they're constantly bickering about what's been unplugged," Margaret crowed.

"I think if it was hooked up where there's not a lot of activity your problem would go away. Not to say that it wouldn't happen from time to time. But it would definitely not be a weekly or monthly issue."

"The Wi-Fi on my phone just popped up! You're the best Joshua, thank you."

"You're quite welcome. And between me and you, I would move the modem and the router before the kids get home from school."

Margaret laughed and agreed that Joshua's suggestion was a novel idea.

"I'll have my husband do it this evening."

Joshua continued the conversation just long enough to add his notes in the system. He was grateful that the call ended on a good note. As soon as that call ended, there was another.

Beep-

"Thank you for calling SC&D, this is Joshua. How can I help you?"

"I'm locked out of my phone and I need you to unlock it," a male voice said.

The account that showed up belonged to Mindy Vaughn, a Snook cellular service customer.

"I'd be happy to help you with that. Can I have you verify the name associated with the account and the last four digits of the social?" Joshua asked.

"I don't have it but I'm actually the account holder."

The man's voice was hoarse, and he kept clearing his throat.

"I follow you, but we have to maintain a standard of security."

"Look, just get me someone that can help me, now! Or I'll have your fucking job."

"I'm sorry, who do I have the pleasure of speaking to?" *Another asshole.*

"Joshua, is it? Get me your fucking boss or I will come down there and get stupid."

Joshua sat doodling on a scrap sheet of paper and rolling his eyes. Not even two minutes into the conversation the unknown asshole was trying his patience. He considered the history of the account and saw that an anonymous guy had called twice before, demanding information about Mindy

Vaughn's account. As far as he knew, this guy might be a jealous boyfriend or even a stalker.

"If Ms. Vaughn is there, maybe she can verify the account."

"Look, buddy, I need to unlock the fucking phone!"

"I get what you're saying, sir. But if it was your phone and your account, wouldn't you appreciate us not freely handing it out?"

"It Is my phone, and my account! Get me your boss, now!" The angry man croaked.

Joshua noticed an instant message on the lower right side of his monitor.

"Send him to extension one-twelve. I'll deal with him."

It was Carol, listening in on Joshua's call.

"Please hold sir, I'll transfer you to my supervisor."

A few beats of silence went by before Carol took the call.

"Thank you for calling SC&D, this is Carol, how can I assist you today?"

"You can start by firing that asshole and then you can unlock my phone."

"To whom do I have the pleasure of speaking to?"

"John."

"John, are you of any relation to the account holder? Mr. Vaughn perhaps? Usually, spouses have their significant others listed. If you can tell me the last four of her social, I'll be happy to update that for you. Or even your last name if it's different from Ms. Vaughn's I can add a note for you for future reference."

"It's John Doe, now unlock the fucking phone."

She dug deeper into the account, the man was indeed calling from Mindy Vaughn's landline, at 2123 Spring Creek Drive, and the month prior someone called from a private number requesting the same action. "I'm afraid we're not going to be able to help you unless you can provide the security information," She politely said.

"I know your boss, Jeremy Michael, and when I tell him how you're treating me, he'll give your ass the fucking boot."

"Be that as it may, he will have to terminate me for following procedures. I'm flagging this account and sending Ms. Vaughn a message about your continued attempts to access her phone. Also, I think Mr. Michaels is in the office today. If you hold I'll transfer you to him and maybe he will unlock the Snook cell phone for you."

"I'm going to find you, bitch!"

John Doe began a slow tirade of threats and ramblings. Carol kicked her feet on top of her desk, focusing on his voice. She opened a compact mirror from her purse and gazed at it with an entranced squint. A pair of hazel eyes glared back as if they were studying something.

She made two copies of John Doe's audio file. She attached one copy to the notes on Mindy Vaughn's account and sent the other copy to a training file.

"Child's play at its best." The voice beyond her conscience echoed.

She stared into space before eyeing a stress ball. She tossed it against the wall in her office before sending an instant message to her team. A reminder of their 11:30 meeting.

Without warning, the stress ball went sailing and connected a perfect bulls-eye to the back of Joshua's head.

He turned around to the sight of Carol pointing at her headset and mouthing the words "What the hell," along with an extreme eye roll.

"That guy is a shmuck," Joshua mouthed back. "That's why you get the big bucks, and I'm keeping this ball," he snickered, bouncing it against his cubical wall. Which was the backside of Phyllis's cubical, who stood and gave him a Guillotine stare.

"I'm going to shove that ball up your ass!" Phyllis murmured with her mute button down and looking seriously pissed.

"I'm open-minded, I'll try anything once," Joshua remarked.

Her angry face morphed into a quick outburst of laughter.

"You're an asshole," she mouthed and smirked.

Joshua kissed the palm of his hand and blew it in her direction. Her chuckle turned to a hard stare when she met Carol's gaze as she sat back down. But something strange with Carol's eyes caused her to stand and look again. She could have sworn one of her eyes were hazel, but when she did a double take, they were both brown.

Carol continued listening to John Doe's ramblings for another full minute, which seemed like an eternity. "Mr. Doe, if there isn't anything else I can help you with, I'll need to end the call. Or would you like to hold for Jeremy Michael?"

"Fuck you whore," he said in a slow gangly voice.

The next thing he heard was the SC&D recording. "We here at SC&D hope you found everything to your liking. Please feel free to take our customer service survey." And then the line went dead.

It was 11:20 a.m. and Carol's team meeting was due to begin in ten minutes.

"You should research Mindy Vaughn's other half." Was the instant message Carol sent Joshua.

She continued listening in on her team's calls. Scoring them and taking notes for their upcoming one on ones.

Natasha, who sat next to Joshua logged in to a short break as opposed to taking another call. She doodled the name and address of an irate customer, Antonio Rodrigues, that she planned to research and transfer into her book of retribution. She would later use one of her fraudulent social media accounts to befriend him.

Chapter 5

A stress ball soared back and forth as Davis and I sat facing each other with our feet propped on top of our desks. We were wearing empty holsters and discussing the events that led us to modified duty.

"This shit is unbelievable," I caught the stress ball he lobbed across both our desks. "We solve the case, caught the murderer, minimized the loss of life and further injury and we get desk duty, pending investigation," I said as I lobbed the stress ball back towards him.

"We didn't actually catch the murderer," Davis remarked as he fumbled the sailing ball that bounced under his desk. "It's more like we retired him," his voice resonating from below.

"You're right. I still think we could have done better. If we would have been five or ten minutes earlier, we could have prevented the whole thing."

"When you think about it, had we taken him alive, families of the victims would have wanted justice or vengeance in the worst way."

"Who says they still don't want it? I feel sorry for his parents. Can you imagine what they must be going through?"

"I'm not sure it compares to what the victim's parents are going through. It's not like one kid fought another. You can come back from that. But you can't come back from a senseless killing."

"True," Davis agreed.

Children's lives were cut short because we were late to the game. We'd gone to four funerals over the last week and a half. It's a heart-wrenching tragedy attending a child's funeral. The school took up a donation to bury one of the students whose parents were barely making ends meet. An anonymous donor footed the bill for what they didn't have.

I hated thinking about it and changed the subject. "My butt's hurting from all this sitting. And I hate taking calls with a passion."

"Same here partner," Davis said while he stooped down to retrieve the ball, implementing a hook shot he had not perfected in the eleven days of being in police purgatory. He sat back down and kicked his feet up again.

"Aren't you two supposed to be working the phones?" Hodges boomed.

He made it his business to check on us, two, sometimes three times a day. "And why are you guys wearing holsters? I told you no gear."

"Do you hear any phones ringing, Serg?" I asked, "and our holsters are part of our normal dress."

"We feel naked enough without our hardware," Davis griped.

"If it was up to me you two would be wearing Burger King uniforms or riding the back of the garbage truck," Hodges rumbled, "Find something to do!"

"We're doing it." Davis propped his feet back on top of his desk.

"I gave you two a mountain of reports and loose ends to type up for investigators that follow the rules."

"Done," I said. "Well... Except one, where the guy was carved up behind the old Parkwood Plaza a few days ago. No identification on him so far. The information from the report isn't much to run on. It hasn't been assigned yet. My take on it is he was a vagrant that got out of line with a hooker and got sliced up," I added while handing the report to Hodges, who didn't take it.

"Whatever. Let's go. We're going to have some face time with the Captain," he squawked, motioning Davis and me into Captain Rowley's office. "It's going to suck to be you two in a few minutes," he whispered under his breath as we walked by.

"Detectives have a seat," Captain Rowley said.

Hodges stood to the side of Captain Rowley's desk with his hands interlaced in front of him.

The Captain's head was buried in a file as he read out loud.

"Allegations against said Detectives, Traycee Jackson and Bernard Davis, that's you two," he looked up and made eye contact before proceeding. "Evidence indicates that it is more likely than not that a violation of the OPD policy and procedure occurred on April twentieth." Captain Rowley glanced up and back at the file again. "You two are neck deep in the preponderance of evidence. You failed to follow procedure, orders, and to inform your direct superior of your actions."

He motioned towards Hodges who had a shit-eating smirk on his face.

Captain Rowley removed his glasses and continued. "It's no secret that Mr. and Mrs. Huggins filed a wrongful death suit against the city and another civil suit against you two," he said. "Conversely, Internal Affairs investigation and the allegations about your actions leading up to the definition of the wrongful death of Jarred Huggins was unfounded. The suspect killed four people and wounded another three. Had you two not averted the situation there may have been many more lives lost, perhaps even another Columbine-style shooting. Therefore, it is the Internal Affairs' recommendation that you both be returned to full duty. And we'll talk about you guys being YouTube rock stars with the dog in the car thing later."

He rolled his chair back, unlocked the side compartment on his desk, and grabbed our shields and semi-automatics.

"Welcome back Detectives," Captain Rowley said as he stood and handed us our hardware. "Just so you guys know, Mayor Washburn threw some weighed around, in your favor on this one," he said in a low voice.

Hodges was beyond pissed. His hands went from being interlaced to resting on his hips. He shook his head in a silent protest and disapproval. His lips pressed firmly together as he shot me and Davis a revolting squint. We ignored him and kept our attention on the Captain.

"Get back to work," Captain Rowley said. "What do you have for them, Sergeant?"

I was still holding the file from the Parkwood Plaza homicide. Hodges nodded in the direction of the file.

"Start with that," he grumbled.

"We'll talk about the back of that garbage truck later," Davis whispered as we walked by him leaving the Captain's office.

Chapter 6

Carol's team filtered into conference room B, to bottled waters and healthy snacks. She started the meeting at 11:30 a.m. even though stragglers were still funneling in, due to taking late calls.

"Everyone knows how to deal with a happy customer, it's pretty hard to mess that up. But it's possible," Carol said. She pressed the clicker, displaying a picture of a smiling customer.

"Wallah," a voice sung from the table.

"This is what we want our customers to look like after we've helped them."

Another press of the clicker bought up a picture of an angry customer.

"Unfortunately, this is what they look like when they call us," Carol said. "For a variety of reasons," she added. "An angry customer can have a strong impact on your mental and physical health. Especially if you guys are not relieving your stress properly. Having said that, let's see what your ideas are of relieving stress."

She went around the oval-shaped table hearing what agents did to relieve stress.

"I put that energy into killing them with kindness," Oliver said.

"I squeeze a stress ball," someone said.

"I doodle," Natasha remarked.

"I imagine what they must look like straining, going number two and not being able to get the whole thing out," was Joshua's comment.

Carol shot him the, "did you really just say that?" look, along with everyone else.

Joshua elaborated, "Plain and simple, some of our customers are just miserable people. Every day, we have those customers that, no matter what we do to make things right for them, they will still find something to bitch about. Just the other day I had a customer experiencing a power outage, and was mad at us because her desk top wouldn't power up. Hello, it's a power outage, you dingbat. I was a nice guy and gave her credit for the day, and she was still irate and bad-mouthing SC&D."

Agents around the table nodded their heads in approval and understanding.

"You have a point, Joshua," Natasha said, "I had a guy curse me out and wanted a free month of cell service because his phone was so-called, 'jacked-up.' But he didn't want me to next day him another phone."

Carol listened and watched the group's reaction to some of the points they were making. Then she passed everyone a single sheet of paper from a small notepad. Another press of the clicker bought up audio file one which was immediately paused.

"I want you to write down your thoughts as you listen to these," Carol said. "Don't put your names on it, just your thoughts."

Phyllis marched through the door. Not happy she'd missed the beginning of the meeting because of a long-winded caller. She took a seat on the far side of the table followed by Carol setting a sheet of paper in front of her.

"What's this for?" Phyllis snapped.

"Consider it a penny for your thoughts," Carol mused.

"You couldn't afford my thoughts."

"And you couldn't stomach mine," Carol said as she strolled back to the monitor.

With another press of the clicker, the audio file played. Followed by four more, one of them being John Doe from Mindy Vaughn's account. Each agent wrote something down at one point or another and some wrote thoughts down for every audio file, but Phyllis's sheet of paper remained blank.

Two boxes circulated the table. A smaller box for the comments and a larger one containing gadgets for stress relief. Each team member slid their folded comment into the smaller box and took a stress reliever of their choosing. Carol made a mental note of who took what.

The first unanimous comment read, "He needs to be put in his place."

"We are the service provider and the customer is always right," Carol said. "Let's go around the table and discuss customer-oriented ways to put him in his place."

"We could have been more stern with him," Natasha said, with her eyes down doodling on the scrap sheet of paper.

"How so?" Carol asked.

"Callers have this perception that they can talk to us however they see fit and we have to take it. That's not fair nor is it professional. And it destroys individual moral."

"Okay, so let's go over a few examples of being stern with the customer," Carol said.

"Instead of SC&D going into their wallets to replace a second, third-party router and our modem," Joshua chimed in, "we should have told him to control his kids temper tantrum or put the modem and router where his kid can't get to it. There is such a thing as being too nice. How is it our fault this guy's kid keeps breaking our stuff along with his dad's shit? I get it, being pissed when you can't get online, but to break stuff that you don't even own and expecting us to pay for it?"

"I follow what you're saying, but he's a long-time customer which goes hand in hand with the cost of doing business," Carol remarked.

"Or we can politely inform him to pay a deposit," Phyllis asserted. "Even though we're in the business of serving customers. We're still in the business of doing business. If we did that for every customer, we wouldn't be in business long."

Agents around the table again nodded their heads in approval.

"Good point Phyllis, and a true statement," Carol remarked.

Most the agents at SC&D had been with the company less than six months and were still learning the ropes of the call center business. Phyllis had been there seventeen years and eight of those as a supervisor. She got burned out and tired of babysitting agents that weren't thoroughly trained on customer service, etiquettes, and the do's and don'ts. So, she went back to being an agent. A highly paid agent. And the question about her always lingered, if she had a backbone or if she was a bully.

The second comment read, "Meet him at his house and kick his ass."

"Under what circumstances would this ever be acceptable?" Carol asked as she looked around the table probing faces and eyes.

Out of the 12 agents around the table, Joshua and Natasha had the same nonchalant expression.

"I don't know, maybe the part where he threatened someone's life," Joshua commented.

"That's all it was, a threat, a prescribed verb combined with an adjective to elicit a certain response," Carol remarked. "It's never the ones that talk big that pose a real threat. Kind of like when a dog shows his teeth."

"What was it you said you used to do again?" Phyllis asked.

"I didn't say, but if you must know, I was a contractor for the FBI. Before that, I was a regular Ph.D. grad just getting by on my brains."

The room fell silent until Joshua asked, "Ph.D. in what?"

"Psychology," Carol said. She shifted her eyes to Phyllis, "Summa Cum laude."

Carol then set a large head shaped stress ball onto the oval table. It was light blue with a mean facial expression.

She raised her hand and asked, "how many times have we been mean or unjust to someone only to realize, that we can't take it back?"

Practically everyone raised their hands in admittance.

She went over the explanations about exercise, and emphasized the importance of that release. Also, pointing out the more release you experience the more you want due to the endorphins rush.

"Are you addicted to endorphins?" Joshua asked.

"I get my fair share," Carol answered. "But, the important thing is to release the tension when we get to a certain level of anger or stress."

"And how will we know that level?" Natasha questioned.

"When things that are out of the question begin to make sense. For example, let's say if Phyllis wants to call me a bad word or name. The madder she gets, the more sense it will make. However, if she releases a little stress, her endorphins will help her feel more relaxed. Thus, helping her make a better decision."

Phyllis gave Carol a revolting glare that was met with evil eyes. A blink away from turning hazel.

Carol passed the stress head around the table, asking each agent to perform one stress relieving action on it. There were several punches, some unkind words but Joshua whipped his pen out and added a black eye and two missing teeth before passing it on.

"Joshua, I'm going to pray for you," was Carol's humorous wisecrack. "These exercises relieve stress and not everyone has the same level of stress or stress relief." She told the group.

"I don't like your methods," Phyllis said, "This isn't a Psychology class."

"You'd be surprised how much psychology plays a role in our daily lives. I would like to continue this conversation but, we have to get back to the floor," Carol remarked. "Those of you that have research to complete," she eyed Joshua and Natasha, "don't forget, the more detailed the better."

Chapter 7

After leaving Captain Rowley's office, Davis and I checked out the Parkwood Plaza murder file. We had a few places to visit on behalf of a murdered nameless homeless man. But our first stop was the old Parkwood Plaza on the corner of West Colonial Drive and John Young Pkwy, even though a CSI team had already processed the area. We needed to get a feel of what may have transpired behind what used to be a Winn Dixie, now a dilapidating building that served as a cover for the homeless man's lifeless body. Crime scene tape, blood and a chalk outline marked where it appeared he spent his last minutes of life. But there was no sleeping bag, no cart or knapsack with his belongings in them.

"Did they steal his stuff?" Davis asked rhetorically.

"If they did, they stole every bit of it. But who would steal a homeless man's possessions?"

"Another homeless person. Maybe some punks looking for kicks."

The only thing that made sense was maybe some misguided young punks did this. But why take his worldly possessions? The crime scene tape draped from a metal post, wrapped around a stack of milk crates and went to the side of what used to be a docking bay for trucks. It looked like someone swept up by his body. A portion of sand covered the perimeter of the chalk by the front half of the figure.

"Did they kill him and clean up?" Davis quipped.

"No, they used something to push his body away from the street view," I said. I took a few steps in an outward direction, gauging the angle to John Young Parkway. "That explains why his blood resembles a paintbrush that went dry. The perpetrator, or perpetrators used something to move him from plain sight."

We searched the surrounding docks along with the entire back and both sides of the building for anything that may have been used to move or to push a body, but we came up empty. We took another look at the CSI pictures. We studied them in comparison to the actual crime scene, and everything was identical. I scouted the other side of the gate that divided the building and the wooded area.

"Do you think they're some homeless people sacked out over there?" Davis asked.

"Not sure," I said, I began climbing the six-foot chain linked fence.

"Hey partner, what's this?" Davis motioned at something on the other side of the fence.

It was a push broom laying on top of the brush. I scurried over the top of the fence and jumped the rest of the way down to get a better look when I heard leaves ruffling.

"COYOTES!" Davis yelled.

I was in a snug place between the fence and the bushes, and unable to see. Davis unsnapped his holster, and when I looked; he was training his weapon to my left. I unholstered and slowly moved back to the fence. There were more ruffling sounds. I turned, blindly training my weapon towards the growling and yipping sounds.

"I think now would be a good time to get your ass back over to this side," Davis yelled.

I agreed and with gun in hand; I began climbing the fence until they rushed me. In a hurry to get to the top I dropped my service weapon. They were clawing at my legs-

"YAW! YAW!" Davis yelled at the Coyotes followed by "BAKA, BAKA!"

He fired at a low angle into the wooded area. The noise from his 9mm made the coyotes scamper back into the woods. I held my position on the fence for a few beats before retrieving my gun. After the coyotes ran off, we hoisted the broom over the fence using a branch. We radioed to have a CSI log the push broom for prints. After CSI logged the broom, we canvassed the surrounding area of the three thousand block showing the unidentified man's picture to nearby store clerks and other homeless people. He was recognized as Flann. A few people said they'd seen him from time to time, panhandling the street corners and working the local stores for spare change.

Our next stop was the Medical Examiner.

Chapter 8

The Huggins family sat in the front row of Saint Andrews Catholic, dressed in black and mourning the loss of their son. Although Father Alexander spoke about Jarred's good days and deeds before his series of killings, he would be haunted by his words and judged by the congregation for his part in the home going service. As he eulogized the departed, Jarred's father sat with his arm around his sobbing wife with a sad but angry expression on his face. Jarred had his same oval-shaped face. Although he was watching Father Alexander, his mind was elsewhere.

Flashbacks of receiving the news that his son had been shot in the back of the head by an OPD detective. An automatic closed casket. The funeral director told him there was nothing they could do to make his son presentable. There was too much damage caused by the hollow point. Even though the impact was at the back of his head, the exit wounds of the sprawled-out bullet obliterated Jarred's face.

Thomas Huggins eyes focused on the top of the casket. An eight by ten seventh grade picture of his son. A younger, happier version of him, his mother's favorite picture. A time in his life when the innocence from within paraded on his face. He wiped a streaming tear from his right eye.

Even though his son was the root of four other funerals, he focused on the question of why Bernard Davis had to kill his son. It corroded him from the inside out. Reporters took photographs from a distance as the burial happened.

Jarred's mother tended her sniffles with a handkerchief, pining and thinking of where she could have gone wrong. How could she not know her son's intentions? Her heart went out to the students and families affected by her son's actions. Thomas Huggins had a different frame of mind that ended with the eulogy of Detective Davis. By the same token, Marius Green, Michael Thompson's cousin, fantasized about the death of the entire Huggins family. And he had the wherewithal to make it happen.

Chapter 9

Laura Miller thought it would be just another day after she hung up with SC&D Communications. She argued her frustration out against the service representative, Joshua, that she would complain if he said anything out of place. She bitched, complained and took up valuable time for something so petty as a power outage. Joshua explained to no end that power outages were beyond their control. Still, she kept him on the phone over an hour, demanding three months of free service. When asked to be placed on hold so the matter could be brought to a supervisor, her response was that she would hang up, call back and say she was dissatisfied with the rep. After a one-sided negotiation, she was given a month of free service, which was the best he could do without supervisor approval. Her history showed a track record of calling every month like clockwork, with the promise of doing business elsewhere, unless she got her way. But unbeknownst to her, her victory would be short-lived.

Hours later she would be approached by a man smoking a cigarette outside of a sports bar in Winter Park.

"Hey Laura," an unknown man said in a chipper voice.

"Do I know you?" Laura asked and looking confused.

His voice sounded familiar, but she couldn't quite place it.

"I'm sorry, I didn't mean to catch you off guard. I'm Jay, Nate's father. Our sons play on the same youth football team," he said with a slight smile and a grin to add. "He always wears a blue practice jersey."

"Oh, is that so," she said. She eyed him, still trying to recollect his face and voice.

"we've spoken on occasion," he laughed.

"You're always looking down at your phone, working I assume. Or updating Facebook," he joked to lighten the moment, and it worked.

"Yes, I have to show my friends and family what my baby's doing on that football field," she proudly declared.

"It's Christopher, right? Has he been playing long?"

"This is his fourth year."

"Has he always been a running back and a linebacker?"

"Coach Chip had him on the line when he first started. A few weeks later he switched him to linebacker. Now he's running the ball."

"Coach Chip doesn't have a set position for Nate yet. I think he's still feeling him out," Jay remarked.

"Don't worry, it'll come. It might take a little time for him to get the hang of it."

"I played football many years ago. Believe me when I tell you that, your little man has good mechanics. Coach Chip is coaching him up right. I see Christopher buying momma a house one day?"

Laura's gaze softened when Jay complimented her son. He kept his distance in a continuous effort to not spook her. A work of art, his scouting paid off. Using the poorest athlete on the team to strike up a conversation. The only things he knew about Nate was that he was last in laps and always wore a blue jersey.

"This is Nate's first year, he's still trying to get into the swing of things. I always use Christopher and Riley as benchmarks for what he should do as far as drills go."

"I'm trying to picture your son's face," Laura said, looking down to the side in her efforts to recall him.

"He's the one that's always last on the laps and can barely do push-ups." Jay laughed a slight chuckle.

"I think I know who you're talking–"

Before she could finish her sentence, she was without a voice. A gurgling guttural of blood spilled from her throat. The swiftness of a straight razor had already done its job before Laura could figure out what happened. The person she knew as Jay, then slid the blood-stained razor through her carotid artery, leaving her no chance of survival. With a loss of blood came a light headedness and loss of strength as she fell against a green SUV, eventually collapsing to the ground. She clutched her hands around her neck in a feeble attempt to stop the gushing crimson blood from her carotid artery.

Her angry teary eyes focused on Jay as she mouthed "why?"

He knelt beside her, pulled his phone out and played her SC&D audio file.

Her teary flooded eyes grew wide, with surprise and disbelief before her world grew dark. Her killer carved a series of numbers on her left arm before casually leaving the parking lot.

Chapter 10

We were en route to the Medical Examiner's office by way of McDonalds drive thru.

"Okay, someone pokes fun at the homeless man, the homeless man tells them to go to hell, and then, the homeless man gets dead," Davis said. "And when I say someone, I mean punks".

"I don't know, why wouldn't they just leave him there? Why go through the trouble of moving his body? It doesn't seem like an MO that's normally used around here. Unless he saw something he shouldn't have."

A voice chirped through on the speaker to take our order. Davis ordered a coffee, and me, a breakfast sandwich, hash browns, and an orange juice.

"You do know we're going to the Medical Examiner's office to see a body, right?" Davis reminded. "Uncle Elton made breakfast for everyone this morning, and you're still hungry?"

"I worked up an appetite dodging hyenas," I replied.

"Not to change the subject but, how are Andre and Renee?" Davis asked.

"They seem to be enjoying life as middle schoolers, although Andre's still upset he didn't make the football team."

"Well, that'll just give him more time to sharpen his skill set."

"I also think he's starting to like girls."

"You say that like it's a bad thing," Davis laughed.

"Some of those little girls can be something else," I said as I inched forward in the drive-thru.

"Well, isn't that the benefit to having a sister at the same school? She should have the inside scoop on everything."

"That's what I'm afraid of."

"Worst-case scenario, you go down there and put the fear of God in them."

"I think I'll hold off on that for a few years," I said. "And speaking of the fear of God, how's it going with your crazy stalker ex-girlfriend? Kimberly, I think it was."

"Don't start up about her partner. I might need you to talk to her."

"I'm not getting involved. I told you she was crazy from the get-go. Really, who stalks the damn police? She's got more loose screws than a kitchen table."

"I changed the locks to my apartment last week, here's a key. Just in case."

"Just in case what?" I remarked with a chuckle.

"Maybe you should put out a restraining order on your ex. She's what, maybe 120 pounds?"

"Go ahead, laugh it up but she's crazy. Truly crazy. You'd think me being a cop would prompt her to at least act like she has common sense. She broke into my apartment and went through my stuff."

"I think you're being paranoid."

"She left me a note."

"Tell the truth, you made her crazy, didn't you?"

"I'm glad you got jokes."

"You bought it on yourself. It's because you made her crazy. Isn't she studying for her Ph.D.?"

"Yes, she'll soon be Doctor Kimberly Williams."

"Oh wow. The less I know the less I'll have to testify to."

We pulled up to the window and were handed one bag and two drinks. I handed Davis his coffee before pulling off.

"I don't know partner, this seems like an open and shut case. Some punks killed this poor guy for kicks. Finding them will be like looking for a grain of sand at the beach."

"I think you have a point. After we get the time of death from the M.E. we'll start by pulling surveillance from surrounding traffic cameras and cross-reference them with the violent offender's database. Maybe shaking those trees will give us some fruit to bare," I said as I took a bite of my breakfast sandwich.

Doctor K. Lauren, Kailey, was in the middle of an autopsy, concluding the cause of death for 37-year-old Stewart O'Brien. It seems he was the victim of a carjacking or attempted robbery.

"Good morning Doc," I greeted as we walked in.

"I've been expecting you," Kailey said, her eyes on her hands. She was removing a slug from Stewart O'Brien's chest cavity. "Detective, is that chewing I hear?"

"Just finishing my second breakfast Kailey," I stuffed the last of my sausage egg and cheese McMuffin in my mouth. "You know how I get when I don't eat."

"I think you're the only cop in all of the Orlando PD that eats when you know you have to come here. Sooner or later that second breakfast is going to take up residency in your hips."

"We all have to eat," I remarked, stepping closer to see what she was doing. "Looks like death by gunshot?"

"That's what it looks like from where you're standing," Kailey replied. Her eyes steady and focused on her work. "Who would shoot someone that's already dead?" Was her rhetorical question because the body expired from carbon monoxide poisoning?

"Someone who wants something," Davis said.

Stewart O'Brien was the owner of Wing Pit Barbecue and had a ten-million-dollar life insurance policy. He was found in his bullet-riddled Hummer on the side of the road, a few miles from his house. After removing the remaining slugs from his body, Kailey Pulled off her white latex gloves. Pulling in a downward motion from the right wrist first, followed by the left, making a pocket, housing the right glove, and pitching them into the red Bio-hazardous bin, before slipping on another pair to avoid cross-contamination.

"How do you do that so fast?" Davis asked.

"Lots of practice," Kailey moved to the table containing the homeless man's body. "Meet John Doe," she added before taking a file from the bottom of the table, handing it to me.

I began thumbing through it. "This can't be right," I said, as Davis peeked over my shoulder. "According to this, this guy's name is Anton Flannigan, and he lives in College Park just off of Lake Adair."

Kailey handed me another file containing dental records and fingerprints. "Mrs. Flannigan identified his remains yesterday afternoon. She reported him missing three days ago."

"So why was he dressed like a vagrant? Did they steal his clothes?" Was the question Davis posed.

"I think we're dealing with something a little more advanced than your everyday hoodlums," I said.

The picture in the file was a match to the sprawled-out corpse with a toe tag that still read John Doe. The only difference was a little facial hair.

"What's that on his arm?" I said. "Looks like they tortured him."

"It was done with a straight razor," Kailey said. She lifted Anton's left arm. "I don't know what this means, but it looks like random alphabets and numbers. And he looks a little old to be in a gang, but what do I know? My best friend's a cat."

I pulled out my cell and took pictures of the brutalization.

"How do you know this was a straight razor?"

Kailey ran a latex finger across Anton's neck. "Knives don't have edges this sharp," She pulled the wound apart. "Do you see how fine this line is? This cut would be three times wider had this been a knife."

My thought was there may have been a mix-up in administration. Usually, when someone comes to ID a body, the assigned detective is the first to know.

To make better use of our time, Davis and I split up.

He went to pull surveillance footage from traffic lights and surrounding businesses while I paid a visit to the late Anton Flannigan's wife.

Chapter 11

I pulled up to a white two-story mansion with olive and gray trim, that sat just off to the side of Lake Adair. The driveway was long and straight. At a glance I noticed it housed an F series Jaguar. Upon making my way to the door I noted a gray S-class Mercedes parked in the back of the driveway.

"Can I help you?" A lady called out from a second-story window.

"I'm looking for Juanita Flannigan."

"What's your business? The sign out front says no soliciting," she griped in a pompous voice and giving me an icy glare.

"I'm Detective Jackson, with the OPD. I'd like to have a few minutes of your time," I held up my badge. I recognized the lady as being Juanita Flannigan from the next of kin picture in Anton Flannigan's file.

She disappeared from the second-story window and stepped outside the front door a few seconds later. She looked to be in her mid-forties with salt and pepper hair, a diamond shaped face and sporting a dark tan.

"How can I help you?" She plopped down on the lounge chair by the front door, folding one leg in towards her midsection.

I held up my shield again.

"My condolences on your loss. I'm Detective Jackson and I'm trying to get as much information as I can about what happened to your husband."

"You don't seem like any detective I ever saw," she said matter-of-factly.

"I'm not one for stereotypes."

"What do you want to know detective? That he was a provider, a dedicated man and a visionary who died an insignificant death." She gave me a serious stare.

"Did he receive any threats or have bad blood with anyone prior to his death?"

"My husband was a businessman. Of course, he had bad blood with one person or another from time to time."

"Is there anyone who stands out?"

"That's a long list detective, and everybody had a number. He cut people out of deals and ran some out of business."

"What business was he in?"

"He was an entrepreneur. He owned a few apartment buildings and two used car lots. He closed on another building two weeks ago. It wasn't a big building, but he got it from right under Michael Hoover's nose."

"Michael Hoover, why does that name sound familiar?"

"He's a developer. He buys residential properties, tears them down, and has them rezoned for his business complexes. He wasn't too happy when Anton got the Pennsylvania building. He even tried to buy it from him and when that didn't work he resorted to sending code enforcement after him."

"Such as—" my phone beeped.

I toyed with it briefly, seeing a text from Davis. I stopped myself from mouthing the words.

"Detective, my husband was no saint when it came to business. He kicked people out of apartments, shorted contractors when he could, and sold enough bad cars to have a lemonade stand. But he had people, the kind of people that make things happen, if you catch my meaning."

"These people, the ones he had. Do you think they would want to cause him harm? Or is there anyone that stands out?"

"Your guess is as good as mine detective. But I think news travels fast."

"Why do you say that?"

"The phone doesn't ring as much since Anton went missing and was murdered."

"Mrs. Flannigan, where were you the night your husband went missing?"

"I was at my girlfriend's Condo in Stonebridge Place."

I did a double take to Juanita Flannigan's answer. "Your girlfriend?"

Juanita arched her back, eased her phone from her pocket, fiddled with it for a few seconds and passed it to me. It was a picture of the late Anton, Juanita, and her girlfriend, wearing matching bathrobes. "We had an open relationship. And it worked because we all benefited."

I pointed at the lady in the picture. She was a brunet that was a little on the thick side. "What's the girlfriend's name?"

"Josey, Josey Talon, why?"

"I'll need to speak to her. So, if you have her address handy that would be useful."

She gave me Josey's Stonebridge Place address.

"The clothes Anton wore the evening of his death didn't reflect his status in the community," I said, trying to put it delicately. "Can you shed some light on that?"

Juanita's face mutated from semi-sad to angry. "What are you talking about? He was always dressed to the nine."

"The unit that responded to the call mistook him for a homeless man. His clothes were filthy and weathered."

"Well, I guess that's something else you need to find out, detective. I understand my husband to be a high-profile homicide case. And if you fuck this up, my lawyers will have your ass." She steadily eyeballed the middle of my face.

Her arrogance through her wealth was showing. Although saddened by her husband's death, her fixation of being affluent and constantly getting her way was shining through. I questioned it in the back of my mind. *Was Juanita having a weak moment or was her sporadic behavior a symptom of an unyielding character flaw.*

There are a few things all cops dislike. Assholes, know-it-alls, and people that profess to correlate with your superiors. One of the biggest things is to attempt to intimidate us with money or lawyers. Juanita obviously missed that day in school.

"Juanita Flannigan," I said as if I was going to arrest her, returning the guillotine stare. "I think you got it a bit twisted! Don't go getting simple on me. We both want the same thing. To find your husband's killer."

"Well, we need to make sure that happens fast and thorough."

She obviously had the wrong impression. I turned to leave, striding down the driveway and then I turned and strolled back. "Don't leave town." I dropped my card on her lap before making my way back down the driveway.

"Are you insinuating I'm a suspect?" She asked, to which I didn't reply.

I had my suspicions. She seemed to take the death of her husband in an unusual stride. Or maybe it was just her selfish nature. But in any event, she needed to know this wasn't amateur hour.

Chapter 12

An instant message flashed across the bottom of Carol's screen.

"We need you to go to conference room B." From H. Sosa, one of the SC&D managers.

"Sure, I can be there in five minutes," Carol replied.

She disconnected from the call she was listening in on and headed to the conference room. She had been with the company for six months and had never been invited to the conference room by any of the managers. Whenever they needed to talk, they'd always stopped by her office or had her come to theirs.

What's this about? She found herself facing a deposition from the five members of the managing staff. Questioning how she ran her team and her meetings. Suggestions made by one of her team members sparked concerns about aggressive tendencies towards stress and customers. She sat parallel from the managers and facing Charlie, the 250-pound security guard. His presence was mandatory, whenever managers had a hearing, in case a termination was rendered, Charlie would escort them away from the premises. He stood 6'3' with his anvil-like arms folded across his chest.

"I coach my team to embrace their stress, to channel it in a constructive manner, with regard to our atmosphere. They're not always at liberty to pace around and relieve steam when the occasion arises. Customer's gripe at them quite often, through no fault of their own. My exercises help them alleviate unhealthy tension," Carol explained.

"Give us an example of your stress relief," Ericka, one of the managers, and a close friend to Phyllis asked.

Carol occasionally saw them sharing rides to work and eating lunch together. Both in their mid-forties and from what she noticed, they had the same vindictive mindset.

"It's important to breathe while releasing energy through one or a few physical exercises."

"Why are you passing out miniature heads around the table? I find that alarming," Ericka snapped.

"I didn't pass a human head around the table and say kill the head. I found out how my team members felt about their level of tension. Some had soothing reactions towards the head while others displayed a slight difference of opinion. Those are the ones I know I need to work with and develop."

"I don't like it! It sends the wrong message."

"I like the concept," Jim said. "I think I'll try that with the engineering department. Truth be told, when grids go down, stress goes up."

"What the hell does engineering stress over?" Ericka snapped.

"You name it. If it's not rookies calibrating parts of the system wrong or vendors giving us outdated or refurbished panel boards, it's the guys at the head end getting it all wrong with the smart grid. It all falls on engineering. My guys get calls in the middle of the night, even when they're on vacation. If you don't think that's stressful I don't know what is. Do you have any more of those miniature heads? I want to pass them out to my guys."

"We were under the impression that you were giving Gestapo marching orders," Denise said. "I'd like to talk to you more about how to use those techniques with the social media team. We're constantly being put on the spot with authors of unrealistic requests. Always waiting for us to respond inappropriately, so they can screenshot us and post."

Carol noticed Ericka looking down at her phone and texting. She could only assume Ericka was giving Phyllis details on how the 'thrashing' was going.

"What about the anonymous comments on the cards? And talks of violently assaulting our customers," Ericka griped.

"There was no such talk. Your information is wrong."

"My source is very reliable."

"We read anonymous comments from the team. After which, we went around the table and discussed it. Sometimes people are more honest when they know others identify with how they feel. Haven't you ever been asked a question on the spot and said the politically correct thing, so people wouldn't think differently of you?"

"I don't see where that's relevant. We're not talking about politics. We're talking about poisoning the minds of our phone agents."

Carol crossed her legs and looked Ericka in her right eye.

"I understand where you're coming from. If I were being told untruths by someone I'd known for years, I would believe them too. But I assure you I have my teams best interest at heart."

"What the hell are you implying?" Ericka snapped.

"Excuse me, ladies. I have something here that might shed some light on whatever this disagreement is," Chad, the human resource manager said. He placed a manila folder onto the long oak wood table. "Whenever our employees are being bought to hearings by management, I pull their stats to use as a benchmark of suggestion for coaching, areas needing improvement, citations and sometimes termination."

He looked at Charlie and gave him an approving nod, relieving him from his further presence at the hearing. Chad opened the file and began. "Ms. Roach has only been with us for six months. Over the last four months, her team has led the entire floor in everything apart from call times. So, I'd say she's got a strong handle on team building and should be commended."

Ericka's eyebrows curled, and her face faded to a dark red. She tossed her phone onto the table, crossed her arms in disagreement to the sound of her heel tapping beneath the table. After the meeting, Carol went back to her office.

Hours later Phyllis would see Carol, Joshua, and Natasha taking a smoke break near her car in the second row. Which was parked next to Carol's car. She thought it odd because supervisors had assigned parking spots in front of the building.

Chapter 13

With chatter in the background, Davis sat at his desk checking the footage from John Young Parkway and Colonial Drive. Not only did he see about 40 cars committing red light violations, and a few near misses, but the cameras from the surrounding intersection showed several panhandlers and one Anton Flannigan. He wore a weathered Miami Dolphins hat, a grimy overcoat, and grubby caci pants. He spent an hour at the first intersection until the video displayed another homeless man approaching him. Although there was no audio, Davis could tell the two men were in disagreement. Maybe over Anton hogging the east side of the intersection. Anton, the larger of the two pushed the smaller man towards oncoming traffic, causing the latecomer to leave. He worked the east side intersection for another forty-five minutes before setting up shop at the adjacent intersection.

Ten minutes and what looked like twelve dollars later a white Camry held up traffic near Anton. Words were exchanged and strange body language along with an ominous look from the driver took place. Davis zeroed in on the tag XJL 54S as the vehicle went a quarter of the way into the turn.

A restricted call on Davis's cell distracted his focus.

"Hello, this is Detective Davis." A few seconds went by, and the line went dead. *Maybe a wrong number.*

Anton tended the north-side intersection for just under two hours. By Davis's calculations, Anton Flannigan had to have made over eighty dollars. He noticed the driver of the same white Camry holding up traffic at the southbound intersection. He was looking down at something. *But what?*

A few minutes later Anton continued his rotation to the westside intersection where he approached the same homeless man from before. This time there was no scuffle. Anton handed the man something wrapped in a small paper bag. The smaller homeless man left with no trouble but gave Anton a long-lasting stare as he disappeared from the range of the traffic cameras. OPD's facial recognition was a match for eight of the man's previous mug shots. Terrance Green, who had a rap sheet ranging from loitering to assault and battery.

"Did you graduate from assault and battery to murder?" Davis maneuvered through the databanks to see Terrance green's aliases and last known address.

The databank kicked out Tera Miller, Terrance's sister who lived in Hunter's Creek. The data hit also showed that he was a frequent flyer around Westmoreland drive, a half mile from the old Parkwood Plaza.

A hit on the Camry tag XJL 45S showed it was a rental to Chang Xen. A second look at the traffic cam video showed a lady in the passenger seat and two toddlers in the back. Twenty minutes later corresponding traffic cams showed the Camry heading towards the Dolphin resort. Davis figured they were tourists that got turned around and trying to find their way back. His phone rang again with a restricted number, dismembering the variables to his train of thought.

"Hello, this is Davis," he answered, hearing traffic noise in the background before the line went dead. He dismissed it as a wrong number or weak call signal.

He gathered his information and mugshots of Terrance Green on the way to the six hundred block of Westmoreland and Arlington. He parked at the corner 7-eleven and canvased the area. Moments later his cell rang again.

He pulled it from his pocket, "hello this is Davis," he said in an exhale, expecting the line to go dead again.

"Hey partner, what do you have?" I said.

"Traffic cams show Flannigan in an altercation with a vagrant name Terrance Green. I'm canvassing the surrounding areas trying to dig him up. How's it going on your end?"

"Seems like Anton Flannigan had an interesting lifestyle. I'm en route to question persons of interest. A Michael Hoover and a Josey Talon. The crazy thing is the list could be longer than what we have. His wife said he wasn't the nicest guy to deal with when it came to business."

"I'll give you a call after I find this guy," Davis said.

I found myself at Michael Hoover's Real Estate office in Winter Park, just south of Park Avenue on Fairbanks near Rollins College. His secretary said he was on a conference call and asked me to have a seat. Ten minutes later, she escorted me to his office.

He was a stout man. Looked like he took care of himself. His office was plush, with swanky furniture and a painting of a Bull charging an Elephant on the wall next to his degree from Boston College.

"Good afternoon detective, how can I help you?" Michael Hoover had a strong Boston accent.

"I'm here to ask you a few questions about Anton Flannigan."

"What do you need to know? I hear he's going to be late for his next birthday."

I could tell this guy was a combination of asses. A smart ass and an asshole. I'm a firm believer in reading faces. *People's facial lines tend to grow to their most common disposition. Maybe you could call it facial muscle memory, but Michael Hoover had a silly built-in smirk on his face.* "How'd you hear that?"

"One of his homeless homies told me."

"Do you hang out with many homeless people?"

"Only when it pays."

"And what's this homeless homie's name?"

"Don't know, but he's a black guy," Hoover amplified his smirk and nodded his head.

"So, let me get this straight because you seem like a pretty sharp guy. You know this guy well enough to talk to him but not well enough to know his name?"

"Look, detective, we were trying to close on the same building, but I wanted it for commercial and he wanted it for residential. It's no secret that Flannigan, and I had a difference of opinion. Particularly when it came down to the difference of him making one million and me grossing over six. He was a greedy prick. I even offered him six hundred thousand with an after percentage on top of what he paid for the last building. The math worked for both of us."

"So, you killed him."

"I didn't kill anybody."

"That's what it seems like from the outside looking in. Six million dollars is a lot of money. But back to the homeless man. How do you know him?"

Hoover pulled a cigar from a cedar chest on his desk, clipped it, lit it and puffed it to life.

"Flannigan and I used to be in business together. We'd buy an old building, throw some money in it, and raise the rent. We did that for a few years and made a pretty decent wage. But I wanted to move on to bigger and better things, so I did what I had to do to get to another playing field. Only he didn't want to go in with me. Said it was too risky, and we had a good thing going with the apartment buildings. So, I scoped out a couple of old buildings, had them rezoned for business, moved in a few firms and my business took off like the Space Shuttle."

"Is that so?"

Hoover reclined in his Herman Miller, fiddling with his cigar clipper. "Two years after I take off he comes and wants in. He got pissed when I told him he needed to buy a partnership, or our split would be 70/30. I guess he didn't like my counter offer. I was surprised he didn't try to Jew me down."

"Jew you down?"

"Anton was a cheap, cheap son of a bitch. I wouldn't be surprised if he had ten million in the bank."

"Most people would say that's a good thing."

"Not when you're obsessed with making a big deal over jewing people down. He was the type of guy to go to a Burger King and want the Whopper half price."

"Thanks for the history lesson, back to the homeless man. How do you know him?"

"A few months ago, I get a call from one of my renovation guys. Says he sees Anton standing at the intersection of fifty and John Young, shaking a cup. I don't believe him, so he sends me a picture, and I still don't believe it. So, I go down there and lo-and-behold it's him. Wearing shit clothes and shaking a cup. I call his wife Juanita to make sure everything's okay and she assures me it's all gravy, but I'm not buying it. I ask to meet her for dinner, to check out her disposition. But that could be an act. I tell her my wallets missing and she doesn't hesitate to pay the tab."

"What's that got to do with the homeless man?"

"I make another trip down there and asked a real homeless guy about him. The black guy, I think his name is Terry or something. He says Anton showed up about five months ago. He referred to him as Flann. So, I make a deal with him, fifty bucks and a cell phone with an excellent quality camera. I have it rigged to where he can only call me because I want to see what's going on. Sure enough, he sends me video after video of Anton, or Flann, pan-handling for cash."

"Let's back up. How do you have his wife's phone number?"

"We'd have cocktails on occasion. Me, Anton, Juanita, and her girlfriend."

"You knew about the girlfriend?"

"Of course, they were inseparable. For an older gal, she was a hot piece of ass."

"I'm going to need you to focus. Where were you on the evening of April 28th?"

"The magic played the Timber Wolves, I was entertaining guests in a few Presidential suites."

"Can you prove it?"

Hoover went to his coat rack and fished around the inside pocket of a leather jacket and handed me a valet stub.

"This only proves your car was there."

"After the game, I went down and said hey to Marcus George Hunt. Asked him how he likes it here?"

"You know Marcus George Hunt?"

"He's from Boston. I hooked him up with a builder."

He also handed me his guest list, also from his coat pocket.

"These are the other businessmen and women I entertained," Hoover said as he regained his posture of reclining with his feet propped back up on his desk.

"Is there anything else you can tell me about Anton Flannigan?"

Hoover sat with his head arched up, blowing perfect O rings from his cigar. "Nope, but if I think of something I'll give you a shout."

"I'm sure you will." I flicked my card onto his desk. "Don't leave town."

Chapter 14

The sun was out in full force while Andre and Renee walked home from school.

"Somebody asked about you today," Renee said.

"Yeah, who was that?" Andre asked.

"The same person you've been bugging me about, Kira."

"What'd she say?"

"She asked where you were. We were making small talk before Rodney showed up and tried to put the moves on her."

The conversation went flat line after that. Flashbacks of Rodney's recent treatment of Andre plagued his mind. The run-ins, and the indirect nudges while passing him in the hallways. What he really disliked was Rodney muscling in on his conversation with Kira. Rodney was never alone. There were always two other teammates with him.

Andre and Rodney were best friends a year ago. Both played youth football, but when Rodney made the freshman team and Andre didn't, their friendship took another path. Rodney's circle became bigger while Andre's shrunk. Life as a freshman wasn't shaping up to his expectations.

The walk home was a little quieter after Renee's public service announcement. Andre's mind continued to wonder, the rest of the way home. They arrived home to the sultry smell of a delectable Pot Roast. which was something they often took for granted.

"I wonder if mom arrested any bad guys today," Renee said.

"Who knows, maybe she'll have another exciting story for us," Andre said.

Renee could still hear the solemnness in his voice.

"What's going on with you and Rodney? You two used to be best friends."

"Nothing, we just do our own thing."

The rumbling sound of a Charger pulled into the driveway.

"Sounds like moms' home," Andre chirped.

I was greeted with my normal hugs and kisses when I walked inside.

"Where's Uncle Elton?" I asked.

"He was gone when we got here," Renee said.

"There's a Pot Roast in the crock pot," Andre declared after removing the lid and taking a whiff of the aroma.

"He's probably at the park with the rest of those old men playing chess, cards or telling jokes about each other," I assumed.

"How was school today? Do you guys have homework?"

"Did it in class," Renee fired back.

"I have an Algebra assignment," Andre said.

"Let's get her done. No time like the present."

Andre took a fork out and proceeded to do some early sampling of his Uncle's roast.

"Are you feeling okay?" I said. "Looks like your picking at Uncle Elton's roast. Are you trying to hear his speech again?"

"YOU MESSIN WITH A MASTERPIECE!" Renee and I said in unison, imitating Uncle Elton's voice and his favorite phrase about his cooking. We all joined in a good laugh.

"Mom, I'm hungry," Andre groaned.

"That's why we have snacks, so get one. Because if Uncle Elton sees you in that crock-pot with unwashed hands he'll probably have a stroke."

Andre reluctantly put the lid back onto the crock-pot.

"Mom how was your day?" Renee asked.

"At least I have one child that loves me," I joked, pinching Andre on his side.

"Let's see, I got hit on by an old man wearing a Confederate shirt, I interrogated two perps and talked to a grieving widow."

The front door slid open and Uncle Elton walked in, smelling like Old Spice and sporting his dark navy Kangol hat with matching shirt, slacks and shoes. "How's everybody doing?" He put his Kangol on the brass hat rack by the front door. He pulled a black and grey iPod from his pocket and untangled the ear-bud wires. "Andre, I need you to doctor on this iThing. It won't play my Miles Davis, Coltrane, or Stevie Wonder. I'm beginning to think it don't like black folks, because it played the

Bee Gees over and over. I need to trade this in for a Walkman."

"What's a Walkman?" Andre asked as he looked at the iPod and pressed a couple of buttons.
Here you go Uncle Elton, your good. It'll play all your songs now. You had it on repeat, so it would only play that one song over and over."

Uncle Elton pressed the play button and "Part Time Lover" by Stevie Wonder began to play. "Now that's rug-cutting music!" he rejoiced.

"What's rug cutting music?" Renee asked.

"It's what old people say when they liked the beat to a song," I told the kids.

"It's what the boogie makes you do," Uncle Elton said.

"The boogie?" Renee asked.

"Yeah, it makes your feet move!" Uncle Elton said in a growling excited voice.

"It travels through the air, into your ears, down your spine and makes you move your feet to the beat. Not like that bippity-bop, some of you young people listen to."

"It's called rap," Andre said as he laughed. "And it's head bobbing music."

"That head bobbing got some of y'all youngsters shaking your brains loose. Kind of like the sound a bb makes in a metal can."

"Guess what Uncle Elton?" Renee asked.

"What's that sweetie?"

"Andre's got a girlfriend," she sang.

"Andre has a girlfriend?" Uncle Elton repeated in a high pitch voice.

"I don't have a girlfriend. We're just friends."

"Ain't nothing wrong with a young man having a lady friend. Is she special?"

"She's—"

"—He has a crush on her," Renee chirped.

"I don't have a crush on anyone, she probably likes this bonehead we go to school with," Andre muttered.

"Okay guys, let's wash up for supper." My voice echoed down the hallway as I came from the study. "We'll talk about Andre's love life later," I joked.

"Mom, not you too," Andre said as he passed me in the hallway.

"That was just getting interesting," Uncle Elton said.

My husband, Wayne, was away in Afghanistan on a military assignment. I wasn't sure what he did for the government, but he was married to his job. All I know is that he's part of an eight-man team. Our living situation with Uncle Elton came about over the last two years. The elimination of a threat that was too close for comfort in Wayne's eyes. Which was the last time we were all together. Aside from dealing with life and death on my own job, I also think about that dreadful knock on my door from Marines in dress blues. I don't particularly care for the idea of Andre not having his dad around to cheer him on. To speak into his life and boost his spirit when he's down. Although Wayne's best friend, Sean, checks in on the kids from time to time and keeps up on their current events. Not to mention Uncle Elton and his band of dirty dozen buddies does Andre worlds of good. On the flip side, there's no telling what that group of crazy old men are teaching my baby. Truth be told, I think I'm better off not knowing.

Chapter 15

Davis smelled the aroma of dark roast coffee as he rolled over to get a few extra minutes of sleep. Although his body's timer was accustomed to waking up at 7a.m., his Sony rooster hadn't yet crowed nor was he in any hurry to press the issue. When it came to waking-up, his alarm clock played second fiddle. But he hadn't made morning coffee, and he lived alone.

His eyes popped open and his senses came alive. He sprung to his feet, gripped his gun, chambered a hollow point and crept down the hallway. He stood fast in the corridor ready to work the action on his semi-automatic. He inhaled a deep breath and rushed into the kitchen in a combat crouch.

"Nice boxers," I said.

Davis exhaled, easing the hammer back down and grabbing a cup of coffee.

"If I didn't have a key, I'd still be outside honking the horn or ringing your doorbell. You sleep like a rock."

"That's why we're partners. Where's the cream?"

"I had the last of it. Use milk and sugar. Oh, I'm sorry," I laughed, "I forgot, bachelors don't have milk."

Davis dug into the refrigerator and pulled a half bottle of Yahoo from the back. He coupled it with sugar in his coffee and took a few sips.

"That's the ticket right there," he said as if he'd made a new discovery for mankind.

"That's disgusting."

"This shit here is the breakfast of champions." Davis held the cup up as if it was a trophy.

"One champion is going to be minus a job if he doesn't get dressed for work. And where the hell did you get boxers with OPD on them? They're cute," I said.

"I got them from Henriques."

"Who's that?"

"Isabella that works the east side. Her mother made them for a few of the guys," Davis said as he strutted around the kitchen showing off the boxers.

I continued sipping my coffee, shaking my head.

"You're a hot mess."

A message came through telling us to go to the Medical Examiner's office. There was something we needed to see, which gave us time to go over case details since they wouldn't be in for another hour.

"Did you ever track down Terrance Green?"

"No, but I have a lead. A few of the homeless guys says he's frequent around the old Arena every Thursday at twelve, like clockwork. If I don't find him there by then I'll put a few units in play and rope him off."

"We need to see if he ties into what Michael Hoover told me. Greens is in possession of a cell phone with footage containing evidence. We need him rounded up as soon as possible."

An hour later I was back at the Orange County Medical Examiner's office, while Davis continued the hunt for Terrance Green.

Kailey was going over notes when I walked through the door. "I have something to show you," she said, without looking up, she strolled over to table Seventeen and pulled down the white sheet that covered the body of Laura Miller.

"Are you kidding me! Another one!" I said.

"She came in last night from Winter Park. I believe Detective Burk worked the scene and maybe looking further into it," Kailey said. "She has the same lacerations on her left arm as Anton Flannigan."

"And you say the investigating officer is Burk?"

"Yes."

"I know Sam, I've worked with him occasionally. He's very thorough," I turned to leave the office. "If you find anything else, hit me on the hip."

I Bee-lined down the hallway outside to my squad car and had dispatch patch me through to Detective Sam Burk.

"It's been a while Traycee, how's it going?"

"Taking it day by day Sam. How's the family?"

"They're surviving cop life. Is Hodges still giving you shit?"

"Every day."

"I'm sure this isn't a social call. Is this about the Laura Miller murder?"

"Yes. I need to see where it went down."

"Meet me at the Spatz. Near the Winter Park Sinkhole, on the corner of Denning and Fairbanks."

"I'll be there in twenty minutes."

Knowing nothing about Laura Miller, I wondered if any of the suspects could be connected to her homicide. *Could it have been Michael Hoover, Juanita Flannigan or Josey Talon? Or maybe Terrance Green was getting more out of the deal than Michael Hoover led me to believe.*

I used the database to cross-reference their names. The only thing that came up was a mutual social media friend between Juanita Flannigan and Michael Hoover. A Marsha Seymour, who lives in the Panhandle.

I pulled up on the back side of the Spatz parking lot. Although the CSI team had already finished processing the crime scene, the yellow and black tape was still up. Burk was stooped down in a corner, staring over the gravel terrain.

"If you keep that position, you'll find it hard to get up."

Detective Burk slowly stood, straightening his legs with a slight stretch. "Traycee, how are you? It's been a long time."

"It's been about three years. Good to see you, Sam."

"This is a strange crime scene."

"This gravel had to have made it tough on the CSI's. What do you make of it?"

He pulled a small pad from his back pocket and flipped to the middle. "Laura Miller, age 36, a nine-year-old son named Christopher. She was recently divorced and worked at a hair salon in Eatonville. My guess is that the perp came in from the back-right side, avoiding the light, and crept up behind her." He handed me his phone with pictures of the unprocessed crime scene.

I took a few steps away from the scene while studying the photos. I came up with a few scenarios of what may have happened.

"Did the cams pick up anything," I called out to Berk.

"The last thing it shows was her walking behind an SUV belonging to a Mark Stephan. Him and his girlfriend, Julie found her. They knew her. She was here with some of the other parents from the youth football team. They said she left because she had to work early."

"Did CSIs move her before photos?"

"No, they took still lifes before processing."

"I'd like to see the camera footage from inside the bar."

"You want to do it now or I can have it sent to you."

"Have it sent."

"This perp knew what he or she was doing. They waited for her," I eyed the parking lot, then I walked across the street towards the Winter Park Sinkhole.

"What are you looking for Traycee?"

"Proof that our perp was waiting. He wouldn't hide-out in a car. That would be too suspicious." I scooped up two cigarette butts with a piece of paper, folded it around the edges and logged it into a small envelope. "I believe our perp was hanging out in this area," I motioned to the adjacent parking lot. "Maybe it's nothing but let's see if we can get a DNA match or at least a sample. I believe they waited until she came out and then approached her."

"Sure, keep me in the loop."

"Will do."

I went back to Kailey's office to have another look at the lacerations of Laura Miller and Anton Flannigan. Before I entered the office, I received a call. It was Davis, he was bringing Terrance Green in on murder charges. He had an ETA of ten minutes. I did an about face back to booking where I met him to question Terrance Green. We bypassed booking and headed to an interrogation room.

I sat across from him looking over his arrest file. "Looks like you've been busy lately." I set a glass of water in front of him.

"I'm just trying to survive, and you guys come harassing me."

"Tell us something we don't know Terrance. Or else we'll have to arrest you on suspicion of murder."

"Murder! What you talkin bout?" his broken language flared.

"The murder of Anton Flannigan and Laura Miller," I said, studying his face.

"I don't even know those people!"

Davis pulled Terrance's phone from an evidence bag, slid the screen to unlock, and pulled up pictures and videos of Anton Flannigan. "This is what we're talking about. From where we sit it seems like you were watching him and waiting for the perfect time to make your move."

"You talkin bout Flann? You say he's dead? I didn't kill him. I didn't kill nobody."

"What do you think the judge will say, when we show him the footage of you two getting into an argument over who will stand at a red light and panhandle?" I said.

"He was supposed to be there for an hour and he stayed for two. We had an agreement," Terrance said as he took a drink of the water.

"What kind of agreement? And what was in the bag he gave you?" Davis questioned.

"He knew I liked Snickers bars."

"How do you explain these pictures and videos?" I rallied back.

"Some rich guy gave me that phone, and he gave me money to take pictures of Flann. I think he might have been into some weird shit. But he gave me good money, so I did it. I didn't want anything bad to happen to Flann, and I told him. He said he just wanted pictures, so that's what I did. I didn't kill nobody."

"What did he want with the pictures?"

"Like I said, I think he was into some weird shit."

I handed Terrance the phone. "Call him, tell him we're looking for you on suspicion of murder."

He sat chained to an eye bolt not knowing what to think of his newfound situation. He glared at Davis and me before reluctantly pressing the call button. Hoover's voice mail picked up.

"Leave a message," I said.

"Hey, it's me, Terrance. I need help. The police are looking for me on suspicion of murder of the guy you had me take pictures of." He pressed end and set the Samsung eight on the table.

"That's a nice phone. I have a job and can't afford a phone like that. Let me guess. He gave it to you because you have a nice personality," Davis said.

"All he said was that he wanted pictures of the guy."

"What can you tell us about Laura Miller?" I asked.

"I don't know no Laura Miller."

I put the file back into the manila folder. "Fine, have it your way. Hoover must have given you a lot of money to take two murder raps."

"I keep telling you, I don't know no Laura Miller."

"If you say so."

Terrance Green was booked and taken to a holding cell, pending investigation. I sent the Samsung eight and the glass he drank from to ballistics, hoping to get a DNA match to one of the cigarette butts from the Winter Park crime scene.

My next order of business was Josey Talon. I made the trip to the Stonebridge Place Condos in Metro West. I rang the doorbell until a lady walking her dog told me she didn't expect Josey back anytime soon. Josey was a flight attendant and was gone for weeks at a time. *Information Juanita Flanigan neglected to tell me.*

Still, there was no return call from Hoover, nor were there any matches of DNA or prints from

Terrance's glass corresponding with the cigarette butts from the Laura Miller scene. I was playing a waiting game. With no concrete leads. I sat for an hour reviewing sports bar footage and traffic cams to see if there was any relation in cars driving fidgety. I tagged a few red-light runners and one speeding offender I planned to consider. A black 1970 Boss 302 registered to a Gary Smith. A hit on the database said he was a co-owner of cycle world and lived on Palmer Avenue. It was a long shot, but I wasn't leaving that stone unturned.

Anyone with any type of criminal mind or common sense would park away from the sinkhole and the playground, and drive through the surrounding neighborhoods undetected by traffic cams. The traffic camera between Denning and Morse captured a dark Dodge but could not get the tag. Another episode of a dog chasing its tail. I made a run to pay Gary Smith a visit only to find out his son took the Boss 302 for a joy ride. He even pulled up the low jack to show the movements and whereabouts of the car the night Laura Miller was murdered. I thanked him for his time before making my way back to the drawing board.

**

Natasha and Carol stood, looking under the hood of a Charger in the plaza, down from the Bahama Breeze in Altamonte. In a dim-lit area, across from the dumpster and out of the range of security cameras. Their arms were crossed, and they were looking worried until finally, a man in a '74 blue Nova pulled up. He couldn't help but admire Natasha in tight jeans and Carol's painted on black dress.

Natasha waved him down as he drove by. "Excuse me, I have a friend that has a car just like that," Natasha said. "You wouldn't happen to be Alphonso Rodrigues? My social media car guru. I'm Natti."

"Guilty," Alphonso said with a big smirk. "Does this monster belong to you?" He motioned at the Charger.

"It's my friends," she pointed at Carol.

Alphonso sat in the Nova, undressing them with his eyes, thinking what a lucky man he was. Natasha knew he would be there from his social media page. Drinks with friends.

"It won't crank."

Alphonso got out and peeped under the hood. "Give the key a turn."

Carol turned the ignition, and the Charger began to cough, the same time Joshua crept out and stood to the side.

"Try it again," Alphonso said above the coughing engine.

Only this time there were the sounds of familiar voices coming from the stereo. It was the call he had made almost a month ago, being rude and using obscenities.

"What's that?" He yelled. "Is this some kind of joke?"

"No, this is my version of customer service," Natasha said as she slid her finger from one side of her throat to the other. The same time Joshua ran a razor across Alphonso's throat.

Unable to call out for help or run, he would die listening to the rest of his call center recording.

***

Josephine Francis was leaving the Bahama Breeze when she sensed a nearby presence. She hurried to her car. With trembling hands, she dropped her keys onto the dark asphalt, in a shallow puddle. Stooping down, she blindly felt around for her keys. Her growing caution turned to frustration. But it hadn't rained that day. She became disgusted when she pictured it might be a pool of motor oil or urine. Finally, she fingered the keys from the murky puddle. She took a Kleenex from her purse to dry her hands and keys, using the light from her cell phone to pinpoint her car key. There was a gurgling sound the instant her eyes zeroed in on the blood-soaked keys in hand. A shriek of horror consumed her. She dropped her cell phone, keys, and purse, scampering to the nearest light only to stumble over what she thought was a log or a spare tire. Getting back to her feet she used it as leverage only to face the gruesome discovery of it being a dead body. Gasping for air and hyperventilating, her mouth made the motion of a scream. Being asthmatic, offered her constricting throat little air to add volume to her scream. On the verge of passing out, she wobbled back towards the restaurant.

Chapter 16

It was a quarter till seven, and we were eating dinner.

"You rarely eat your asparagus Andre. What's gotten into you? Not that I'm complaining, but wow. You didn't let it breathe," I said.

"It tastes different when Uncle Elton makes it mom," Andre said.

"Everything tastes different when Uncle Elton cooks it," Renee chimed, as she took in a forkful of his roast.

"Hey, I can cook a few good dishes too," I said as if protecting my honor.

"Kids your mother is a genius at baking. She can make peach cobbler and that banana nut bread just like your aunts. If you ask me, I think they gave her their recipes."

"Well, no one's asking you," I joked. "And they did give me their recipes," was the salt I added.

"I can see that, because every holiday you get your own banana nut bread and peach cobbler while the rest of us have to share. Scandalous, I tell you. My own sisters plotting against me."

"I want to learn how to cook like you when I grow up Uncle Elton," Andre said.

"You know, women like a man that knows how to cook," I said.

"Speaking of women, how's your friend doing? Kira, is it?" Uncle Elton asked.

"It's not looking too good. She's been hanging around this bonehead at school," Andre griped. His voice took on a depressed tone. "They see each other pretty much every day."

"She's a cheerleader, and he plays football," Renee said.

"That don't mean nothing," Uncle Elton said. "She's probably just being nice."

"That's what I'm afraid of," Andre said.

"I'm gonna give you your first lesson on women," Uncle Elton said.

"This ought to be interesting," I chirped. "Don't go telling my baby none of your wild Vietnam stories."

"Hush woman, right now y'all sitting at the man table."

I propped an elbow on the table resting my chin on my hand and rolled my eyes upward.

"I saw that," Uncle Elton said before redirecting his attention back to Andre. "Now, the thing you always want to do is pay close attention to them. Because some of them are like wild horses. You got to sneak up on them to get their attention. Or, for example, does she ever speak to you when you're not looking?"

"Yes sir."

"Does she ever bring the conversation to you?"

"Yes sir."

"And this bonehead character. What does he mostly talk about?"

"Your guess is as good as mine. I try to avoid seeing them together."

"They talk about football and the plays he's in on. He's always boasting about himself," Renee said.

Uncle Elton shifted a look towards Renee.

"That's gonna get boring quick, fast and in a hurry. Don't no woman want a man that's stuck on his self. She probably don't even look him in his eyes when he's talking."

"Oh my Gosh! You may be on to something Uncle Elton," Renee said.

"She didn't look at Rodney one time after acknowledging him the other day on the way to fourth period."

"The eyes are the gateway to the soul young man," Uncle Elton declared.

"Rodney's been trying to start stuff with Andre in the hallway. Trying to show off for everyone, like bumping into him and standing in his way," Renee said.

Andre kicked her underneath the table.

"I bet he'll settle down if you hit him with a two-piece," Uncle Elton said.

"Yeah, a two-piece," Andre got excitement.

"Do you mean hit him with chicken?" Renee asked.

Uncle Elton held up his fists. "These two dukes is a two piece. One to the body, and one to the head." He demonstrated a few air punches.

"Okay you two, it's time to hit the sack. Andre, your Uncle has your best interest at heart. But there will be no two pieces, wings or short thighs given out at school."

"Okay mom," the excitement dropping from his voice.

"Unless you're provoked to defend yourself," I said and winked an eye at him, causing him to perk up with a smile.

Chapter 17

My phone rang from a number I didn't recognize.

"Hello, this is Jackson."

"Good evening detective, I'm Commander Noles with the Altamonte PD. I'm sorry to call you this late in the evening, but I need you to come to the Bahama Breeze on 436."

"What's going on out there?"

"There's been a murder in which the victim's throat was slashed. I understand you've been working these homicides."

"I can be there in twenty minutes."

I ended the call and had Davis meet me at the "Bahama Breeze". We arrived minutes apart. It was 11:02 p.m., and the Altamonte CSIs had just started processing the crime scene. A uniformed officer directed us to Commander Noles. Noles, in his mid-fifties, was a tall thick man that sported a salt and peppered crew cut. He stood next to Officer Michaels who was first on the scene. Proper introductions were made while he escorted us around and pointed out particulars.

"This isn't our jurisdiction, we're OPD," I said to the commanding officer.

"It is now detective. Your names came up on the Joint Homicide Investigations Team, otherwise known as the JHIT squad," Commander Noles said.

"How nice of them to let us know. Who's this down from?" I asked.

"Not exactly sure, historically it's done by a panel of captains and I.A. Who knows, it may be the top brass at work trying to get a handle on this neck slashing thing."

"Aren't we supposed to have paperwork reflecting a joint task force?" Davis asked.

"Again, historically yes," Noles said.

"We'll sort that out later," I told Davis. "So, what's going on here Commander?" I said as we approached the middle of the crime scene.

"Detectives meet Alphonso Rodrigues," Noles motioned towards the lifeless body and slipped on a pair of reading glasses. He stepped into the light and looked down at a small pad.

"His body was found around ten o'clock by a Ms. Josephine Francis. He was an auto mechanic that worked at Sanford Motor Sports. He was found about 30 feet from his Nova. It seems like he had the misfortune of pissing off the wrong person."

The first two fingernails of the his left hand were slightly damaged, which may have been understandable since he was a mechanic.

"Who are your CSI's commander?" I asked.

He motioned, "Rodrigues, no relation to the victim, Peterson and the lead is Dr. Vincent Collier.

He's as good as they come. A Ph.D. in Forensics and another in Biochemistry," Commander Noles said as we continued to walk.

"Didn't I see him on the news a few months ago?" I asked.

"You may have detective. He's kind of popular when it comes to forensic pathology."

"If memory serves me correctly it was a federal case. Is he a Fed doing you guys a favor?"

"It's the other way around, he does the Feds a favor from time to time. He used to work in Washington, but being from Florida, this is where he hangs his hat. That, and he wanted to be near his mother after his father passed away a few years back."

With latex gloves on and stepping carefully into the dim-lit crime scene, I had forensics dust the surrounding vehicles for prints. But, there were no fingerprints or splatters of blood in any other areas of the parking lot. A quick peep over the video techs shoulder displayed surveillance footage of a green Camry seen moving by Antonio Rodrigues's body.

"Jarvis, I need you to run this tag," I reached over his shoulder and pointed at the green Camry on the screen.

Startled that I called him by name, he gave me a puzzled look.

"Your name tag reflects from the screen, I'm Detective Jackson," I extended my hand.

"Good to meet you, detective," Jarvis gave me a firm handshake.

Davis and I knelt at the body of Alphonso Rodrigues while Noles stood.

"This will be a fun thing to explain to the Chief," Davis exhaled a deep breath.

"Don't worry about the chief, he's been in situations like this before, as a detective," I said in a reassuring voice.

Davis moved Antonio Rodrigues's body onto his left side, just enough to pull his wallet from his back pocket. "Damn, this man has a wife and three kids! Check it out," Davis passed me the wallet.

The picture folds fell opened, apart from the rest of the wallet, spilling out pictures of his family.

"Has anything been disturbed?" I asked.

"Nothing's been touched," Noles said.

"Is Josephine Francis our only witness?"

"For now, yes. The EMT's had to calm her down. She's got acute asthma and recovering from a nervous breakdown. So good luck interviewing her."

"This is absolutely the worst part of the job," Davis said.

"The worst part of the job is to not catch this maniac." I commented.

Lieutenant Jarvis walked up to share more news. "The Camry belongs to a Millie Thompson who lives off Reinhardt Road in Lake Mary. Born in 1940, a retired schoolteacher, active in the community and a part of the senior outreach program at Bethel Baptist. I'll take a stab at this and say she's not your killer. She was in attendance here tonight for a wedding rehearsal dinner. Everything checks out with her. She left around 10 p.m."

"Thanks, Jarvis," I said. I stood from my stooped down position with my fingers interlaced around the back of my neck, looking down and thinking, *I'm between a rock and a hard place, nodding my head from side to side.* I sighed out in an exhale, "Can things get any worse?"

"Look alive partner, here comes Hodges with his want to be H.N.I.C. ass."

Sergeant Kirkland Hodges was pretty much the asshole of assholes. The kind of guy whose own parents probably didn't even trust him. He was a shady character to real cops and an ass kisser to I.A. and politicians. Forever trying to further his career at the expense of my fellow blues. He also ran with a shady entourage. I'd have to say; his super power was being a dick.

His blacked-out Crown Victoria rolled into the plaza parking lot, thru the perimeter tape and parked about fifteen feet from the crime scene. Hodges and Deitz got out and walked into the middle of the perimeter with Steak N Shake drinks in their hands and talking to reporters. The audacity. Even though Hodges was lead Detective, he was more like the lead schmuck, and his partner, Deitz rarely spoke.

"If it ain't the Mod Squad. To what do we owe the privilege this evening?" Davis said. He walked towards Hodges and Deitz chuckling and added. "We were just thinking about you. We need to know your take on this."

"Doesn't Central Florida's finest have it under control," Hodges grumbled.

I cornered Hodges from Davis's direction. Those two in the same vicinity was an instant recipe for an argument or worse. I led Hodges to

Alphonso's body. "It's the same MO But unlike the other victims, two of his fingernails were damaged and no lacerations on his left arm."

"How long have they been processing the scene?"

"Close to three hours."

"I'm going to need copies of everything pertaining to these murders and second, the chief wants us all in his office for a 9 a.m. briefing."

Hodges and I talked over details and possible motives. Hodges was a prick, but he also was a source of good knowledge of over 28 years that could shed light on the recent murders. Not even he knew what to make of this string of murders.

Hodges mentioned it being crimes of passion. Each of the victims had their throat slashed. So far, the tally was two men and a woman in various parts of central Florida. None of the victims had anything in common. A white male age 52, a black female age 36 and now a Spanish male age 41. All murdered in the same manner with no common denominator.

I sat on the hood of my Charger smoking a cigarette and thinking. If I should go to the Rodrigues residence sooner or later. I was leaning towards getting it over with as soon as possible. Hodges interrupted my thought with talks of known perps and their MOs. So far this had the making of a serial killer on the loose. The third murder just shy of a week. And by definition, we were chasing a serial killer. We were concerned that things would start heating up. One murder is one thing or even two that could slip by the media as regular homicides.

But a serial killer would be the spark of an interesting news story if investigating reporters were on their toes. And they were. They were on the far side pointing cameras from behind the caution tape. A third murder with the same MO was a recipe for something the OPD didn't want... National news.

It wouldn't be so bad if that's all it was. But aside from that, this could blow way out of proportion in different ways. The fact that a wacko is running around with a straight razor could stir up a real nightmare. Not to mention the impact it could have on the budget. We're stretched thin enough with working other homicides.

We didn't need Hodges to tell us that the chief would want to see us in the morning. We've been doing this long enough to know that politics always has a game plan. A special briefing with the mayor, address the issues and kiss a few babies. Thinking that Hodges and Deitz wouldn't be at tomorrow's briefing was out of the question. The two senior detectives have never worked a case with potential for so much publicity. They would do anything to get there shot, because of their addiction to news cameras and mics.

As he left the crime scene Hodges reminded me about the copies of the murder files again.

Officer Michaels was en route to the Rodrigues residence. His third month as Altamonte PD. I called him before he arrived at their house. "Hold off on your visit to the Rodrigues residence. I'll deliver the bereavement. Besides, I'd like to ask a few questions and maybe get a head check on the situation."

There was a sigh and an exhale of relief on Michael's end of the phone.

"This would have been my second time delivering shocking news," he said.

Chapter 18

My GPS led me into the Bakers Crossing subdivision in Sanford. A brick-paved road around two right corners and a third left brought me to 672 Bloom Street. Sitting on the front porch of a taupe house trimmed in white and brown was Mrs. Rodrigues, smoking a cigarette. She took a puff and stared as I walked up the long curvy driveway.

"Good morning Mrs. Rodrigues. My name is Traycee Jackson with the OPD. I'm afraid I have some—"

Before I could utter another word, a gun materialized out of thin air. And it was in Mrs. Rodrigues's hand. She sprung to her feet pointing it at me. "I don't care who you are. You tell my cabron husband to keep his whores away from me and my kids," She said, her voice arcing a heavy Spanish accent. "I am surprised. I didn't think he like black womans. So, you better be leaving now."

"I'm a policeman, Mrs. Rodrigues," I said as I slowly lifted the side of my blazer, showing her my shield and Sig. "Alphonso Rodrigues was murdered last night. His body was found in the Bahama Breeze parking lot in Altamonte."

Her face morph from angry to sad. She eased the hammer back into position and placed the gun on a table. *Was she planning on shooting Alphonso or his new girlfriend?*

She eased back into the wicker chair and took a long puff of her cigarette. "Did you said your name was Traycee?"

"Yes ma'am, Traycee Jackson."

She sobbed, and tears streamed down her face.

"We haven't been together for the last five months. He move in with his girlfriend and her roommate. The judge said he could pick the kids up to visit with them once a week. The last time he came to get them he brought his whore," She said, continuing to sob. "What happen to him, Officer Jackson?"

"He died from a knife wound. I don't mean to be out of line Mrs. Rodrigues, but can I ask you where your kids are?"

"They spent the night at my brother's house."

"Any reason for that?"

"Yes, we have three boys and my brother has two boys. They get together with their Uncle and cousins almost every Friday night."

"Can I ask what you were doing last night?"

"I was here playing Farmville and Candy Crush."

This visit was shaping up to be something a little more unexpected.

"Sounds like you two had a bitter break up."

"If that's what you call it. One moment he was here and the next, I get papers for his visitation."

"Do you know of anyone who may have wanted to cause him harm?"

"He liked to gamble a lot."

"Did he owe any debts?"

"I don't know, no bills ever came to the house. But there was this lady one time when we were out that keep staring at him. She was with two guys and he walked off to talk to them. I never ask him about it or bring it up."

"Can you tell me what they looked like?"

"It was an older black lady with two guys. One black and one was Spanish."

"How long ago was this?"

"It was a couple of months before he move with that puta."

"Do you think one thing had anything to do with the other?"

"I don't know. But they was looking at him like they was in on something together."

"Can you be more specific?"

"I see the look on his face when people would make him for somebody else. He squint his face like he don't know you. But he no do that with the black lady. They talk a few minutes."

"Do you feel like they were the type that would cause him harm?"

"I don't know."

More tears cascaded down her face, until she broke down, resting her face in the palms of her hands. I waited until she wiped her eyes. I gave her a card and asked if she thought of anything else to please give me a call.

Chapter 19

I left the Bakers Crossing Sub-division trying to wrap my mind around what Mrs. Rodrigues said and didn't say. I was curious why she would sit outside with a loaded handgun. A woman scorn who just lost her husband. This whole thing stinks to hell because of motive. It may be a good thing this serial killer got to him before she did. It had probable cause all over it.

I was enjoying the silence of my car. The rumble of the engine and the sound the tires make while rolling down the highway. It's along the same tranquil feeling as raindrops flurrying against a tin roof. It would be short-lived because my phone rang. It was Katlyn Chandler, an investigative reporter, and friend. Like all reporters, she wanted the scoop on what was going on, which was something I couldn't help her with.

But she gave me a heads up about a live report due to be given at noon, which was news to me. As far as I knew I was due to meet with the chief for a briefing on last night's homicide. It turned out that three of the commissioners that live in the sectors where the murders happened want microwave results along with microwave arrests. Giving a live report is only the first step of their plan from what Katlyn said.

Another call came in. It was Davis asking for an ETA I told him about twenty minutes and gave him a quick update on what Katlyn shared with me. I didn't have to tell him to keep it hush, but I did ask him to keep an eye out for Commissioners in the building.

Fifteen minutes later, I made my way into Chief Spencer's office to find the mayor, his assistant, Hodges, Deitz, Commissioner Beckwith, and Davis. As soon as I walked through the door, my phone rang again. It was Kamille from vice with a potential witness. At the risk of keeping my business remaining my business, I stepped back out into the hallway and briefly conversated and told her I would call back. I shut my ringer off and went back into the chief's office.

"Glad you could make it," Hodges grumbled.

"Sorry, I'm late gentlemen I was interviewing a victim's family member."

"Mrs. Rodrigues?" Commissioner Beckwith said, her voice arching a curious tone.

"She's the wife of the late Alphonso Rodrigues."

"How'd it go?" Bernard whispered, leaning towards me.

"It was enlightening enough to where I'll have to do a follow-up."

"How many follow-ups are you planning to do detective? Because so far you have zero scheduled for all the victim's in your murder book," Hodges boomed.

I nonchalantly reached for my Tic-Tac container and popped a Xanax. "I have follow-ups for two out of three of the victims. Laura Miller is from North Carolina with no local family members. Her son is in child services waiting for her sister to get him."

"What about the Flannigan file?"

"He started out as a missing person's case, but he was killed near the old Parkwood Plaza," I said. "The map behind his murder report gives that away. I still have to speak to Josey Talon who's a flight attendant and frequently out of town."

"There's no map in there," Hodges grumbled.

I grabbed all the murder books from him and thumbed through them, looking for a map I didn't expect to find. "I need you to find that map. There's information relevant to these cases. I don't recall giving you permission to go through the reports on my desk. You asked for copies and that's what you got."

"Maybe you haven't noticed but I'm the senior lead detective. I can do whatever I see fit to solve crimes."

"Does that include losing vital information?"

"We're not here to discuss that detective," Commissioner Beckwith chimed in. "We're here to discuss results."

"Aren't you supposed to be someplace rigging votes? How about you leave the cop shit to us, and stick to what you do best!" I snapped.

"Detective, that's enough," Chief Spencer interjected.

"With all due respect sir, she doesn't need to be here. We're trying to solve crimes and apprehend killers, not give inside intel for her fellow constituents or social media."

"Maybe you should play your part and let her worry about hers," Hodges said.

"So, I guess it's safe to assume that you're driving Ms. Daisey in that blacked out wagon of yours. I can understand why the mayor is here, this is his city. But why are you all wanting to discuss police business around someone who's been accused of selling information to news outlets," I said.

"Nothing was ever proved, and I resent your allegations detective," Commissioner Beckwith snapped.

"Like I said, leave the cop shit to us!"

Mayor Washburn sat in silence, taking everything in. He gave a nod to his assistant who then scribbled something on a sticky note and handed it to Chief Spencer.

Chapter 20

"I wanted salt on my fries!" The one lady said to the server, and quite loudly.

"We keep extra condiments at all the tables, ma'am." The server said, motioning at the salt.

"My drink isn't cold, it looks watered down and there's a thumbprint on my burger. You suck at your job. I'm not paying for this," the lady in the grey blouse and orange pants barked as her friends encouraged her by laughing and egging her on.

"That's your old drink ma'am, the new one you asked for ten minutes ago is over here." The server said, motioning towards her new drink.

"Are you challenging me? I'd like to speak to your manager."

In the midst of conversation, Carol, Natasha, and Joshua were doing tequila shots when Joshua saw his last supervisor, Sherrie, walk in. She was holding hands with Jason, an agent who got a promotion that should have gone to him.

"There goes that conniving bitch," Joshua said.

"I think I'll go over and take their pulse," Carol remarked. No sooner than they sat down Sherrie walked back outside clutching her phone to her ear.

Jason eyed Carol from across the restaurant while she walked over.

"I didn't know you two were a thing," Carol murmured with a smile.

"Not really, more like beneficial friends."

A waitress served them a Vodka Tonic and a Screwdriver. Carol took the Screwdriver and slid the Vodka Tonic towards Jason. "How did you know I liked Vodka Tonics?"

"Lucky guess," she said. "So, how's the new position treating you?"

"It's a lot to take in but I'll manage."

Just then the conversation took a U-turn.

"I like Sherrie, but she has no idea what I want, although I spelled it out for her."

"Has it ever occurred to you that some women have their own agenda?"

Jason's eyes went vacant, marinating her statement.

"Well, in that case, I guess I'm just playing the game to get ahead. Women do it all the time."

"You mean sleeping their way to the top?"

"In this case, yes. She has a secret reputation not everyone knows about."

"That she's slutty, I know. Just watch your step with her."

"Between me and you, she's a done deal. This is my way of showing gratitude."

***

Four months earlier…

"You have the highest scores of all the agents on the floor. That's three months in a row now," Sherrie said.

It was Joshua's monthly review. He had a knack for solving I.T. issues but hated being bitched at by customers. The truth be told, his skill set would take him a long way on the commercial side of SC&D, which is what he was aiming for.

"I hear they have a few openings on the commercial side. I've been contacted by two of their supervisors about making the jump. They said it would be a three dollar an hour raise. And with your blessing, I'd like to go be all I can be," Joshua said in an uplifting voice.

"I'm not going to be able to release you at this time."

"Why not? You just told me I have the best scores on the floor. Jason got in and I didn't?"

"Let's worry about ourselves, and how do you know Jason got in?"

"Because everyone's congratulating him. A guy I help on a daily basis. How's that fair?"

"I need you to help keep the team balanced," Sherrie said.

"Are you offering me a position?"

"Nothing different from what you're doing right now. I need you to help us reach the top seat before you go elsewhere."

"You mean hold me hostage, until you get a bonus."

"I don't see it that way."

"I'm trying to earn a paycheck and you're wanting to hold me back, so you can get a bonus and a pat on the back."

"My recommendation is for you to remain on my team until further notice. If it's any consolation, the newbies like the way you explain things to them."

"Isn't that your job?"

"My job is to have agents that get good scores."

"I was bought in with the understanding that I'd be a shoe in for the commercial side, because of my background."

"Did you get that in writing?" She pompously peered at Joshua.

"I'm going to Ms. Morgan about this."

"She'll call me. Then I'll confide in her about a would-be rock star with good scores and an attitude problem. And despite his performance, he's bossy, arrogant, and is anything but a team player."

"I was depending on that raise."

"Maybe you should downgrade your car. That's a Hellcat, isn't it? Maybe a used Honda Civic would better fit your price range." She added another partial stare down as she smirked.

"Don't be so sure of yourself," he whispered. "Now that Jason's gotten what he wants, maybe he'll do an upgrade and get a woman with some class. I'm not who you think I am."

"Excuse me!"

He peered at her with daggers.

Joshua had no intention of telling her about his hefty trust fund or that his father was Doran Smitz, a wealthy business owner with ties on both sides of the law.

Chapter 21

"I need you kids to change out of those school clothes and meet me in the backyard," Uncle Elton told Andre and Renee.

"The backyard?" Andre asked.

"Yes, we're going to go over a few things, and shake a leg, we don't have much time."

Renee and Andre strolled into the backyard as soon as Uncle Elton voiced his request.

"You two are still in your school clothes."

"Well duh, we just came from school," Renee said.

"I guess it's just the same. I don't want your mother getting wise to anything. Slip these on." He handed them a set of sparring gloves.

"What's this?" Renee asked, "Why are we putting on these funny mittens?"

"There for self-defense. Just in case you have to serve up a two-piece."

"A two-piece?" Renee asked while Andre and Uncle Elton made faces and extreme eye rolls.

"Boxing lessons!" Andre said, "We went over this the other night. Uncle Elton's going to teach us how to lay hands."

"Eww, no thanks, I'll watch," Rene said.

That being said, Uncle Elton began teaching Andre the basics in hand to hand. They were working on footwork and jabs when they heard the rumble of my charger pull into the driveway. Uncle Elton stashed the gloves in a box mark "poker stuff" in the tool shed out back.

"Hey mom, how was work today?" Andre asked.

"Okay, what have you two been up to?" I asked.

"What have we been up to?" Uncle Elton chimed.

"Yes, what have you two been up to?" I motioned at Uncle Elton and then Andre. "Because you're sweating and you're out of breath. And Besides, Andre, you never ask me how work was."

Uncle Elton placed a hand on Andre's shoulder just as he was about to speak.

"Traycee, I'm just showing the boy some drills. Just in case," Uncle Elton admitted.

"Just in case what?"

"I'm just giving him a few self-defense pointers."

"And what type of pointers would that be? I don't want him learning how to hurt people."

Uncle Elton told Andre to wash up for supper. He waited until he was inside before continuing.

"Traycee, I'm just teaching the boy how to avoid a fight with some style. You saw his head dropped when Renee was talking about that bully. It ain't good for a young man to get shamed at the schoolhouse. I'm just showing him some options so he don't damage his pride. Especially in front of his young lady friend."

"And what exercises will help him avoid a fight?"

"Little things like posture, footwork, and rules of engagement."

"You make it sound all fine and dandy Uncle Elton but—"

"—I used to be a young man once upon a time. I think because we're older we get used to avoiding bad situations. We forget how hard it is for young people. I'm not saying fighting is the answer. But it's always good to have an ace in your hand. And besides, it didn't work out too bad for you now, did it?"

"That was a whole different story."

"You're right. And now this is your son's story. Did you not think this day would come?"

My phone chirped an unfamiliar number, a few minutes before Davis pulled up, where he was greeted with the swift news. "I got a call from a Captain Beckham from the Sherriff's Department in Seminole County. We need to hightail it to Heathrow."

"I can just imagine what this is going to be," Davis said.

We road sirens and rack lights all the way.

"This is a first," Davis said, as we pulled into the multi-million-dollar neighborhood.

"A lot more eyes will be on us. This killer has been moving around Central Florida like bad germs. And now they're here, in the middle of high society."

I toned it down to rack lights only when we entered the subdivision. After driving through a maze of turns we pulled into an Alaqua Drive address. There were squad cars parked up and down the road and three CSI vans in front of the house. We hung our shields around our necks and walked up the circular driveway.

"Detective Jackson and Davis, I assume?"

"Yes, and I gather your Captain Beckham," I said. *I noted a uniform walking out of the front door with a handkerchief covering his mouth. It was normally something to overlook but a second glance proved that whatever awaited us on the inside was more than a homicide. The front of the officer's uniform was covered in vomit.* "What's the rundown Captain?" Beckham led us into the house after we slipped on latex gloves and booties.

"You guys will need more than gloves," Beckham handed us masks. "We're not sure yet but at a glance we think the body has been here just around a month, give or take a few days. So, it's kind of ripe in here."

CSI's in white coveralls were conducting batteries of tests.

This was more than a murder. There were way too many CSI's here. I followed Captain Beckham through a door with stairs leading down to a basement.

There was a mildew smell coupled with a strong stench of a decomposed body. Beckham slowed his descent, giving Davis and me not so much of a glance at first.

"Detectives, meet Timothy Smithers." Then he stepped aside.

There were the remains of a tortured man, filleted and sewn into a recliner. Dizziness overpowered my equilibrium, I stumbled up the stairs gasping for air. I made it outside, to the side of the house just in time to remove my mask and vomit.

I've seen my share of dead bodies. Some that rival the atrocity of the late Timothy Smithers. But this one was different. I knew this man from a life I left behind.

Chapter 22

Back at the table, Natasha eyeballed Joshua.

"What are you doing on that iPad?"

"I'm giving our loud mouth friend a dose of karma," Joshua nodded at the neighboring table.

"Too late for karma, they're getting ready to leave."

"Wait for it." He said in an exhale. He continued navigating the iPad through the Applebee's server. He installed a logarithm with a 30-second delay, giving him the authority to accept or decline credit and debit payments.

The server whose name tag that read Katie approached the neighboring table with embarrassing news. "Ma'am, do you have another form of payment? Your card was declined." Saying the latter part louder so everyone could hear it. Katie stood, smirking and waiting for the lady in the orange blouse to say what everybody says when they get such news.

"Run it again!"

"We ran it three times, and they all declined," Katie said. She handed the Visa card across the table, in front of her friends.

"Are you jerking with me? Get your manager!" The rude lady squawked.

The manager stood a few feet behind Katie. Observing the interactions so she could better gauge the situation. She was a short, pale, bean-pole older lady with red hair, that was graying on the left side.

"Hello ma'am, I'm the manager, Abby. We ran the card three times, and the system gave us the same response each time. I am sorry for the inconvenience. Do you have another card you might be willing to use?"

She pillaged through her purse and dug out a Discover card. She gave little effort in handing it to Katie, causing her to stretch and fully extending her arm to get the card.

"Let's not screw this one up," the lady griped as if she was disciplining a young child.

Katie gave her a bold smirking glance as she left to run the Discover.

"You guys have that look like you're up to no good," Carol said as she sat down and sipped her drink.

"Just dishing out a little karma boss lady," Joshua said while he continued to manipulate the billing system.

Natasha nodded to the neighboring table. It took no time for Carol to catch on to what was happening.

"What's going on with Jason?" Natasha asked.

"Just a quick head check and the pulse on his 'so-called' relationship with Sherrie."

"So how is it?"

"They need life support," Carol glanced over to see Sherrie sitting back down, and from the looks of things she made an inquiry about Jason's Vodka tonic.

"I'm gonna sue this crappy place!" A voice boomed from the neighboring table.

Katie came back with news of the Discover also being declined.

"Can you add her bill to my card?" A friend sitting next to her asked.

Katie and the manager took the card only to return moments later with news of it being declined.

"I just used that card for my drinks. It's got a limit of ten thousand," The friend chirped.

Abby stepped forward. "I ran it myself and the system declined it. I apologize, and I know it seems redundant, but you can use another card or pay cash."

Joshua chuckled.

"That's a novel idea," Katie said under her breath as she stood back in the cut smirking to no end.

"I'll pay it in cash!" The lady snapped.

Her bill was forty-two dollars. Which she only had twenty-two of. Katie stood next to the manager, turned her head and gave a slight chuckle disguised as a cough, which caught the lady's attention.

"Is something funny!" She barked.

"Excuse me, I was clearing my throat," Katie said with a smile on her face and another chuckle, watching the group piece the remaining balance together.

"I guess they won't be leaving a tip," Joshua mumbled and laughed just loud enough for Carol and Natasha to hear.

"She needs to be pissed at whoever dressed her this morning," Carol said.

"In other world news, I still haven't been able to get a positive bead on our John Doe yet," Joshua said, while navigating the ipad to different social media platforms.

"It'll come, I have a feeling it's just a matter of time," Carol said.

Part Three
HAUNTED BY ASSASSINS

Chapter 23

Davis excused himself and followed me out of the basement. Once outside he did a visual sweep where he found me in a slumped over position, wiping vomit from my mouth.

"Are you okay partner?"

"I Just needed some air." I threw up next to a pile of bricks and dirt. Where Smithers must have been having work done.

Davis snickered, "Looks like you missed the dirt."

"These killings are bigger than we think," I muttered while running my sleeve over my mouth.

Chances are there's more than one Timothy Smithers. But this one I knew. From a different time, and a different circle of life. In the two years that Davis and I had been partners, I never withheld anything. But information about the Dark Circle would have unlimited consequences. The circle I knew Smithers from, would accompany me to the grave.

Davis kicked a portion of dirt from the mound over the vomit. "Looks like you had Burritos," he joked.

"You're an ass," I replied faintly under my breath, "It's chicken."

I pulled the Tic Tac container from my pocket and dry swallowed two Xanax.

"I was just thinking it might be time for a Tic Tac or two," Davis said.

Little did he know. What looked like Tic Tacs to him was my growing Xanax addiction.

"What's going on here?" An all too familiar voice boomed. It was Hodges walking around the side of the house.

"This guy's like a cockroach. He always comes out when you have company," Davis murmured.

"He definitely needs a hobby or a companion," I whispered.

"Is everything okay detective?" Beckham asked. But he was looking in Hodges direction.

"Yes, just needed a little air," I told him before heading back to the basement.

Hodges fell in line, following us into the Alaqua mansion.

Captain Beckham turned and headed him off. "We need you to wait outside sergeant."

Hodges gave him a surprised look.

"We called Jackson and Davis because their J-Squad. More importantly, they have been working these cases which may be related," Beckham said.

Hodges growled, "There is such a thing as professional courtesy."

"The courtesy was asking you not to bombard our crime scene."

Hodges grazed a hand across the bottom of his chin, looked around and made his way back to his cruiser, where he sat listening to radio calls to save face.

"Is everything okay Jackson?" Beckham asked.

From what he observed there was a paleness to my complexion.

"I'm fine captain, just needed some fresh air," I said. Without offering any explanation for my abrupt exit. *Because unwarranted explanations can lead to probing questions.*

I took the lead back down to the basement. On the way down, I stopped at the last step causing a chain reaction. Davis bumped into me and Beckham bumped into him.

"What's the problem detective?" Beckham asked.

"No problem captain, all good," I said, motioning the CSI's to leave the basement. One was taking photographs, and the other was dusting for prints and working the black light for biometric oils.

"We need the room gentlemen," I added, in case they missed it the first time.

They both looked beyond me to Captain Beckham who gave an approving nod. After the basement was clear I closed my eyes, placed a death grip on the railing to maintain my balance. I was still woozy but felt I needed to embrace this butchered horror of a murder scene. Still, with my eyes closed, I removed my mask and took in a subtle breath followed by a gag, and a much deeper breath after that. The smell of old bile and exposed bowels filled my nostrils causing my throat to purge. But I fought it back down.

"You okay partner? Put your mask back on." Davis said to which I didn't respond.

Listening to the dead calm, I unconsciously tapped on the railing to steady my nerves. I focused on breathing the horrid air and inoculating my senses to the gruesomeness that lay ahead. Once my breathing was under control, I focused on what I'd seen on the first go around. The stench of dried up blood and a man's filleted body sewn into a recliner.

I opened my eyes and stepped down into the basement. The blood on the floor had dried to a thick gummy coating of maroon slosh. Which wasn't the worst part. Timothy Smithers body was riddled with thick and thin gashes.

"Is this what death by a thousand cuts looks like?" Davis muffled under his mask.

His phone rung from an unavailable number. When he answered, the line went dead.

"Who was that?" I asked.

"Must be another wrong number," he replied.

"Looks like they tortured him," Beckham observed.

I commented at a closer look, "Not only did they torture him, but it looks like practice."

"Practice?" Davis questioned.

"Yes, practice," I pointed at the cuts. "These cuts start small and shallow and then they go long and deep."

An empty IV was taped to his arm.

"We put a rush on the toxicology workup," Beckham said.

"You're only going to find two drugs in his system," I said.

"Is there a reason you don't think more drugs were used to aid in the torturing detective?" Beckham asked.

"His furniture is neat, no sign of a struggle, and no scratches on the walls or turned over chairs. He was drugged, placed in the recliner and then injected with an IV painkiller. Your tox will show two different drugs. And he was definitely tortured." I shined my Maglite on his face. "Look at the creases around his eyebrows. He was pissed and making an extremely angry face. He was cannon fodder for the homicides we've been seeing around town," I commented out loud.

"What the hell! Is this fishing line?" Davis strummed at the shiny thread with a pen.

"Not only that, but this recliner can be set to vibrate," I said.

"That would suck!" Davis chirped.

The basement had all the full-on toys. A fully stocked wet bar, three sixty-inch flat screens, four swiveling Lazy Boys with custom-made massage controls, a strobe light and two stripper poles.

"With a house like this, you don't have to leave home to have a boy's night out," Davis said. "This basement is pimped out."

"That's probably what put him in this predicament. This isn't a crime of passion or the heat of the moment. This was well thought out and finessed. I'd be willing to bet that this torture lasted well over a day."

"And how do you figure that, Nancy Drew?" Davis asked.

"All that brown stuff in between and on the sides of his legs that ran down the recliner and all over the floor is not just blood and guts. It's the bowel movements bought on from the torture."

"Whoever did this, gave him just enough drugs to ease the pain so he wouldn't pass out." I closed the restroom door, displaying the full-length mirror. "If that wasn't enough, imagine seeing an image of yourself sewn into a recliner, naked." I said, motioning to the mirror.

"So, what makes him different from the rest of the victims?" Davis asked.

"Aside from pissing off the wrong person. That's the million-dollar question," Beckham murmured.

"Timothy Smithers was the mark of an assassination. The kind of assassination that sends brutal messages," Davis commented.

"I agree with you to a certain extent. Because most messages along these lines are often done for the public to see," I suggested. "I'm going to need you to pull all incoming and outgoing phone numbers and all contacts, programmed and not programmed. As well as anything fishy with his bank account and emails. I don't think this was over money, but you never know," I said.

"This guy was a politician of some sort, right?" Davis asked.

"Judging from this house he was a big shot at something." Beckham motioned to the pictures of the late Timothy Smithers and other well-known political figures.

Just then a uniform came down. A special agent, Caroline Oakley wanted to speak with someone in charge.

"Any takers?" Beckham announced to me and Davis to our silent responses in the way of slight nods.

"I'm sure they're here because of the victim's professional status. And I'm sure the less they know the better for us it'll be," I said.

"I'm way ahead of you detective," Beckham replied before he walked out to meet with the special agent.

"Look at this mark in the blood." Davis knelt and shone his light. "What the hell is this?"

I knelt beside Davis and clicked my light on the mysterious half-moon shape surrounded by blood. I knew exactly what it was. But for the time being, I kept it to myself.

Chapter 24

A man sporting a dark suit and an earbud escorted Captain Beckham to a black, blacked-out Escalade. The rear window rolled down as he approached the SUV.

"I was expecting detective Jackson," A pale brunet, in her mid-forties with shades on said. "Captain Beckham I assume. I'm special agent Caroline Oakley and this is my constituent Wylla Wasp."

The door opened, and both ladies stepped out. Caroline was thin and wiry while Wylla had somewhat of an athletic build and was taller. She was a beautiful, dark-skinned ebony, maybe mid-thirties, with a serious disposition. She wore a black tapered business suit with double shoulder holsters on the outside. Her two-nickel plated pearl-handled Smith and Wesson .40s caught Beckham's attention. She had an awkward facial expression as she studied Captain Beckham.

"Detective Jackson is indisposed at the moment. I'm the ranking officer. How can I help you, agent Oakley?"

She took a step closer and whispered in a seductive tone. "No offense Captain but I'd much rather speak to the woman who knows what's going on, than a man, who's simply in charge."

"This must really suck for you then," he replied and began walking away.

"Detective Traycee Jackson born May 12, 1976, married to Wayne Jackson who's in Afghanistan on a string of suicide missions. Two kids, Renee and Andre. They live with their Uncle Elton Smith Thompson born February 4, 1957. Former golden gloves champion 1979-1982. Marines special ops 1974-1995 with four medals, one of them being a Navy Cross. He's also a semi-retired member of MI6," Wylla barked which caught Beckham's attention or was he startled, because up to that point she hadn't said anything.

"What was that?" He mused. "I almost had you figured for a mute."

"Now that I have your attention Captain Beckham, would you like to know what's not in the system about Traycee Jackson?" Wylla spewed, her eyes wide and eyebrows arching all the way up.

"Actually, no, I don't have an interest in what you're selling. From what you're saying, her family is full of bad asses. So, you may want to tread lightly with what you think you know."

"What I have up here can make you Central Florida's top cop," she said, pointing at her temple as if she had the cure for cancer.

"News flash," Beckham leaned in to whisper. "What the hell makes you think I want to be the top cop? I have more than enough shit to deal with at this level. Truth be told, I've been thinking about culinary school lately. Cute guns by the way. Do they come in purple?" He motioned two deputies towards him. "Make sure they stay away from my crime scene."

"It's important that we see this scene," Agent Oakley said. "And more importantly, we need you to pull Jackson from this case."

"Now why the hell would I do that? Is the FBI offering help and resources?" Beckham asked."

"We can't offer you any support right now but would like you to consider our request. This visit is strictly off the books."

"No-can-do agent Oakley. Over the last six years we've requested your help eight times and have never even been granted the courtesy of sending someone down here to help us out. So we started relying on the local JHIT which has been working pretty well so far. Now if you'll excuse me, I have a murder scene to wrap up." Captain Beckham put his mask on before entering the house.

As the Escalade was pulling off, a tapping on the window prompted it to stop. The back window slid a quarter of the way down.

"Can I help you, Sergeant Hodges?" Oakley said, which threw him for a loop, because he wasn't in uniform nor did he have his creds visible.

"How do you know me?"

"It's my job to know everything."

"It doesn't seem so in this case, but I can help you," Hodges said.

"Now why would you be willing to help me?"

"Let's say we have mutual ambitions."

"To what ambitions are you referring?"

Hodges faced the crime scene. "There's something in there they really don't want anyone to see," he said, adding an emphasis on the word, "really." "I've been here just under two hours and only six people have gone into the house so far. One of them came out covered in vomit."

"I'm impressed, Sergeant. You get an A plus, for stating the obvious."

"Don't be, but try to keep up. Jackson and Davis work for me, which means I have access to their files."

Two fingers holding a business card protruded through the slight opening in the window. "I'll be in touch, but for now, here's my contact info."

The Escalade disappeared into the falling dusk as it left the Heathrow subdivision.

Chapter 25

Back inside the Smithers house, Captain Beckham went over a series of checks and balances with two CSI's before going back down to the basement.

"That didn't take too long," Davis said.

"Typical Fed stuff. Black suits, black Escalade, naturally curious and hidden agendas. Special Agent Oakley and her constituent" he made quotation marks with his fingers "wanted to see you for your take on what's going on here. They also wanted me to boot you from this scene."

"Her constituent?" I questioned.

"A sharp-looking lady named Wylla something... Wylla, Wylla, Wylla Wasp."

I unholstered, rushed upstairs through the double doors. I did a sweep in a power stance, training my Sig for anything suspicious. Davis was on my heels backing me up.

"What's the play partner?" He called out with a confused look.

"SHOOTER!" I yelled. "TAKE COVER!" I called out to the deputies before dropping into a combat crouch.

With a two-fisted grip on my Sig, I sprinted up the driveway expecting to be fired upon. I trained my Sig from left to right registering all variables. I took cover behind a CSI van before sprinting up the block, training my Sig on every car, tree and house I passed. But the black Escalade was gone.

"Looking for someone detective?" Hodges boomed to which I didn't respond. I eased down on the hammer and holstered my Sig.

Captain Beckham stopped me as I made my way back up the drive-way. He whispered, "I've been doing this job a long time. I get the feeling this Timothy Smithers and Wylla Wasp might be above our pay grade."

"That's not even the half of it, captain. I can assure you she didn't have visible creds and packed pearl twins."

He gave me an incredulous look, squinting his eyes. "Is there anything I should know detective?"

"On second thought, I might have mistaken her for someone else," I murmured.

He gave me another look before returning his attention to a CSI holding paperwork.

I couldn't tell Beckham, Wasp was Dark Circle. A female network of professional killers, which meant she might have been contracting for the CIA with an FBI escort. I dry swallowed two more Xanax.

After wrapping up with the crime scene, Davis and I endured a quiet ride back to Orlando. I lit a Newport as I pulled onto I-4. I took a long drag and blew a hefty cloud through the opening in the window.

"I didn't know you smoked," Davis sneered.

"I don't. I saw one of the uniforms sneaking a quick smoke and bummed one."

My mind was a mile a minute, with nervous energy, restlessness and tapping my fingers on the steering wheel as I sped down the highway. Davis kept an eye on the road but most importantly he had a look of playing the recent events back and forth in his mind.

The ringing of his phone broke the quietness. "This is Detective Davis." And then the line went dead. "Probably someone trying to sell something." He blurted before acknowledgment of the eight-hundred-pound gorilla. "That Smithers scene was a first."

"It's a first for you and the Seminole Sheriff's Department," I said, pulling off of I-4 and accelerating onto Lee road.

I didn't mean to say it, it just came out.

"Don't you mean a first for all of us?" He questioned.

I pulled into the 7-eleven and parked. I took another long drag of the Newport.

"I meant exactly what I said," I sputtered.

A homeless man in a dingy overcoat approached my window from a milk crate, where he was sitting with a dog, asking for spare change.

"We're cops. How would you like a few days in jail?" I bellowed.

He was a husky, bald dark-skinned man with a scruffy salt and pepper beard.

"Nothing wrong with three hots and a cot Miss. Lady. Last time I was in county that air conditioning was humming," The homeless man said.

"We can't help you, sir. And furthermore, you're loitering. You're going to have to move," I snapped.

The homeless man lifted his beverage "I'm not loitering, I bought a drink." A beer wrapped in a paper bag.

"Ya gotta love it," Davis chuckled.

"You're kidding me, right?" I scolded, took a deep breath and slowly exhaled. "Sir please, just go sit back down and drink your beverage," I said. "Before I shoot your ass," murmuring the latter part under my breath.

"Back to what we were discussing," Davis said. "I either heard you wrong, or that cigarette is the shit."

"You heard me right, and this cigarette IS the shit. I should go over there and apologize to that bum and ask him for a drink of his beer."

"Why are you so shook?"

"Because Timothy Smithers wasn't who everyone thought he was. The circles he ran in were that of a different type of law, and above ours."

"Are you saying he was above the law? No one's above the law."

"That's exactly what I'm saying. Guys like that are untouchable, and above our pay grade. Timothy Smithers wasn't just a lobbyist. He used to work with the Special Activities Division. The kind of unit that the government doesn't issue uniforms to. With certified nightmares for connections. The kind of guys that'll make the president get a face lift."

"He's not untouchable anymore. Someone needs to fire his security team," Davis quipped. "At the risk of sounding more intrigued by you than normal. How do you know this?"

Davis's last statement had not registered with me. It was his prior statement although a swing at light humor that got me to thinking. *If Smithers kept the same routine with his security, he had to have been killed on a weekend. Which were the days he gave them off!*

"Is everything okay? I can actually see your wheels turning," Davis commented.

"BAKA, BAKA, BAKA!" We were taking fire from a man dressed in black near the passenger side of the cruiser.

Patrons scattered and ran for cover.

"GET DOWN!" I yelled. I opened the door and rolled onto the ground.

Davis unholstered, placed his barrel flush with the door and returned three rounds, backing the shooter up behind a cement spackled trash can.

A child who couldn't have been over five years old, left his mother's car from the gas pump and ran into the crossfire. His younger sibling chased after him.

The homeless man, with no regard for his own safety, ran into the crossfire, turning his back towards the oncoming bullets. "Hey young fella, come to Uncle Payne," He said, scooping the young boy up and out of harm's way. "ARNOFO PROTECT!" The homeless man commanded, pointing to the sibling toddler that was following his brother from the gas pump. The dog scurried and knocked the toddler to the ground and covered him. "ARNOFO STAY!" He commanded again, and the Labrador Retriever stayed put.

Their mother cried out from behind the glass window of the 7-eleven in horror.

"Oh, Lord my babies. HELP! HELP!"

It took three patrons to hold her down from running out into the flying lead.

"DAVIS, SAY SOMETHING!"

"I'm still here," he uttered faintly.

More rounds were fired into the passenger side of the cruiser. Some hitting, some missing. Davis cleared the remaining particles of glass, reclined the seat and returned fire in the direction of the assailant. The shooter took another position behind a grey minivan. I rolled to the rear of the cruiser into a prone position, resting my Sig over my left arm. I returned fire towards the top of the van.

Davis was safe until slugs penetrated the side doors hitting the front panel of the cruiser. Customers pumping gas disbanded in all directions. One customer almost ran into a guy riding a Harley as he bolted across the four-lane highway.

"WE CAN TALK THIS OUT!" I shouted to the shooter.

His answer was two more rounds of hot lead.

"Send rounds under the van," the homeless man said in a tone, just low enough for me to hear.

I eyeballed the shooter's tech boots through my sights. Oddly, there were a set of black pumps a slight distance behind him. And they were attached to someone who wasn't running. They were standing and casually watching.

Another round to the passenger side of the cruiser averted my attention. I scoped my spot, let out a slow breath and fired a round into the heel of his boot.

"AHH SHIT!" He wailed out in pain before going down.

I rolled to the opposite side, switching gun hands and bridging with my right forearm. Our eyes locked under the minivan and the cruiser.

"DIE! DIE! he yelled while training his gun at me.

He had me dead to rights with a line of sight to my head for a split second before a round left the chamber hitting his throat and severing his spinal cord. He involuntarily released the pistol. His angry, teary eyes locked with mine. His head slowly rested in a puddle of blood, and his eyes remained fixed on me until they turned vacant.

In my peripheral I noticed a black Escalade pulling on to Lee road as it left the scene. I trained my Sig at it, about to fire, until an involuntary gasp snapped me out of my daze. I up and rushed to the passenger side of the cruiser to an unresponsive Davis, riddled with bullet holes in his arm, leg, chest and a head graze.

"OFFICER DOWN! I REPEAT, OFFICER DOWN IN THE EIGHT HUNDRED BLOCK ON LEE ROAD AND ADANSON, THE 7-ELEVEN!" I boomed into the radio. "DAVIS, DA-VIS!" I shook him to get a response. But all I got was a long hick-up and gurgling sound.

"His lung is collapsing," the homeless man said.

I trained my gun at his face to back him up.

I shouted, "GET THE HELL AWAY FROM US!"

I eased down on the trigger, bringing just enough pressure towards the firing pin.

Sounds of the toddler made him give an order to his dog. "ARNOFO, CRATE."

The shaggy dog licked the toddler in the face and returned to the milk crate him and the homeless man sat at.

The homeless man raised his hands.

"Your partner is going to die, unless you put your finger in that hole to stop the bleeding, but more importantly, stop his lung from collapsing. That hiccup sound is his lung trying to get air."

I kept my gun trained at his head with tears streaming down my face. *For all I knew, he was here to finish the job, and him and the man in black were partners. No way was I not going to kill this guy.*

The sounds of sirens roared closer. My eyes shifted in search of a first responder, which was all the time it took for him to grab my Sig. He emptied the clip, cleared the chamber and stuck his finger in the hole in the side of Davis's chest.

I began hitting him. "Get the hell away from him!"

He took everything I could dish out, and grabbed me with his other arm, with a fluid like dance motion using my own arms to restrain me.

"It's going to be okay officer," he assured before letting me go.

Units and first responders arrived and took over.

"That was quick thinking man. You saved this cop's life," a paramedic cheered.

"Just got lucky, she did all the work," he said before joining his dog at the milk crate where he continued drinking his beer.

"You and your dog saved my children, mister. Can I do something for you? Do you need somewhere to stay?" The overwhelmed, overjoyed mother bawled. Her two kids gave Arnofo hugs and playful scratches.

"We're fine miss," the homeless man said.

The deceased assailant had no identification but would later be identified as Thomas Huggins, father of Jarred Huggins, Anderson Rains High School shooter.

After Davis was squared away, I observed the homeless man. *How did he do what he did?*

"I'm gonna sell this video to the news and get PAID!" A hefty-sized, twenty-something year old told his friend as he replayed the video. "Look at this shit. That lady cop freaked out and was going to shoot everyone."

The homeless man made his way to the two young men, verified what they were watching and low and behold, the kid recorded everything.

"On second thought, I'm gonna post this to my social media, and sell the rights."

The homeless man grabbed the smartphone and flipped through pictures and videos to find the footage. The two younger guys exhibited a failed attempt at wrestling the phone from him as they curse and continued their efforts.

"Hold it right there," I said with my gun to the homeless man's head.

"You're just a common low life. You're probably one of those vets that uses his skills to take advantage of people. Give me the phone," I said.

"I saved your partner's life," he griped.

"Spread'em."

He motioned to my cruiser, "You mean on this car with all the bullet holes?"

"We'll see how funny you are at 33rd, and we euthanize that walking fleabag."

The homeless man whispered, "These guys are trying to add to your collection of greatest hits."

"Do I look like a singer?"

"If the footage on that phone gets out, you'll be famous in a way you don't care for. I suggest you erase the last video. Or else it'll be next to the one with you trapping the dog in the car, so I know you like animals, Detective Jackson…Hurry before the phone locks," he mumbled.

Who the hell was this guy? And when did homeless people start watching internet?

"Can I get my phone back miss lady?" The young man asked.

"I need you two to back up," I said.

I flipped through the pictures and videos and deleted the last two before giving the phone back.

"You two need to see that patrolman. He's taking witness statements," I motioned towards a uniform.

I ran my hand along the homeless man's shoulder blade and felt a holster. I unholstered, holding my Sig to the back of his head. "If you flinch, or if

157

this coat blows the wrong way, I'll fill the back of your head with some hot shit." I removed two .45s from his double shoulder holster and a third .45 from his left ankle. "You're just full of surprises," I pressed the barrel of my Sig to the back of his head, hoping he would move, cough or even clear his throat. But he was way too calm.

"I was trying to help," he said.

"By having three .45s. Tell it to the judge. Right hand behind your back." I slapped one side of the metal bracelets around his right wrist.

Captain Livatt caught the side of my eye while I was putting the left cuff on.

"Detective Jackson, I see you've met Payne Cayde."

Chapter 26

Payne Cayde and Arnofo sat outside by the dumpster behind the Dead Shot gun range. They split a whopper with cheese while he went over the razor murder files. He masked them inside an old magazine he'd dug from the dumpster. He paid particular attention to the location of each homicide. The case files were given to him by his captain, in the wake of Davis being shot.

"That bum and his dog are always back there," a guy in a blue and white plaid shirt said, while he and another guy unloaded a crate.

"That gives me an idea," his associate in a white t-shirt said, calling out towards Payne. "HEY YOU, want to make a few dollars?"

Payne folded the weathered magazine and put it in his breast pocket. "Sure boss, what you got?"

"We need help with these crates," white t-shirt said.

"Arnofo stay."

Payne up and rushed over to give the guys a hand with the large wooden crates, stamped with Russian markings. He counted 16 awkwardly weighted crates. Plaid shirt gave him twenty bucks after the crates were loaded onto a long flat dolly.

"How would you like to make a few more bucks?" White t-shirt asked.

"Sure, do you have more crates? I have a friend that can help."

"No more crates today. But I'll throw you a few extra bucks to watch this back area," White t-shirt motioned with one hand, and with the other, he dug in his pocket and handed Payne a fresh twenty-dollar bill.

"Is it okay if I split the job with a buddy? Don't get me wrong boss, I'm grateful for the chance to earn money. It's just that I sweep up outside of some of the other stores around here."

Plaid shirt gave Payne a second look and went back into his pocket. "I'll tell you what, there's an extra ten spot in it daily if you or your buddy put the trash in the dumpster whenever we set it outside this door."

"Thanks, Mister, you got yourself a deal!" Payne said with a big smile as he went back to sit with Arnofo.

"Aren't you hot in that overcoat?" Plaid shirt called out.

"Not really. I take it off to cover my dog when it rains."

Payne and Arnofo had been staking out by the gun ranges dumpster for the past three weeks. Plaid shirt and white t-shirt gave him an in, as far as confirming the Deadshot gun range was dealing in outlawed guns.

"Hey Payne, what's shaking?" A homeless man named Kenny asked. He walked up pushing his cart and stopped to give Arnofo a friendly scratch behind his ears. "Good afternoon Arnofo. Who's the big boy?"

"Kenny, my main man, I have a job for you," Payne said. He reached into his pocket and gave Kenny the $30. "We have a deal to put the trash in the dumpster and keep the back lot clean. Depending on the trash days it could be as much as $30 a day."

"Are you for real?" Rodney said with excitement in his voice. "God is good all the time! The lady in the grey house on 45th told me she wants me to cut her grass and water her lawn every week now, because her lawn people ain't dependable. Man, things are finally looking up."

Kenny, in his mid-fifties, left his home state of Texas with the promise of a job at a Fortune 500 company that fell through. After his savings ran out, he was forced to live on the streets. But there were lots of homeless people up and around Orange Blossom trail, each one with a different story. The thing that set Kenny apart from everyone else is that he was friendly and helpful to everyone.

"How's the car running?" Kenny asked.

"Aside from not having insurance, like a busted chainsaw. I'm just waiting on it to die. I have an oil leak, a radiator leak and it's hard to steer," Payne said.

Payne had a 1969 GTO that was once blue. There were traces of blue around the rust and bondo that had not yet corroded. The crappy looking GTO was a part of his facade. Under the hood was a 6 liter, V8, 400 cubic inch engine. A chain welded under the hood gave it the sound of being an old out of shape clunker. That, and the clothes and toiletries in the back seat.

Chapter 27

It was six thirty and I was sitting in the Publix parking lot, across from the Heathrow guard shack, smoking a Newport with my eyes fixed on the gated entrance. I drifted off into space, wondering how the Smithers play went. How did this murderer gain access to his residence without being seen?

The footage from the guard shack showed nothing strange or any anomalies.

Was this the work of the Dark Circle? Was the question gnawing at my mind. I hadn't noticed my hands were clutched on the steering wheel until I released the tension. I raised the Tic Tac container to my mouth, dry swallowing a Xanax. I was snapped out of my daze by a call from Captain Rowley, wanting me in his office ASAP. At speeds over 90 mph, I was pulled over by a trooper. So deep in thought, I hadn't noticed my rack lights weren't working. Courtesy of Thomas Huggins. Slugs from the recent firefight damaged my cruiser's control panel. After showing the trooper my creds, I was on my way.

I pulled into the station just a little after 7 a.m. Captain Rowley was finishing up his conversation with another Captain.

"Detective Jackson, I'd like you to meet Captain Livatt."

We exchanged salutations and shook hands.

"I already know Detective Jackson. Her reputation precedes her. Rowley, I have to run," Livatt looked down at his watch. "I have an 8:30 a.m. with a human trafficking group. Are we still on for golf next weekend?"

"Sure," Captain Rowley said as Livatt left for his meeting.

Captain Rowley directed his attention towards me. "Walk with me," he held the door open and we went down the long hallway. "How's everything? Are you holding up okay?"

"Yes sir, everything is okay," I assured.

"How's Davis?"

"Still in a coma, Doctors are hopeful he'll pull through."

"What do you think of the flowers from the department?"

"I didn't see them, Cap, I called and spoke to Doctor Morrell," I said, slightly lagging in pace. "I don't like hospitals."

Captain Rowley stopped mid-stride. "I can understand that. There's lots of cops that don't like hospitals, and I get that. Do you think if you were laid up in some hospital bed, that Davis would visit you?"

I nodded, a sad expression morphed across my face. "I know Cap. It's just going to take some time."

"I get it. I know from experience it's awkward and scary," Cap said. He walked into the break room and poured a cup of coffee. "Between you and me, Hodges and Deitz are gunning for your case."

"He showed up at the Heathrow scene and was told to back off."

"What else happened? Hodges claimed you overreacted to something, pulled your piece, and ran down the street like a psychopath."

"I didn't overreact. We were being watched, and I didn't have time to explain."

"Well, he's your superior, so keep him in the loop."

"His idea of being kept in the loop is taking credit for our work."

Captain Rowley leaned inward towards me, "You're J-Squad now. The last thing you need floating around is that you don't work well with others. I know that's not the case, but give a squeaky wheel all the oil it needs. Hodges report about you will carry weight, with him being one of your superiors."

A few beats of silence went by.

"Have a cup of coffee. You look like you need it," He said, pouring dark roast into a Styrofoam cup.

I closed my eyes and inhaled the aroma before taking a sip. I savored the smell as opposed to the taste.

"Don't you take cream and sugar?"

"Normally, yes, but not today."

We started back down the hallway to Cap's office.

"Listen, with Davis out of action and Hodges gunning for your case, I made a move on your behalf."

"What move was that?"

"I'm pairing you up with another partner until Davis gets back on his feet."

"I don't need another partner Cap. That means I'll have to babysit some new guy who probably just passed his detectives test and thinks he's God's gift to solving crimes."

"This guy comes highly recommended. He's a new guy, but, he's been on the job for a while. Vice, narcotics, homicide and the trafficking division."

"Can't he decide which team he wants to be on?"

"He doesn't have a preference from what I hear. Until three years ago, he was New Orleans PD."

I stopped walking. "what kind of nutcase are you sticking me with? He's still learning the area."

Cap looked me in my right eye, "I need you to give this guy a chance Jackson."

He held the door as I walked back into his office.

"Do you know how long it took for me and Davis to gel?"

"Most cops would thank me for doing this. You're a good detective. I think you can catch this knife killer with the right support. I don't know if you're aware, but murders are up eight percent. I don't think I have to tell you, but a serial killer on the loose in Central Florida Is not only bad for the community but also our local economy, with this being a tourist state."

Captain Rowley sat at his desk and took a few sips of his coffee.

"The news outlets are making this guy out to be Jack the Ripper."

There was a knock at the door.

"Can you get that? I just sat down for maybe the only five minutes of the day."

"Are there any more surprises?" I asked as I opened the door. And there stood Payne Cayde in a pair of weathered Dickies, a Hawaiian shirt, and a weathered overcoat. I glared at him with guillotines, my head tilted sideways. I slammed the door and sat back down in front of Cap's desk. "It's for you."

Cap massaged his right temple, "Jackson, please, play nice."

"Tell me this is a joke Cap."

The door glided open and Payne walked in. "Good morning Captain," Payne said, shutting the door behind him.

"Detective Jackson, meet Payne Cayde. He's your new partner."

"We've already met Captain," Payne eyeballed me.

"How do you two know each other?"

"She tried to shoot me last week."

"Why am I not surprised," Cap said, pillaging through his middle drawer, in search of his bottle of Tylenol.

"YOU WERE INVADING MY SPACE!" I got out of the chair and stood in front of him.

"I was trying to help you and your partner."

"I had it under control!"

"You were freaking out."

"BOYS AND GIRLS THAT'S ENOUGH!" Captain Rowley yelled and held up a few sheets of paper. "You have been assigned to work with each other. You don't have to be best friends, but you do have to abide by the professional code of conduct that you are sworn to. REMEMBER? That oath thing you took, right before they made you cops and gave you guns... Oh shit, you both have guns." Captain Rowley lowered his head and ran his fingers over his eyebrows.

A few beats of silence passed.

"Jackson, I need you to bring him up to speed on what's going on."

"I've been going over the reports at my stakeouts," Payne said.

I sassed, "Did you spill beer on it?"

"I was working undercover."

"You're a lawsuit waiting to happen!"

"That's funny, I hear the same thing about you!"

Captain Rowley bought his cabinet drawer all the way back and slammed it shut, interrupting our banter.

He held up the bottle of Tylenol. "I've had this same bottle going on two years now. The last time I took a couple aspirin, was when that school shooting happened a month ago. The time before that," he massaged his temple again, "the hostage situation, when you didn't wait for backup, went into the warehouse downtown, shot up the two suspects and came out with the hostage."

"I'm sure you'll be needing a new bottle soon."

"You sound like the marrying type. Are you related to Action Jackson," Payne mumbled under his breath, just loud enough for me to hear.

I glared at him, grazing my hand across the butt of my Sig.

"I don't need an ulcer guys. This time next year I would like to have this same bottle of aspirin."

Chapter 28

Phyllis religiously took the same route to and from work. Semoran, left onto McCullouch Road and left onto Lockwood Boulevard for the home stretch. She hadn't paid attention to her two passenger side tires. A loosening of her valve stems caused air to trickle out.

She lost control after veering onto Lockwood. A turn she'd maneuvered countless times. The passenger side tires swayed, slingshotting her car towards an oncoming vehicle. Over-correcting landed her on the roadside at an angle. After the near miss, she sat with the engine idling and both hands clutched on the steering wheel, trying to catch her breath.

"Where's a cop when you need one," she sputtered aloud.

A helpful bystander pulled up behind her with flashers blinking.

"Thank God," she sighed.

In the rear-view, she saw a figure with a cell phone and a pen approaching.

"Thank you, thank you," she sighed again.

The driver's side window rolled down when the Samaritan addressed her.

"Is everything okay?"

She didn't make out the face, due to the darkness of late evening.

"I lost control," Phyllis uttered.

"Have you called anyone?"

"No, I'm waiting for my hands to stop shaking."

She zeroed into the hazel eyes on the Samaritan's face. "What are you doing here!" she yelped.

What she perceived to be a pen sprawled into something shiny.

She floored the gas. The lopsided car swayed down Lockwood reaching speeds of 60 mph.

She felt a wetness on her neck and chest. A sickly attempt to call out for help would prove she had no voice as a light-headedness came over her. Instant pain plagued her neck while she glared at her blood covered hands seconds before a full-on impact into a tree.

Chapter 29

Elizabeth Overstreet, forty-nine years old and an SC&D customer began her descent towards self-destruction.

"Why am I calling you guys every week about my lack of service?" She scolded.

"I apologize for the inconvenience, ma'am," Joshua said.

"I want someone out here right now with a stronger modem."

"You have our strongest modem ma'am. The issue could be related to your router. You may need to switch channels."

"This is a brand-new router, so try again, you jerk off."

"Excuse me?" Joshua remarked.

"You heard me. If you want to keep my business I'll need two months of free service and another modem, since you guys can't seem to get it right."

Joshua didn't respond right away. He pulled out his phone and snapped a picture of his monitor, capturing all of her personal information. He pulled her address up in a maps application before logging in to social media. Her and a friend, Nancy

Robbins, an SC&D customer also, were daily walkers at the Apopka Vineland Trail. He used his SC&D resources to look up Nancy's address, just in case. Her social media showed her standing by a grey Honda Civic on occasion.

"A two-month credit would require supervisor approval."

"You're getting on my nerves. It wasn't a problem for the last person I dealt with. They did it right away."

Joshua had long seen the notes dating back a full year. Elizabeth Overstreet was given a partial credit due to a signal outage. The notes and logs showed her calling every one or two weeks. He knew that telling her this would be cause for more griping. But at least she would know the calls were tracked and logged and it would possibly guide her to stop the frequent calling and demands.

"Our records show you getting a partial credit four months ago for an outage in your area. You must be mistaken about the last person giving you a two-month credit."

"Are you calling me a liar? Put your superior on."

"No ma'am, I just think you're mis—"

"—I need your full name, your supervisor and manager's name, right now!" She snapped with an arching tone. "Put your manager on the phone!"

"We're not allowed to give out our personal information ma'am."

"That's bullshit! You have all of my personal information."

It was the birth of bad intention that the angry, powerful woman had for Joshua. She had a reputation of getting people reprimanded, even terminated from their places of employment, and for much less. She had a history of using her husband's wealth and title to get what she wanted. She could give two shits about people needing a roof or food on the table as long as her rage was fed.

Yes, you bitch, I do, along with everything else, Joshua thought.

"I demand your full name, and I need to speak to someone in charge."

"Yes ma'am, please hold." Joshua placed her on a silent hold, where he could hear everything she said, unlike a normal hold with music playing.

Elizabeth Overstreet crowed, "Who the hell does this asshole think he's dealing with. Trailer-trash ass will be out of a job by lunchtime."

Joshua sat back, kicked his feet up and thought, exactly how to make use of his newly acquired information. He sent Carol a text before the transfer went through.

"SC&D this is Carol," she said after getting the rundown. "How can I be of service Mrs. Overstreet?"

"You can start by firing the asshole that was on the phone," she barked.

"Can you be more specific? Did he use bad language, was he rude or unprofessional?"

"He was all the above. And to top it off he called me a liar about my services not being up to par. And I'd like to lodge a complaint."

"I can help you with that," Carol hit a few keys on the keyboard, "I'm starting a report." She wasn't typing anything, merely punching keys for Mrs. Overstreet's benefit.

"He makes your company look bad. Because of him, I'm considering taking my business elsewhere. And I'm warning you, if I take my business elsewhere so will other customers. My husband is a well-known business figure, and I have a large social media following, so tread lightly."

"What can we do to keep your business, ma'am?"

"Aside from firing that asshole? You can give me a new modem and my two or three months of credit for the poor service I've had to deal with. And I want a guarantee that he won't be working there after today."

"It's against the law and an invasion of privacy if we were to release that information to you," Carol said.

"I don't feel comfortable with him having access to my information. Now if you can't help me, you either need to pass me to someone that can, or I'll do business elsewhere after my husband's office sends your company a legal letter. Your business and jobs will be on the decline when I share this with my ninety thousand followers. You're not the only game in town," she barked.

Carol's eyes went from brown to light hazel in a blink.

In her most sincere voice. "I understand what you're saying, Mrs. Overstreet." A few seconds went by while more keypunching was going on.

"Tell you what I can do, I have your email address as eoverstreet@scd.com, I can send you an email that explained what happened in a roundabout way. But I can't just come right out and say yay or nay on his job status after his panel review. But I will let you know if the issue at hand has been rectified, Fair enough?"

"I can work with that. Now what about my modem and three-months of credit?"

It was a two-month credit, you grimy bitch! Was Carol's passing thought. "It's already been done. We have you scheduled for a new modem on Thursday and you have three months of free service Mrs. Overstreet, and I apologize for your inconvenience." *You lying, conniving bitch.*

"Don't disappoint me... I'll be looking for that email."

"Of course, Mrs. Overstreet."

Chapter 30

It was a cloudy day, with on an off showers. Andre sat on a bench outside, parallel to the basketball court. He pulled papers from his book bag and double checked his Algebra.

"Is that what the smart people do during lunch?" Kira mused.

"Just giving it the once over before I turn it in," Andre said. "Besides, I hear you're the Brainiac when it comes to Algebra."

"I wish. I'm struggling to keep a B. We can't all be gifted."

The rain thickened, becoming more intense as it hit the ground. No rain fell on Kira and Andre, sitting under the overlay. But their lunch was over, and like the rest of the students, they would have to make a run for it.

They trotted toward the 200 building as the rain fell harder and more deliberate. Andre's left foot was kicked from behind him causing a misstep, ending with him falling to the puddled filled ground.

From out of nowhere Rodney wrapped his arm around Kira. "He'll catch up, he stopped to tie his shoe," Rodney said.

Concerned about getting her hair wet, Kira continued to the 200 building.

Once in the hallway, a confrontation took place.

"Is that how you get the girl?" Andre said, before taking an offensive posture towards Rodney.

They stood toe to toe as Andre dripped water from the puddle onto the floor.

"I can't help it if you have two left feet." Rodney pushed him up against a locker. "Now we know why you didn't make the team," he said, amping up his voice to attract attention.

Kira was ashamed of the spectacle that was taking place. She lowered her head and disappeared into the crowd.

"What's it like being overrated?" Andre said.

He stepped closer, standing face to face with Rodney.

"Overrated?" Rodney pushed him again. "I'm the starting running back of the squad you couldn't make."

The two-stood face to face in a crowd of students egging them on. Even though Andre was mad and displeased with what happened outside, he felt a fist fight with Rodney would be more embarrassing than not making the team or being tripped in the rain. He parted the crowd and made way for the boy's rest room to dry himself off and spend some alone time.

Chapter 31

Elizabeth Overstreet normally walked the Apopka-Vineland trail every evening before dark with a friend, Nancy, who could not make it due to car trouble.

No biggie, Elizabeth thought when she received Nancy's text. After a few light stretches, she slipped on her earbuds, queued up Lady Gaga on her playlist, and began her brisk walk. On average, she walked between three and four miles a day, using circular breathing to maintain a good pace, inhaling through her nose and out through her mouth. She pumped up the volume to the "Fame" album and was in her zone.

Two miles into her walk she caught a dark figure in her peripheral. With no other walkers in sight, she became alarmed. Deeper inhales and exhales aided her in longer, quicker strides. But the dark figure had not fallen behind.

In a panic, she turned around for more of an obvious look, stumbling and almost falling to the ground.

Conversation and laughter of two women headed her direction served as both a relief and comfort.

Call it women's intuition but Elizabeth's eyes and facial expression conveyed a sense of nervousness and fear.

The two ladies could tell something was wrong by the way they locked eyes. "Hi, would you like to be our third?" The taller of the two asked.

"Well, it is time for me to turn around," Elizabeth said. "Sure, the company would be great." She made a U-turn and joined the two women going in the opposite direction.

The man maintained his direction but adjusted his hoodie.

"I was glad to see you two come along. That guy was giving me the creeps," Elizabeth sighed.

"He had that, up to no good look." The shorter of the two women said. "I'm Natti," She added.

"And I'm CC," the taller of the two said.

"Nice to meet you, I'm Elizabeth. Do you two walk this trail much?"

"We normally walk the West Orange trail," CC said. "What mile are you on?"

Elizabeth looked at her fit bit. "I'm on my last mile."

"We have two more to go. You're more than welcome to tag along," Natti said.

"I'd be glad to. That would actually put me ahead of my steps for the week."

They walked, talked and laughed for another mile and a half, sharing conversational details about themselves. Until Natti alarmed CC and

Elizabeth that the man in the black hoodie was back and walking at a hurried pace.

"This path leads to the playground side of the parking lot," CC motioned, veering down a path through a wooded area, followed by Natti and Elizabeth.

"Anything to get away from this creep. Does anyone have a cell?" Elizabeth asked.

"Just my iPod," CC said, followed by a shrug and a nod from Natti.

"What's this guy's problem?" Elizabeth grumbled.

"Shhh, hold up, I think he's gone," CC whispered.

They stopped moving, listening for oncoming footsteps or rustling leaves. Their surroundings were silent for a few beats until a sketchy voice filled the air.

"Is he playing a radio? What the hell is that?" Elizabeth asked as they eased through the wooded path, looking around.

It was only a matter of seconds before the voice became shockingly clear. Elizabeth's conversation with Joshua and Carol. Joshua stood at the exit to the wooded cul-de-sac, swinging ignition wires from Nancy's car.

"What the hell is going on?" Elizabeth mumbled.

A set of hazel eyes met her confused gaze. "We'll give our regards to your ninety thousand followers," CC said.

A Paralyzing panic and terror overcame Elizabeth as the three-closed in.

Chapter 32

Shirley Murdock was the next customer in the SC&D black book. Her call was passed through to Carol as an escalation. Unhappy with the service, due to her own negligence. Her Dell laptop screen wouldn't power on. Instead of calling Dell she decided it would benefit her to call SC&D for a repair. The first agent that took the call, Kellie, told her they didn't repair computers. She recommended looking into calling Dell or maybe a local computer shop for repairs. None the less, Shirley demanded they send a service man out at once to fix her laptop.

The agent calmly explained to her that they were only her service provider. They didn't do repair work on any devices.

"My computer won't turn on and if you won't send somebody out, I want a refund for this month's bill. I pay you all a grip of money for my stuff to work!"

"I'd be happy to help you with that Ms. Murdock. Can I place you on a brief hold? My supervisor may be able to offer more help." In a pleasant voice from Kellie.

She understood that not everyone was up on technology. Some people didn't know communication companies didn't do repair work on devices. She didn't like that Ms. Murdock was so rude. Kellie went on record as to referring her to a supervisor. She'd done a good job on the call. With the threats, allegations, and ridicule, she remained professional and courteous.

Listening to the boring hold music made matters worse on Shirley's end of the phone. The feeling that nobody cared began to sank in. Whoever took the call next would be in for more abuse. She didn't care about cursing out a supervisor. Getting into an argument was her goal. All supervisors were on other calls and the hold time was near fifteen minutes.

"Thank you for calling SC&D this is Carol; how can I assist you today?"

"You can give me a God damn refund and send somebody here to fix my laptop. I've had enough shit from you people today!"

"I'd be hap—"

"—I don't want to hear what you'd be happy to do. Just fucking do it!"

"What seems to be the prob—"

"—Don't play stupid, you know what the problem is. I've been on this phone for over an hour, trying to get my computer fixed, bitch!"

Every time Carol talked Shirley interrupted. She was purposely waiting for her to talk, so she could cut her off. To the point of Carol being quiet. To where Shirley asked, "Hello, are you still there?"

At that point Carol just let her talk. She didn't bother offering a comp diagnostics voucher, which is what she usually did. But in this case, she thought *absolutely not.*

Twenty minutes into the call Shirley was still bitching, complaining and threatening about what she would do if she didn't get someone out there right away.

"I can find out who you are and where you live! Don't test me! I don't even like you high and mighty bitches."

"Ms. Murdock I'm afraid we're going to have to end this call. I apologize for any inconvenience that SC&D has caused you. We can't send anyone out to fix a faulty computer screen."

"Whatever bitch!" Shirley barked.

"I want to speak to someone in charge, now!"

There was a brief silence. Carol's eyes blinked from brown to hazel. "Well ma'am, I am in charge and I'm flagging your account! I see you have a history of calling my agents and giving them hell about things they have no control over. You've been in collections for the last five months and before that, your account was a write-off. So, we can do this one of three ways. One, you can pay your outstanding balance to avoid service interruption. Two, you can return our equipment, or three, we can send a representative with a police escort to your house to pick up our equipment. So, what will it be?"

There was a long silence. In the background, Shirley could hear Carol typing.

"I want to speak to someone else, Shirley griped."

"I'd be happy to help you with that. Should I transfer you to billing?"

"Fuck you, bitch! It ain't gonna be funny when I find your ass!" There was a loud crash on Shirley's end before the line went dead.

Carol finished typing her report in the notes section of Shirley's account.

Shirley Murdock's social media page would prove to be useful information.

Mad enough to be dangerous, and just careless enough to be in danger, Carol thought.

Chapter 33

"Nine-one-one, you're being recorded. Is this an emergency?" Margaret-Rose, Orlando dispatch said.

"There is a body at the Apopka Vineland trail," a calm female voice said.

Margaret-Rose didn't know what to make of the call. *Was it someone playing a prank or what?* Another red flag was that her system didn't display the entire number of the caller, only the area code displayed in the number section.

This was going on Margaret-Rose's seventh year as an emergency dispatcher and she had never come across this combination before.

"May I have the number you're calling from?"

"There is a dead body here and you're worried about my phone number?" the faint voice said before hanging up.

Chapter 34

Payne, Captain Rowley and I were going over particulars.

"How are we supposed to go from location to location?" I motioned at Payne. "Do you even have a squad car? Are we supposed to ride with that fleabag you call a dog to crime scenes?"

"His name is Arnofo. Riding around with him in my car would be better than going around town in that shot up hooptie you call a squad car. Last I saw, your control box had two holes in it and you're leaking something. Your sirens and rack lights probably don't even work. Who are you going to pull over with that clunker? Just so you know, my squad car is top of the line."

Captain Rowley lowered his head and massaged the back of his neck. "I hope this isn't a bad idea. I'm hating the fact that you two wear multiple firearms."

Our phones chirped a message from dispatch about another homicide.

"Have to run Cap," I said.

"Looks like a homicide on Apopka-Vineland," Payne said.

Captain Rowley dry swallowed two Tylenol and chased them with his coffee. "I need you two to not shoot each other today. Can you manage that?"

"Not making any promises Cap," I said before leaving the office.

Payne gave a slight nod, checked the rounds on his shoulder holster and walked out behind me. We took separate cars and pulled up to the Apopka walking trail minutes apart. A patrolman, who's name tag read Harris, escorted me to the crime scene.

"What do you have so far?" I asked.

"Elizabeth Overstreet, forty-nine, reported missing by her husband, Robert Overstreet three days ago. Her car was parked up front. None of her belongings were disturbed. Purse, phone and a change of clothes were in a bag on the passenger's seat."

"Did you run insurance, bank statements, emails and text messages?" I asked while slipping on a pair of white latex gloves.

"Doesn't look like they were having money troubles, He's part owner of a bank. Her emails are comprised of women's groups and charity organizations she funds. The last text she received was from a Nancy Pelgro. She was unable to meet her for their usual power walk. Her car wouldn't start."

"Did you follow up yet?"

"Not yet."

"What's her information? I'll do the follow up," I said.

Payne walked a part of the trail with Arnofo. Making mental notes of spots where assailants could hide. He noted possible shortcuts, until he walked into the crime scene marked with yellow and black tape.

"Hang back Arnofo," he commanded, to which Arnofo sat by an oak tree.

He lifted his badge to the outside of his shirt, just enough for the perimeter patrolman to see it before he ducked under the tape. He pulled a pair of latex gloves from his pocket and slid his fingers through the narrow openings.

"Are those claws not fitting?" I questioned.

"Here we go again," he mumbled, fitting his hands to the gloves and interlacing them for a snug fit.

Elizabeth Overstreet's lifeless body laid on her left side. Hands bound behind her back with ignition wire. And a gaping slice across her throat, where she bled out.

"I guess this is where she expired," Payne said.

"Yep," I agreed. "Pale on her right side, and the blood that didn't escape from her wounds, settled and turned dark blue against the left side of her body."

"There were a few people at this party," Payne pointed at her face.

"She was restrained and punched." I ran my finger along the edge of her jaw. "It's dislocated."

Payne knelt and opened her mouth to the sight of broken fragments of teeth. "Get a picture of this," he told a CSI.

"These small handprints on her neck suggest it was a woman," I said, grazing my hand over her neck.

Payne pointed to a series of footprints and zeroed in on one. "Looks like a size eleven. This same divot was near broken branches on the opposing side of the trail."

"That suggests they waited for her. Hiding out and waiting on an accomplice to guide her to this spot." I backed away from the circumference. "Those size elevens don't go past this point," I motioned to an imaginary circle. "She's about five feet eight and looks pretty fit. She should have been able to get away from one person with hands that small. There had to be at least two accomplices," I backed up a little further to lean on a tree. I felt light headed and couldn't catch my breath. I dry swallowed a Xanax while I studied Elizabeth's body.

"That's not a bad thing when it comes to tracking them down," Payne said. "Someone's going to want to make a deal."

I zoned out, remembering how The Dark Circle operated, a study of people, their immediate family, and their habits.

A ringing brought me back to the reality of the crime scene. I answered my phone. "This is Jackson." But it wasn't my phone. The ringing came from under Elizabeth Overstreet's left side.

Payne moved her from her left side and the ringing became louder. He motioned for me to retrieve the phone. I answered, thinking it would be a relative or a friend. But there was something strange about the phone. The battery was ninety-six percent full and yet Elizabeth was reported missing three days ago. The average phone would not have that much battery left.

I pressed the talk button. "Hello," I said into the mic.

"Hello," a sultry voice answered.

"May I ask who's calling?"

"You can call me CC. But more importantly, why are you answering this phone?"

I dolefully said, "I'm afraid there's been an accident."

"Accident!"

As we talked, I fumbled through the phone searching for anything. There wasn't a contact list, pictures, texts, incoming calls or numbers previously dialed.

"What type of accident?"

"Mrs. Overstreet was murdered," I said.

"Oh my God, that's dreadful," CC gasped.

"Do you know if she was having issues with anyone?"

"Yes, she had a false sense of security."

"Excuse me?"

"Detective Jackson I presume," the female voice became bold and more declarative.

"Who the hell is this?" I snapped.

"Your counterpart."

"Counterparts work together."

"We are working together. Haven't you noticed?"

I looked at the phone as if this CC would materialize in front of me. There were no incoming numbers on the display. It was a Tracfone, and it would be hard if not impossible to trace.

"Are you responsible for this?" I asked.

CC's voice morphed into another tone and speech pattern, "I'm responsible for answering calls of humanity."

I felt like I was talking to another person. "What does that even mean?" I scarfed.

"I'm helping society."

"By killing innocent people like a coward?"

"By putting a question mark in the minds of those who don't realize the limits of their security."

"You're a psychotic lunatic."

"Haven't you ever been mad at the same ones you're sworn to serve and protect, detective? Think about it. Maybe someone who thinks the rules doesn't apply to them, or someone who wants to be above the law."

"I don't know whether I'll lock you up or put you down like the sick animal you are."

"Temper, temper detective," CC warned.

"When I find you and your circle of cowards, things will get dark, very quick."

"I'll be in touch," then the line went dead.

"Who was that?" Payne asked.

"A lunatic," I said, placing the phone in a zip-lock bag. "Check this for prints right away," I told a CSI.

I ducked under the tape and left the crime scene. Even though we were outside, I needed some fresh air. Payne made eye contact with Arnofo, pointed in my direction which Arnofo followed me. Minutes later, the dog led him to my location. I was slumped over, leaning on a tree, hyperventilating and trying to catch my breath.

"There's a little more going on here than what meets the eye," Payne said.

"I think I'm coming down with something," I said.

"So, you had to come here to be sick or catch your breath?"

"I had to regroup and gather myself. What's it to you, anyway?"

"What else is going on with you? What's this circle of cowards?" He made quotation marks with his fingers.

I sprung up from my slumped over position, charged Payne and grabbed his shirt. "Like I said, what's it to you. Don't worry about whatever you think you heard. This is my case. As far as I'm concerned, you're a second-rate cop, trying to fit in wherever. You can't even commit to a department."

"There's more than what meets the eye, detective."

I released his shirt and went back to the murder scene, where I found Hodges snooping around.

"Detective Jackson, I've been looking for you? Where'd you go?" Hodges queried.

"I was canvassing for clues."

"What's this about a phone you recovered? And who'd you speak to?" He held up the plastic bag containing the phone.

"CSI couldn't pull any prints from it, so I'll hold on to it, and conduct my own investigation. The next time it rings, they will be dealing with me," he took the phone out of the bag and slipped it in his side blazer pocket.

"That phone is vital to this case. I have a rapport with the person on the other side."

"As your superior, I'll feed you information as I deem necessary. This is a high-profile case."

"If anyone other than me answers that phone there's no telling what could happen. You may put more lives at risk."

"Let's look at it like this. What I say goes if you want to remain a member of JHIT. Let me know if you find anything else," Hodges said before walking off. "Oh yeah, give my regard to Davis." He said with a smug look on his face.

Arnofo growled and ran a zigzag pattern whizzing by Hodges. To keep up with him, Payne collided into Hodges knocking him off balance.

"Excuse me sir, trying to catch up with my dog," Payne said. He brushed Hodges's blazer off before continuing after Arnofo.

"Watch where you're going, this is an active crime scene," Hodges grumbled.

Until then, he had only seemed Payne from a distance in a crowd. He suspected Payne was homeless or a construction worker taking his dog to the park on his break.

"Sorry sir, he gets excited," Payne said as he continued down the path after Arnofo.

Payne walked up after Hodges left the scene. "What was that about?"

"The usual load of crap from a sergeant who takes credit for everyone's work!"

"You're just getting along with everyone, today aren't you?" he said. He stepped in front of me and held up the Tracfone.

"What's this?"

"Slide of hand. He's going to be pissed when he finds out he doesn't have the phone."

I gave him a baffled look, "What are you saying?"

"This is your show Jackson. I'm just here to help." He handed me the phone. "I'm sorry about what happened to your partner and I hope he's back on his feet soon. From what I hear he's a hell of a cop." He turned and trotted away with his dog.

Who was this Payne Cayde? I wondered. I eyed him and his dog until they disappeared.

"Detective, we got a partial thumbprint from one of the ignition cords," the lead CSI said.

"Is there a name to go with it?"

"No hits yet."

"That means they've never been into custody and haven't been convicted of a crime."

Chapter 35

Altitudes, a bar on the roof in downtown Orlando was frequent to many wanting to wind down and relax. Shirley Murdock and friends, Bernadette, Michelle and Janice had drinks on the second floor as they people watched.

"It's been a while since we've all had a drink together," Michelle said. "Thanks for the invite." She added, looking at Shirley with her glass raised in a toast.

After a few more drinks, Michelle and Janice went down to the first floor to ogle the local talent.

"They're going down, let's go up," Bernadette suggested.

With drinks in hand, they found themselves at the third-floor bar ordering another round.

Feeling slightly buzzed, Shirley flirted with Helga, the bartender that made her Margarita. "That's smooth and strong, just how I like it," She said.

"Glad you like it, I aim to please," Helga wiped down the side of the bar near Shirley.

"We all love pleasers," Bernadette said before ordering two Tequila shots.

When they got them, they toasted to happy landings, the only thing they ever toasted to, even as underage drinkers.

"Bottoms up," Bernadette declared, then the two downed their shots.

And Shirley replied, "Bottoms down," they finished, slamming their tops face down onto the table.

They ordered full drinks afterwards to sip on.

A tall, dark, slender lady approached the bar and ordered a Cosmo. Her black and green body-hugging skirt with matching black heels caught Shirley's attention. She leaned on the bar with her foot on the metal runner while she ordered a drink. She had a velvety voice of dominance and confidence. Her perfume smelled like pure seduction, an arousing woman with long hair, a lean waist, and athletically stout legs.

"Excuse me, I like your perfume, what is it?" Shirley asked in an indulgent manner.

She couldn't control staring at the lady's hypnotic brown eyes. Her gaze moved from her eyes to her neck, stopping at her chest.

"I'm sorry, I didn't mean to stare."

"It's okay; it's a compliment, thank you." She said with a welcoming smile. "Is that a Margarita you're drinking? I love Margaritas!"

"Yes, it is, and I'd be honored if you had one with me," Shirley remarked.

"Sure, why not? I'm game." She pulled up a chair and sat down, taking a long drink of her Cosmo. "It's Chanel," she whispered.

Shirley leaned in and took a subtle whiff of her new friend's neck. "I like." Then she eyed her drink. "Will you be okay drinking that, and a Margarita?" She asked, sounding concerned. She got the feeling she was being invited to look. After all, her new friend was displaying encouraging body language.

"I'm good. Can you handle a Cosmo?" She commented, shifting her body towards Shirley.
"I'm CC. Do you come here often?"

"I'm Shirley. I've been here once or twice. What about yourself?"

"I've been here on occasion."

Helga returned and took their orders. CC ordered a Cosmo and a Margarita. Shirley looked over and gave Bernadette the nod, to which she went to the third floor to hang out with Michelle and Janice.

"I saw you and your friend toast. So, what should we toast to?" CC asked, sliding a Cosmo towards Shirley and with a slide of hand, she dropped something in Shirley's drink.

"I like happy landings," Shirley raved.

"How appropriate."

After more drinks and conversation. "How are you getting home?" CC asked.

"I'm thinking about an Uber. I'm pretty sure my friends are gone."

CC leaned in, "Don't be silly, I'll give you a lift, and then I'll let you make me a cup of coffee, or maybe even a nightcap." She caressed Shirley's thigh.

Chapter 36

The next morning...

In her panties and bra, and duct taped to her dining room chair, Shirley awakened to the smell of cigarette smoke. CC sat across from her, gazing into a compact mirror and puffing on a Newport.

"What's going on?" Shirley asked, and looking bewildered. "Why am I tied up?"

"That's simple. You're tied up because I want you to be."

She took a long pull of the Newport. "Pitiful. You have no idea who I am, do you?" CC placed the compact mirror on the counter and picked up her cell phone.

"What's this about?" Shirley's voice was frantic but still, she couldn't help checking CC out as she sat across from her in matching panties and bra. They were black lace with mint trim. She briefly wondered if they had sex. She smelled CC's Chanel on her neck and shoulders.

CC sat with her legs crossed, tapping her left foot on the floor, cueing the audio file on the phone. "Do I sound familiar?"

The cell phone she cradled began to talk. Her eyes were fixed at Shirley while the SC&D call played. The look on Shirley's face was confusion and wonder. Her facial expression morphed to shock after recognizing her voice.

"Why do you have my call with the data company on your phone?" She asked in a curious, yet hysterical voice.

Surprise reeked, and the silence grew as the voices became louder.

CC leaned in again. "Have you figured it out yet?" She straddled Shirley, gazing into her eyes. She pulled her head back by the hair and gave her a kiss. "I'm the high and mighty bitch," she whispered. She tightened her grip on Shirley's hair and blinked her eyes from brown to hazel.

"Oh my God! What's wrong with you?" Shirley cried.

"Not God, it's Carol, but you can call me CC." She paused and kissed her again.

With her free hand, she caressed Shirley's neck. The caress became a light squeeze and then a choke. Shirley wiggled her hands and feet in an attempt to get free. A hard stream of urine gushed from between her legs and down the chair.

"That's disgusting." CC eased a straight razor from the left side of her panties and slid it open. She slowly sliced from one side of Shirley's throat to the other. With her life coming to an end, Shirley shook and spasm until her carotid artery was dry of blood.

Chapter 37

Payne and Arnofo would find it difficult to find eyes where eyes didn't exist. Over the last few days, they mingled in areas where vagrants were frequent near crime scenes. They talked to dozens of transients, trying to get leads. At 2 a.m. they found themselves on Colonial and John Young when they came across a vagrant named Dexter. He claimed to have seen Anton Flannigan being murdered.

He described a dark sports car casually easing out of the John Young side of the old Parkwood plaza. "They weren't making any mannerisms. They stood over him until he stopped moving," Dexter said.

"They?" Payne asked.

"Yes, they. It was at least two people. They stood him up and then he fell and wobbled around. I thought he was drunk and maybe they were helping him. I didn't know he was dead until the next day."

"Whatever became of his nap sack?"

"Don't recall him ever having one."

After talking to Dexter, Payne went to the west side of town. A little after 3: 15 a.m. he parked behind the Publix building on 436.

"Is that your car?" A lady in torn weathered clothing and a nap sack asked.

"This car is the last of my worldly possessions. It's the only thing I have worth anything. And as you can see it's not worth much," he murmured.

"At least it works," the older lady said.

"By the way, I'm Payne and this is Arnofo."

"Nice to meet you two, I'm Ofelia."

"Good to meet you, Ofelia. I try not to drive during the day because of insurance and registration. It gets hot at night so we're looking for something to eat and a cool place to lay our heads. Do you have any suggestion? We were thinking about checking out that dumpster by the Bahama Breeze".

"Young man, that's not a good idea. A man was murdered in that parking lot just two weeks ago. My friend saw the whole thing. He said they slit that fella's throat from ear to ear."

After getting a few details about her friend, Winardo, Payne asked for a quiet, cool place for him and Arnofo to sleep. She walked them across Semoran Boulevard and down Palm Springs Drive while giving them the mini-tour.

He hadn't noticed until she walked under the light pole, but she was maybe in her late fifties or early sixties. She was a tanned, fit-looking older lady. She took off her ball cap to scratch her head; she had long salt and pepper hair.

She pointed at the "Bahama Breeze" restaurant, "That's where that poor man got killed. Winardo says he was in the cement enclosure back behind the dumpster, watching the whole thing."

"Seems like the right place to be if you want hot food. Do you know if they lock it at night?" Payne asked.

"The restaurants around here are kind of hit and miss."

Chapter 38

My breathing was shallow and labored. Beneath a black ski mask, my eyes shifted in different directions through the crosshairs of a Swarovski scope. From high ground, the scope danced from an old lady in an overcoat to a man in an Armani suit. There were passerby's' in all directions near a busy intersection. A pearl Maybach rounded the corner. In the back was a man in a business suit sporting sunglasses, talking on a cell phone.

The scope floated from the man in the Maybach to a policeman at a stoplight, followed by two guys riding full Hog Harleys.

My breathing was more labored but controlled. I tossed and turned. I slowly inhaled through my nose and exhaled through my mouth. With black tactical gloves I cradled an AR-25 sniper rifle, with an all too familiar index finger, nestling a sensitive trigger. I swayed the crosshairs from the rider on the left to the rider on the right, who wore a shirt that read "kiss me, I'm Irish." I took a breath, slowly exhaled, then I squeezed. The AR-25 made a single spitting sound, hitting the rider on the right in the back of the head. His body turned to

Spaghetti. The momentum of his cruiser sent him on a collision course into a concrete barrier.

I woke up, drenched in sweat, breathing heavy and strained. I looked around trying to gather my bearings. My heart was racing, my eyes wandered around the room, finally settling on my gold shield resting on the nightstand. I hadn't noticed, but I was clutching my .380. I eased the hammer down and placed it back under my pillow.

Chapter 39

Payne called to meet at the Burger King in Altamonte on highway 436. He needed to show me something.

Who the hell was this Payne Cayde? Was the question plaguing my mind on the way to Burger King. Who has a dog as a partner? As far as I knew, OPD only had K-9 dogs for sniffing out drugs and bombs. I pulled into the vacant parking lot to find him sitting on an old GTO.

"I have a potential witness," he said.

"Okay, are they invisible? Because I don't see a witness."

"We have to find him, but we can't look like cops because he's a vagrant. So shed your hardware. His name is Winardo, and I don't want to scare him off."

"Okay, where is he?"

"That's the million-dollar question. We have to put some leg work in where vagrants sack out."

We started by the Publix around all the business buildings, then the convenient stores and apartments.

The whole time I was expecting him to put a leash on his dog. "Shouldn't you have a leash on him?" I asked.

Him and his dog stopped walking and gave me an incredulous gaze.

"Would you put a leash on your best friend?"

"What if he bites someone, or runs off?"

"If he does, it will be because I tell him to. His name's Arnofo, and believe me, he's a better judge of character than most people."

"What's your story?" *I finally had to ask.*

"I was Southside New Orleans, Narcotics, vice squad, homicide, and missing persons division. What do you want to know? You name it, I've done it."

"How do you come to be in Orlando, Why not Atlanta or Miami?"

"Because Disney's here. Arnofo and I like the parks."

"How do you get a dog into the theme parks?" I asked, tilting my head sideways, squinting. Expecting him to tell me he knew someone that worked there.

"I put a service vest on him and we walk right in. We make a day of it every few months."

"Most people have families to do that sort of thing with."

"Been there, done that, now Arnofo is my family."

"I get it, it's taking shape now. Divorced, wife won't let you see the kids. So, you move here and bury yourself in work up to your eyeballs."

They stopped in their tracks and Payne held up his shirt, revealing bullet wounds riddled across his stomach and chest.

"My family was murdered by a group of masked cowards, in a staged home invasion. Technically, I'm still dead. I didn't move here just for Disney and my birth name isn't Payne Cayde."

Now I was the one frozen in my tracks and speechless. "Does anyone else know this? Why are you telling me this?"

"Captain Livatt and now you. And you know because it's okay with Arnofo."

"What the hell are you involved in?"

"This is a conversation for another time, detective."

We were further down Palm Springs drive when Arnofo spotted two tents behind a mom and pops store.

"Arnofo, play lost," Payne commanded.

Arnofo lingered to the area of the tents, crooning a low whining hum.

"Let's get a cup of hot coffee," Payne said, leading the way into the mom and pops spot.

"What about your dog?"

"It's time for him to earn his keep."

By the time we got two coffees and walked out, Arnofo was being fed Vienna sausages by a homeless man sitting in front of a red tint behind the store.

"Arnofo, where have you been?" Payne said. "I'm sorry mister, has he been bothering you?"

An older man looked up with a toothy smile.

"No, he was just keeping me company," he said as he fed Arnofo another Vienna sausage.

"I'm Payne and this is Traycee, thank you so much for finding our dog. His name is Arnofo. As you can see, sometimes he follows his nose."

"I'm Willie. Good to meet you. Are you new to the area?"

"We're just passing through, trying to get the lay of the land, the do's, don'ts and where not to go at night."

"People around here won't bother you as long as you're polite. You can pretty much go anywhere."

"No go near the Bahama Breeze restaurante," a man with a strong Spanish accent said as he crouched out of a blue tint.

Payne introduced us to him.

"Mi llamo, Winardo."

"We passed the Bahama Breeze on our way here. Do they have strict security?" I asked.

"I see a man killed last week. They put the knife across his neck and leave off in the car."

"Road off in a car?" Payne asked.

"Si senor, the tag say 'BEWARE.' I sit by the gar, the gar, what is word?"

"The garbage," Willie said?

"They no see me because I was by garbage dumpster. A gringo and two mamacitas."

"A man and two women?"

"Si Senora."

"What did they look like?"

"They look like you, but the gringo was blanca," Winardo said.

"You mean the women were black, and the man was white?" Payne asked.

"Si senior, very dangerous."

"What kind of car did they have?" I asked.

"Dark car, fast. The mamacitas get his attention, and the man cut his neck. They no rob him."

"Is it safe over here?" Payne asked, looking at Willie and Winardo.

"As safe as it gets. We're out of the way and there's always traffic trickling by. And there is a security guard working the apartments across the street at nights. Sometimes we run errands for him, on the count he can't leave," Willie said.

My next order of business was to pull footage from surrounding traffic cameras. So far, this killer was a ghost. And now a report of a man and two women makes for an interesting equation.

Chapter 40

Wayne Gordon called the Data company with an excessive amount of arrogant, belittling banter. His words were nothing short of combative. Natasha loathed being held hostage on his forty-five-minute call. Unable to get a word in edgewise, she focused and dug deep into his account. She glared at his address of 1122 West Beck Drive. Wayne continued talking down to her as if she were a child. She sat, doodling his address on a scrap piece of paper.

"If you had a college degree, you would understand what I'm explaining," Wayne said.

The time wasted on the call he didn't specify a particular issue. He called out of the blue to complain about paying for his service.

"Mr. Gordon, is there anything I can help you with? I can't control your having a bill every month."

"I've been one of your customers for almost two years. That alone should entitle me to a few months of free service."

"Managers and supervisors are the only ones that can make that call sir. If you hold I can transfer you."

"I don't want a manager or a supervisor!" He snapped. "I know it's within your power to give me something. I had a friend call last week and got two months of free service."

That's what they say when they can't get their way.

"If you were more intelligent, you would understand how word of mouth would help your business, and also help you get a good review from me," he said. "Now that I think about it, my girlfriend's SC&D cell phone might be interfering with my router. Which makes it your problem."

He then contributed to the issues he was having. He was an asshole using whatever means.

After the disclosure of his girlfriend's cell number. It was pieced together that he was the mysterious John Doe. The last agent to leave notes on the account was Joshua, followed by Carol.

"Found your John Doe, AKA Wayne Gordon," she texted Joshua and Carol.

In an exchange of texts between the three, disclosed his picture, name, social media page and his physical address of 1122 West Beck Drive. Which were all cross-referenced with Mindy Vaughn's social media accounts.

***

Days later, he was called from an unknown number along with threats from a voice impersonating Jack Torrance, Jack Nicholson's character in "The Shining".

He was advised to leave town, which he didn't heed. Thinking it was a game his thought was, whatever. He began the tough guy routine about what he would do if confronted. He'd finally mouthed off to the wrong people. The attention grabber was the verification of his 1122 West Beck address. Only then did he think there may have been truth in what was being said. He continued mouthing off, taking the call as a joke, or a wrong number, despite the correct address. He ultimately dismissed it as someone playing with the phone book.

Before the call ended, he was told, "We'll be paying you a visit."

Wayne tried to get a word in edge-wise, but the call was over. He was surprised that someone took a disliking towards him.

In his mind, he was a good guy, the kind of guy to be out at a nice restaurant and find a reason to give the server a hard time. He thought it was fun and had no consideration for other people's feelings or respect for their jobs. Now the shoe was on the other foot. He thought about who he had pissed off. And that list of people was a few pages long. He didn't possibly know where to start.

Days went by and nothing happened. He believed it was a prank from someone playing on the phone. He'd gone over the call a few times in his mind thinking what he could have done to de-escalate the situation. He even stopped being a prick to people for an entire day. When nothing happened, he thought he should have given the pranksters a piece of his mind. He dismissed the call as being made by some punks that had nothing better to do. After all, he pranked people as an adolescent for thrills and kicks, compliments of the yellow pages.

The dark Hellcat was parked in front of his neighbor's house one early evening. Down the street next to a limestone two-story house. No one was the wiser due to a neighbor's ongoing party. Natasha and Joshua sat in the Charger, talking and smoking, while people walked up and down the street partying. The longer they sat, the more ideas came to mind.

A beige Jetta backed out of the 1122 West Beck driveway, pulled out of the subdivision and drove down the main highway. The dark Hellcat kept a safe distance behind him. Wayne Gordon had no clue he was being tailed. He pulled in to the Publix near Colonial and Dean. Minutes later he came out with a few bags.

As he drove off, his eyes focused on a slip of paper under his passenger side wiper blade. It was wavering and about to blow off. Curiosity would play a role in his fate when he pulled to the roadside to retrieve the mysterious note.

It read, "Gotcha!"

"I just made fifty bucks," Natasha said. "I said it was the oldest trick in the book."

Wayne gave her a confused, yet surprised look, eyeing her latex gloves.

"Excuse me?" He snapped.

Joshua, with dark sunglasses, latex gloves, and a pistol, stood opposite of Natasha. "I'll take those," he took Wayne's keys and pressed the trunk button. "Get in," he told Wayne.

Once in the trunk, his mouth, wrists, and ankles were duct taped before Natasha drove off in the beige Jetta. Joshua followed in the Charger. They parked in a dark secluded area with lots of trees. Wayne, sensing the car had stopped moving began to panic even more. Joshua and Natasha stood at the rear of the Jetta listening to him moaning. He was so tough on the phone. His cocky, demanding demeanors seem to turn to fear and for sure uncertainty.

They removed part of the duct tape from his mouth as he lay in the trunk.

"Who are you? You have the wrong person! Let me out!" He cried.

"You know who this is, punk. Think, you dumb ass! Your mouth has been bouncing some good-sized checks," Natasha squawked.

"I tell you what, since we're fair people. If you can tell me who we are and apologize, we'll let you go. But, if we have to tell you who we are, your punishments going to go from zero to sixty, real fast! Killing you will be the least of your anguish," Joshua said.

Immediately Wayne knew the voice. He remembered it from the phone call. He sounded excited; he talked quickly and frantically; he was sure some sort of mistake was made. As far as he was concerned, he had done nothing to anyone. But the mistake was on his part.

He was told to listen to Natasha's voice, and still; he didn't recognize it.

She pressed play on her phone. "Thank you for calling SC&D this is Natasha; how can I help you today? Sound familiar?"

A sweaty Wayne Gordon squinted through two blinding flashlights. "Oh my God. You did all this because of a service call? What's that for?" He half pointed a finger at the rope, honey and the straight razor in Natasha's hands.

"It's for whatever name you want to give it. Vengeance, retribution, payback but mostly, it's to make you dead," she eyed him.

He was forced from the trunk at gunpoint, blindfolded and walked deep into the woods. He begged to be let go as they walked. Finally, they came to a spot.

They bound his hands behind him, tied him to the tree and duct taped his mouth again. A rope went around his ankles and the base of the tree, and one last rope circling the tree and his neck. He would be okay as long as he continued to stand. The wind blew, the leaves flew around making a heavy rustling noise. Natasha wanted payback, and she was getting it. But that wouldn't be enough.

"Looks like you're at the end of your rope, John Doe," Joshua said, as he stepped back, admiring his handy work.

Natasha cracked the seal on the honey and poured it from the top of Wayne's head and over his torso. She took the straight razor and gave him several long slits to which he grunted, unable to part his lips or cry out. She was careful not to slice too deep into his femoral or carotid arteries. "I recommend you keep pressure off of that left leg. Every time you put pressure on it, it'll bleed like crazy. As for your neck and chest, well, it's going to suck to be you pretty soon. You've been well seasoned, and your endorphins is an extra added bonus."

Joshua peeled back the duct tape. "Any last words?"

"Please, don't do this! I've learned my lesson, I'm sorry! I'm sorry!" Wayne cried as tears fell from his face.

"Yes, I know you are," Natasha said as she caressed the side of his face, and then she slit him again with the razor. "If we hear you yell out, we'll come back and make you wish you were never born," she said as they disappeared into the darkness of the woods.

Chapter 41

I received a call from Captain Rowley telling me to high-tail it to Colonial and Dean. Another murder with a similar MO.

On the way out, I walked through the living room to find my furniture was rearranged. And the culprits were facing each other.

"What are you two doing? You're up kind of early," I said.

"Just working a little Krav Maga," Uncle Elton said. He averted his attention back to Andre. "Always watch their feet. Their feet will tell you what you need to know. When they move to shove or punch, they'll always take a step to put weight behind it. And will most likely strike with their dominant hand."

"Hi mom," Andre greeted.

"Hi baby," I kissed him on his forehead. "I'm in a rush this morning. Make good decisions and be responsible with what Uncle Elton is teaching you. I have to run. Bad guys ain't gonna catch themselves. And you guys put my furniture back or I'll arrest you when I get home," I said before leaving the house.

I rode rack lights all the way to Dean and Colonial.

An unmarked squad car blocked to the side of a wooded entrance near a CSI van. Officer Jemirez made his way to my cruiser.

"Follow the yellow brick road detective," He said with a surprising, New York accent as he pointed at the yellow and black crime tape. "I think you may be late to the party, Hodges and Deitz came in about ten minutes ago."

"I was told we were the only ones beside you and CSI that got the call," I said.

"I heard the same thing. I'm new on the job here from New York. Hodges threw rank at me when I questioned him, and I didn't want to make unnecessary waves, with being the new guy. I'm sorry detective."

"That's okay, I'll deal with him," I followed the crime tape.

Out of the corner of my eye, I saw what appeared to be two FBI suits from afar looking in my direction. They could have been there for a few different reasons. But I had a growing body count to get to the bottom of, and I wasn't going to put much thought into their presence.

At the end of the tape was a God-awful stench radiating from a carcass strapped to a tree, identified as Wayne Gordon. His head was slightly severed. Blood from his neck attracted the local wildlife. That, and the honey they poured on him. His body was nibbled on by everything from fire ants to raccoons. He was slowly hung as the strength in his legs gave out. That, and animals chewing on his neck, didn't help his situation.

I caught a glimpse of Hodges talking to one of the CSI's. *What did he tamper with this time? And why is he here?*

"So, what do you think Jackson? It looks messy." Hodges said as he loomed closer.

"I think whoever did this isn't worried about getting caught. This was an impulse thing from something that's been building. It was two people, and one of them probably didn't want to go through with it. What's your take?"

"I think they're sick junkies pressing their luck. It's a rush for them to see how much they can get away with. Like the rich kids that go into Macy's for the rush of stealing. These victims are random people caught off guard," He said, sounding like he was giving a eulogy.

"CSI says postmortems been around a week."

The lead CSI motioned for me. He was standing by an older man with a small dog sitting next to him.

"Can you give me a few minutes Hodges?"

"No problem. Seems like you have it under control, we're going to head out." He took a few steps and turned back around. "I can't seem to find that phone from the Overstreet Scene. You wouldn't happen to know anything about that, would you?"

I gave him a slight gaze, so he could better come to an appropriate conclusion.

I hadn't noticed before, but Deitz was standing near the far side of the crime scene.

I made my way to the CSI and the older man. He and his dog have walked the same path every day for the last six years. Max, his Beagle, discovered the body of Wayne Gordon when the smell led him and his owner, Mr. Gillman, to the horrifying site.

As we talked, it came out that my partner put a few things inside a plastic bag when nobody was looking.

"Mr. Gillman, my partner is not here." I said.

"Then who was that feller you were just talking to?" His voice, curious and southern. "I suppose this is police business, but I watch a little TV, and I don't think you're supposed to walk around putting things in plastic bags. That other feller didn't think I was paying attention because I was tending to Max. But he was trick or treating pretty good with them bags. He gave them to the heavy-set feller while everyone else was looking at broken branches and footprints." He pointed to Deitz.

"He's a detective Mr. Gillman and I'm sure he had a good reason for collecting those items. *A reason I also would like to hear*. Mr. Gillman, can you tell me what direction you and Max came from when you arrived?"

Lifting a stick, he pointed in a diagonal direction that led the long way to Dean Road. "We came in from over yonder. Max charged us straight through those trees. I thought he smelled left-over food."

"Did you see anyone else back here sir?"

"No ma'am, this whole area was bone clean of people. I shooed away a couple of raccoons. I had to get this stick at them because they wouldn't stay gone. It's a damn shame how they went to chewing on that boy."

"You're handling this surprisingly well Mr. Gillman. Usually, this stuff makes people lose their breakfast."

"Young lady I'm a Vietnam Vet. I used to wake up to stuff like this." He pointed the stick at Wayne Gordon's body. "You better believe this was personal."

An instant curiosity grew. *What would Possess Mr. Gillman to say such a thing?* "Why do you think it's personal?"

"When I was in Vietnam, the only killing we did was business only. A man's going to be dead if he takes one round to the head or twenty. Some of them fellas would try their luck going into those villages to meet an acquaintance, and get found deep in the woods, worse off than this young man." He motioned towards Wayne Gordon's body. "A lot of times it boils down to simple respect."

"Respect, Mr. Gillman?"

"Yes ma'am, respect! Back in the day, there was quite a few men going into those villages to get involved with a new acquaintance, relieve some stress. Some men treated people in the villages like crap and others treated them like human beings. Nothing bad ever happened to those guys, but the ones that showed their asses got something else."

"I follow you."

"Detective Jackson, I have a feeling when you get to the end of this red-hot flame, that fire will be fueled by gas-soaked twigs, sticks, and big logs of disrespect," he whispered, examining my expression.

"Some people go a long way to get respect. It's a byproduct of integrity."

His look loosened from examining me to agreement. I took a little information from him and gave him my card before finishing up with the CSIs. I walked a few steps and turned around to ask him.

"Mr. Gillman, what was your job in the military sir, if you don't mind me asking?"

"When I got back from Vietnam, I became a 31 Delta, a criminal investigations officer. Good luck Detective Jackson." He said before him and his dog disappeared into the wild brush of the woods.

The alarm on my phone went off which meant I was on the verge of running late for a meeting.

Chapter 42

I found myself sitting in front of a Citizens Review Board thirty minutes later. I was being questioned about the incident that left Thomas Huggins dead and Davis in intensive care. Internal affairs had completed their investigation three days prior.

The citizen's board grilled me with below board questions.

"Detective Jackson, when did you conclude that your partner was in danger?" Stacey Belmore asked. She was a pale older lady who dressed like a librarian. Her family owned a few hotels. It was rumored that she had a few friends that owned media news outlets.

"As I said earlier, Detective Davis, and I were victims of an ambush. Is there something wrong with your hearing?" I said, looking the panel citizen directly in her right eye.

"There's no need to get testy Detective Jackson. We're just trying to sort this out." Mitchell Smith said. He was a semi-retired politician with a reputation of being hard on cops. His life had dwindled down to such last-ditch efforts to stay relevant.

"I'm assuming you have the statements from Internal Affairs," I said.

"Yes, Captain Rowley let us look at them briefly," Mitchell said.

"I have a question of concern detective," Doreen Feely said. A retired executive secretary with over 30 years' experience. "How is it that just shy of two months you and your partner have been involved in two shootings? Both resulting in death." She laid the report on the table and adjusted her eyeglasses.

The bracelet she wore threw me into a trance. It was a brass bracelet with knots around the circumference. The same kind Thomas Huggins wore. It flung me back to the recollection of Thomas Huggins shooting at us. The hateful look in his eyes. Him yelling "Die! Die!" And his soulless, vacant eyes when I killed him.

"DETECTIVE! ARE YOU WITH US?" Doreen Feely yelled.

My eyes shifted from the bracelet to the center of her right pupil, causing her to look away. "In both shootings, we were protecting the public while saving our own hides. I don't see why that's so hard to understand."

"Because over the last two months you and your partner have killed a father and son on two separate occasions," Stacey Belmore protested.

"If they hadn't tried to kill people, they'd still be alive. WE DIDN'T OPEN FIRE! WE RETURNED FIRE! It's that simple!"

"I'm afraid it's not that simple. Regardless of your semantics, the public and a grieving widow want justice," Doreen said. "This is a public out-cry."

The other civilian board member, Gary McJacob, sat quietly scribbling on a sheet of paper. A retired Navy man and for the most part kept a level head.

"Maybe you all should ride out with a cop some-time. Instead of passing judgment whenever some-thing negative happens," I said.

"Why would we put ourselves in harm's way? You are the ones that are sworn to protect and serve," Doreen Feely snapped.

"Far be it for you to know what really goes on in the field. Maybe you'd adjust what you say about cops."

"What are you insinuating?" Belmore crowed, putting her pen down and eyeballing me.

"Was I not clear enough. You think—"

"—That's enough ladies. I don't mean to cut you off Detective Jackson. I sometimes think my fellow board members are at a loss for words when emotions run high." Gary McJacob said, standing and gesturing to everyone. "My opinion is that we all need to support Detectives Jackson and Davis. Just imagine if one of your loved ones was at that high school or the 7 eleven."

"She's a menace with a badge," Doreen Feely boomed. "Tell that to Mrs. Huggins. Let's not for-get she lost her son and her husband to this death duo."

"Are you ignoring the fact that her son and hus-band went on a shooting spree?" Gary McJacob commented.

"He was a misguided young man and needed help. Given the right training they could have talked him down," Stacey Belmore said.

"Maybe you should look those parents in their eyes and tell them that. Or better yet, how about cranking up your S-Class and taking your ass to a funeral or two! Try selling your weak speech to their parents! And just so you know, Catherine Huggins is still receiving death threats behind her son's actions. Does the name Marius Green mean anything to you?"

"Marius Green is a drug dealer that's always on the news. He has nothing to do with this."

"His cousin was Michael Thompson, one of the victims. Need I proceed? Because you act like you got it all figured out. I wonder if I'd be sitting in front of you if I'da killed one of the Green boys?"

A few beats of silence went by.

"Truth be told, Central Florida could use a few more Traycee Jacksons," McJacob said as he turned towards me, giving a nod of approval. "I think our review is over detective."

"She's terrorizing the city," Belmore squawked.

"People like you are why it's hit and miss with us cops instead of a happy medium. A week from now you'll probably leak this story to your newspaper people, and it will be a crappy week for every cop in Central Florida. And the sad thing is, you won't mention how the two deceased woke up with plans of killing innocent people on their last day, which is what it should have been."

In a peculiar way, Huggins trying to kill us eased my mind. Better him than the Dark Circle. Oddly enough or call it a coincidence. Red flags were popping up in my mind about special agent Oakley, her connection to Wylla Wasp. I also wouldn't rule out Hodges feeding them information in exchange for information. It was too much of a coincidence and needed to be looked in to, below board.

Davis sustained gunshot wounds to his arm, head, chest, and leg. After six hours in surgery to remove the bullets, he would need months of rehabilitation.

Chapter 43

No matches for a tag reading "BEWARE" came back from the Florida vehicle database. I was thinking Winardo may have indulged in a drink that evening.

I pondered the theory, gazing at the word BE-WARE written in large letters on a steno pad. Was there any semblance or was I wasting time along with my thought process? My eyes shifted to the files on my desk, but I was deep in space, a limbo of thought. My mind's eye caught the huge central Florida map taped to the wall over two months ago. I looked at and studied it many times since these murders began. It was a broad map with assorted color thumb tacks for each murder victim. Pink for female victims and red for the males. Red and pink yarn went from their perspective colors to establish a radius or a pattern. I couldn't help shifting my thought slightly to Timothy Smithers. National turned international lobbyist. Who else knew about his murky deals? And if he wasn't killed by the Dark Circle, then who?

What other ties did Smithers have that weren't known by the agency? I glass eyed the map with a hypnotic gaze, thinking of possibilities of why the murders may have happened. They lacked swagger, not professional, but not sloppy enough to be random killings. Like the old timer at the Wayne Gordon, murder scene said, "it's personal."

Why would they travel all over Central Florida to commit murders? But maybe it was the other way around. Maybe the map was the clue and all the locations were the guide. My mind's eye was drifting further and further away.

"That's one less bill those prospective companies will collect on," Wynowski said.

The sound of his voice purged me from a conscious daze.

"What did you say?" I said.

As if he had just given me an answer to a pop-quiz question.

"I said that's one less bill those companies will be collecting."

I reached across to my desk sweeping the folders and reports towards me with both hands. The steno pads got mixed up in the shuffle, and upside down. I glared at it and my mind raced. I wrote 3RA-W38 on a slither of paper which is BEWARE spelled backwards. Maybe Winardo could have been dyslexic.

"Wynowski, can you give me everything on this tag and cross-reference these numbers carved into the victim's arms with perspective creditors?" I asked, I feverishly looked through the files noting bills and creditors the victims owed.

"I won't ask what's happening right now, because I'm married, and I know better," Wynowski chuckled, taking the slither of paper.

He ran the plate numbers through the database. "Bingo! This vehicle is owned by Duron Smitz! He owns a crapload of businesses. Some above board, and some not so above."

He looked at the screen for the make and model of the car while we talked.

"It says here he has eight vehicles registered under business names and another six in his name. He seems to like high-end cars." He said as he mumbled through them. "A Bentley, a Mercedes, a Yukon, the one you're looking for is the dark blue Dodge Hellcat." He wrote the name and address on a piece of paper, folded it and tossed it to me. "Let me know how it goes."

I at least needed to get the ball rolling on the Winter Park address. An hour later I was pulling into a long curvy brick paver driveway on Interlachen Avenue. The gate guard gave me a tough time until I flashed my badge. After I was granted access a servant told me that Mr. Smitz would be right down. He had an assortment of fine art accumulated over the years. Looking over the inner decor of his house I paid attention to a Sun Tzu statue. It was positioned in the middle of the foyer on a mantel near a marble chess set. This statue was of the warrior on a horse rising up on his hind legs with his sword rose. It depicted action, war, and rising to power. I knew this statue, I'd seen it one other time before, years ago. Only a few select people in the world would have it. It wasn't anything you could get from a local art dealer. Its origins were abroad. And it wasn't a knockoff, the features of expression of Sun Tzu and his horse were very detailed.

"I got that in—"

"—China." I interrupted before he could finish his sentence. "They sell knock-offs pretty much everywhere, but this is the real deal. There were less than five hundred ever made," I said as I turned around.

Duron Smitz was an older strapping man with salt and peppered hair and a matching goat tee. He gave me a look of curiosity about the Sun Tzu statue.

"Detective Jackson I presume," He said.

"Yes, and you must be Duron Smitz."

"Correct again detective. How can I help you?"

"This is just a routine follow up about a dark blue Hellcat you own."

"How can I be of assistance?"

"It was spotted at a crime scene a couple of weeks ago."

"I was out of town on business detective and besides, my son Joshua drives that car. But I can assure you, he's no murderer," He said, heading towards his bar. "Can I offer you a Scotch?" He asked matter-of-factly, making himself a neat Scotch.

"Thank you, but I'm on duty. And who said anything about murder? Do you know where I can locate your son?"

"He lives in Longwood. I'm not sure of the address but it's off of 17-92."

"I assume he works for one of your companies."

"Joshua is on a different path. He wants to do it on his own. Young people don't know when they have it good." He took a drink of his Scotch. "But I can respect building what you have on your own. It's a certain joy in it. He's taken a liking to all of this new age technology. How do you know of Sun Tzu detective? Few people know the origins of the great warrior. Let alone the number of authentic statues ever made since 500 BC."

"Let's just say I have an appreciation for art."

"I would say that's more than an appreciation." He faced the statue and talked about the struggle he went thru when attaining it. He talked in round a bouts. I knew exactly what he was saying but led on as if I was getting an education. "He was a very interesting strategist," he said. He motioned to a marble chess set that was still in play.

"Who are you playing with?" I asked as a man with a scar across his right eye entered the room.

"Abram," he motioned to the man with the scar across his eye. "Along with other talents, he was a chess champion. We've been playing this game for about two weeks. What kind of detective are you?" He asked.

"Homicide."

"I thought that was you, I've seen you on television a time or two, most recently over the last couple of weeks. So, you're the hotshot that likes dogs and kills kids. I thought you were OPD."

"I am."

"How is it that you're here in Winter Park?"

"My team goes everywhere. Me and a handful of detectives' work multi-jurisdictions."

"Are you the lead dic?" He said with a smirk.

"No, I prefer to get out and make things happen." I eyed him.

"Who's your commanding officer?" He asked in a casual tone.

"My next ranking officer is Kirkland Hodges; he's the lead in my precinct."

"I think I'll call him and let him know what a fine job you're doing."

"I'll be in touch," I called out as I walked to the door.

"I don't think so Detective Jackson," he murmured, finishing his drink in one gulp.

I studied him even deeper, something told me I'd be seeing him again. "Checkmate," I told him, to his puzzled look. "Black Pawns Bishop four captures white Knight five, which makes your ending inevitable," I said.

Abram studied the board with an astound look.

"Detective, do you know the true meaning of the Sun Tzu? Duron asked.

"Yes, I do," I said, and I left it at that.

His question was meant as a below board threat.

Seeing the Sun Tzu bought back memories that needed to stay buried. The basis of the statue to those who owned it was to eliminate every opposition in their path. It went hand in hand with the teachings. Usually, it meant the contracting of mercenaries with special skill sets. In the ancient time, they were called Shinobi which later became the Ninja. Chinese hit men who studied their oppositions before attacking with deadly force.

No more than fifteen minutes after I left the Smitz residence, I received a call from Hodges ordering me to steer clear of Duron Smitz and family.

"They need to be investigated," I told Hodges.

"I'll do that end of the investigation. Duron Smitz is a well-respected businessman, and I will not have you tarnish his name because of something a homeless crackhead said. Once again, I am ordering you to steer clear of the Smitz family. Is that clear?"

"I hear what you're asking," I said, before ending the call.

If the Smitzs' didn't have anything to hide, then why would he call the station? I called Wynowski.

"Wynowski, are you at the station?"

"I should be there in about ten minutes. What's up?"

"I'll see you when I get there, I need a favor."

Chapter 44

I sat at my desk going over pictures and statements.
Aside from that, I hadn't been spending much time
with Andre and Renee. I hated that Andre was being bullied. Though Uncle Elton was there to look
after him, he needed his father and me to cushion
his wounds; to comfort him and keep him on the
right path. Maybe Jarred Huggins could have used
more face time with his parents if that was the case.
Maybe an extra hug and more attention was what
he needed.

I was at an all-time low. I haven't even gone to
visit Davis who was still in a coma. What does that
say about me?

"Jackson, what's up?" Wynowski's voice took
me away from my thoughts.

I looked up in a dismayed manner.

"It's okay kid, I get it," he said, sensing my dis-
tress.

"I'm a piece of shit," I murmured. "My partner,
my kids, these damn murders and Hodges's she-
nanigans is just the icing on the cake."

"Trust me, I know how you're feeling," he said
as he turned my chair around, studying my face.

"This type of work isn't for everyone. But it's for you. You care about things. You're unorthodox, but you get it done. Truth be told, I would have shot that dog," he joked, instantly brightening my mood as I chuckled out loud. *I couldn't remember the last time I laughed.*

"How'd the Smitz thing go?"

"I have to do more digging. That's where you come in. Keep it hush around Hodges or he'll read you the riot act," I said. I handed him an address. "They know who I am, which makes it challenging for me to get DNA."

"It wouldn't be any fun if they handed it right over, now would it?"

"Tell me about it."

I picked up the stress ball on my desk, thinking of Davis.

"So, let's make the world perfect," Wynowski whispered.

After talking to Wynowski I made a beeline to Orlando Regional to see Davis. He was still in a coma, and unresponsive to treatment. His gunshot wounds were still serious. Doctor Morrell explained he had severe swelling on the left side of his brain that would have to go down on its own.

I sat with Davis for a while and talked. Although he was unresponsive, it was still nice to sit and chat with him for a while. I was longing for one of his off the wall comical comments.

"I haven't seen this type of coma in a while," Doctor Morrell said as he entered the room to replace a chart.

"What do you mean?" I asked. "How many types of comas are there and what makes his different?"

"In a coma, the brain goes on vacation and often takes every function with it. Although his brain is on vacation, he can still breathe on his own, when normally we have to put coma patients on a ventilator. In his case, that's a positive. Although he's hooked up to tubes and being fed intravenously, he's still somewhat in a dream state."

"I don't follow you."

"It's unusual for coma patients to breathe on their own. The brain controls everything in the body. The fact that the second nature function like breathing is working is a fantastic sign."

"Could you have the nurse notify me if there's any change in Detective Davis's status?"

I asked, cradling my phone close to my head for an incoming call.

"Sure thing," Doctor Morrell called out as I headed down the hall.

It was Captain Rowley informing me that our body count had gone from five to seven. I sent Payne to the Phyllis Smith scene, and I took the Murdock murder.

Halfway there my car gave out. It seems Thomas Huggins didn't just hit the control box and Davis, but also my radiator. I called a tow truck and then Uncle Elton to give me a lift home. I didn't have time to go through paperwork and fill out a requisition for another squad car. I figured to make use of Davis's Suzuki.

I got strange looks, riding the Suzuki with gun and badge on my hip, but it was nice. The last time I rode was when Wayne and I rented dirt bikes. The kids were small then. There's nothing like the open road. The ability to go as fast as you can handle. I exited I-4, rounding onto LB McCloud, stepped into third gear and fed the throttle before turning into Willie Mays Sub-Division.

"Are you guys switching to sports bikes now?" A bystander called out as I pulled up.

"What the hell is this?" Hodges barked.

"Whatever it takes," I said, footing the Suzuki kickstand down and ducking under the crime tape.

There was a slight stench upon entering Shirley Murdock's house. Inside was another silent story of murder. She was duct taped to a chair with her head draped back. Her eyes were vacant and fixed at the ceiling. Eyes I've seen far too much of. There was a gaping line across her throat and blood on the floor. That, and the weight of her head made the cut open wider. Along with running toxicology, CSI gathered strands of hair for DNA sampling. They put her time of death right at 20 hours.

There were cigarette ashes but no butts surrounding the chair, which almost suggests a professional, or someone with common sense. But there was an indention in the blood. The same half-moon shape found at the Smither's house.

"Our killer is a female," I said out loud.

"Bull shit, no broad did this! No broad did any of these killings," Hodges woofed to which I paid no attention.

Aside from the stench, I smelled a light scent but couldn't place it. There was a sweet fragrance to it. After seeing an assortment of perfumes on Murdock's dresser, I still couldn't narrow it down.

I noticed Katelyn was just outside the perimeter reporting at the scene. I shot her a text that I was inside, and to pan the crowd for potentials just in case.

Shirley didn't have any immediate family in Central Florida. Her cell phone revealed the last numbers called, a text with no incoming number, and a few other contacts about drinks downtown. She was still wearing the fluorescent green wristband used for admission. It was stamped Altitudes.

I sent Wynowski a picture of Murdock and asked him to check surveillance at the Altitudes club for anyone that was with her.

Just as I hung up with Wynowski, I got a call from Payne. "You're going to want to see this," he said.

"Give me twenty minutes," I told him.

I had enough of what I needed from the Murdock scene but asked the lead CSI to send me all photos and findings. I hurried outside where I met Katelyn's eyes with a slight glance and nod. We had an understanding and I would be expecting a CD of the crowd later on.

I hopped onto the Suzuki, lit the candle, click down into first and made love to the clutch as I slowly pulled away from the onlooking crowd. Some recording me as I rode away.

Chapter 45

Wynowski pulled up to a brownstone house with a brick paver driveway in Longwood. Although Joshua's Charger wasn't there, his roommate answered the door. She was a tall, thin, freckly-faced early twenties-something girl.

"Hello, I was inquiring about the blue Dodge that's for sale," Wynowski said.

"I'm sorry, but there are no cars for sale here," she said.

"Is this 809 Spruce Lane?"

"That's this address, but as far as I know there hasn't been any for sale signs on any of our cars."

"I beg your pardon, miss. My wife probably saw a Dodge here and thought it was a Hellcat."

"My roommate has a Hellcat, but as far as I know he hasn't mentioned selling it."

Wynowski scribbled his cell number on a piece of paper.

"Can you have him call me?" He handed her the number.

When the door closed, Wynowski strolled down the driveway, pulled a small yellow envelope from his back pocket and collected a few cigarette butts.

Chapter 46

I pulled in to the Phyllis Smith crime scene on Lockwood. I flashed my creds to the Oviedo PD, ducking the tape and putting gloves on at the same time. I walked around the Hyundai, noticing both passenger side tires were flat.

"Looks like a car parked in a tree," I called out to Payne.

"That's not all it looks like," he mused back, walking in my direction.

The driver's side of the Hyundai was blood-soaked. The car looked like an accordion.

"The airbags didn't do her any good," I said.

I carefully moved Phyllis Smith's head upward. There was a blood-filled laceration across her throat.

"CSIs says the car was doing at least sixty when it hit the tree." Payne motioned to the tree.

"There's no visible evidence that there was a passenger," I said.

"Not unless they bailed before impact," Payne said.

We walked two-tenths of a mile where Lockwood meets McCullouch. He pointed out the tire marks that became rim marks due to swerving into oncoming traffic and over correcting.

"They stopped over here, and a car pulled up behind them," Payne motioned.

"How do you figure that?"

"I've had my share of traffic homicides in the windy city." He stooped down and pointed out two different sets of tire marks embedded in the sand on the side of the road. "My guess is that whoever pulled up behind her, put the accident in play. They rode the passenger side rims all the way to the tree."

When we arrived back at the crime scene, Mathew Smith, Phyllis Smith's husband had just arrived.

"What happened to my wife?" He cried as a police officer guarding the perimeter held him from crossing the tape.

I walked Mr. Smith off to the side. "We're sorry for your loss and we are doing everything we can, to get to the bottom of this. Was your wife having issues with anyone?" I asked.

Before he could answer, Arnofo, sitting in Payne's clunker let off a bark and a short howl.

"That's my time," Payne said. "I'll be in touch."

"Where are you going," I asked as he got in his clunker and pulled off.

"Detective, I'd like to have a word," an all too familiar voice boomed.

It was Hodges, and this was getting a little annoying.

I excused myself from Mr. Smith to consult with Hodges.

"Don't you think I needed to know there was another murder when you left the Murdock scene?"

"I saw you were busy, and I had what I needed from that location. Why disturb you from collecting further evidence?"

"I need to be aware of what you're doing and your findings," he barked.

"Right now, I'm processing a scene and talking to next of kin. So, if you're done trying to micromanage me, I'd like to get back to work." I took a few steps, and something dawned on me. "How is it that you're showing up at all of these crime scenes? They aren't going out over the radio, and they're out of your jurisdiction."

"You answer to me, not the other way around! Remember that detective."

Any other time I would have been pissed. But he was becoming more like the dog that barks at the moon. The only difference between him and the dog was loyalty.

"Detective, another word if you don't mind," He called back.

I turn back around, giving him a humdrum look.

"I'll finish this portion of the investigation. You're relieved from this scene."

"I was in the process of talking to next of kin. I need to finish the interview!" I bellowed.

"Deitz and I will finish it," he boomed.

That was fine with me. I'd already gotten what I needed from the scene.

I slipped Mr. Smith my card. "The lead detective will finish this portion of the investigation, in the meantime, if you think of anything or have questions, please call me."

"DETECTIVE!" Hodges boomed again.

"If you need me, I'll be doing more detective work," I said.

I rode off on the Suzuki thinking about what a talented dog Arnofo was. My curiosity about Payne blossomed. He had a knack for avoiding Hodges. Or maybe he avoided people that hindered his progress.

I arrived at the station, to find two manila envelopes on my desk.

One labeled KC was from Katelyn and the one with the drawing of pizza was from Wynowski. His envelope had a note attached that read, "Bingo, compliments of littering and partial Altitudes footage."

Inside, a smaller envelope containing two cigarette butts with Joshua's address. Along with that, there was a CD. A partial video of Shirley Murdock at Altitudes, having drinks with an unknown woman. The sunglasses and wide fedora she wore suggests she knew where the cameras were. Every time she removed her sunglasses her back was facing the camera.

The second CD showed an assortment of onlookers to which I watched, again and again, trying to see something different, but no cigar.

I sat pondering, there had to be a connection with Joshua Smitz and this lady.

A text from Kailey came through reading "lunch?"

I returned, "sure a quick one."

Chapter 47

Twenty minutes later I was sitting in Chef Eddies, with what we call "The Auxiliary." A close-knit group of women that work in, and around law enforcement. It was hard for all of us to get together due to different schedules.

"Hey girl, I see you've been busy, no time for your friends anymore," Kailey said.

"You don't know the half. These cases have me running in circles," I said.

"My sister should be here in a few."

"I didn't know you had a sister."

"My baby sisters been working for the city for a few years now."

Sharri and Megan walked in at the same time.

"Looks like I'm in danger of losing the, being late title," I joked.

Sharri was an attorney and Megan, a private investigator.

"Where's everybody else?" Megan asked.

"Busy schedules girl," Kailey said.

We ordered and continued our conversation. A few minutes later Rebecca joined us. She was looking seriously pissed.

"Damn girl, tough day?" Sharri said, her voice curving at the end.

"Just dealing with a bunch of assholes today," She murmured. "I hate power-tripping Judges."

"You could have been one of those power-tripping Judges," I reminded her.

"I've been kicking myself in the butt over that lately. You'd think that some of these kids are career criminals by how they get sentenced. Many of them are smart kids that have made one boneheaded decision."

Aside from being a lawyer, Rebecca took lots of pro-bono cases for kids. It was personal with her. As a youngster, her brother was sentenced to eighteen months in prison for being in the wrong place at the wrong time, something that happens far too often among young people. If his public defender would have just done a little more digging, he could have gotten the case thrown out.

"It'll get better Becca," Megan said.

Kailey stood and eyed a young lady from across the room as she approached their table. "I'd like you all to meet my baby sister, Kamille. She works for vice squad."

There were salutations around the table.

Kamille and I crossed gazes.

"You gave us a tip a while ago that helped prevent another Columbine." I raised a glass of water towards her. "Keep up the good work."

"Thank you, Detective Jackson."

"Traycee," I said.

"Columbine!" Kailey shrieked.

"Just one more reason why kids shouldn't play with guns."

"So how is everything going with the cases," Kamille asked.

"Cat and mousing and dealing with resistance."

"That would be Kirkland Hodges?"

"How'd you know."

"Word gets around. The consensus in my department is to treat him like the flu."

I thought back to Payne disappearing when Hodges showed at the Smith scene.

"That puts a few things into perspective."

The TracFone in my pocket rang. I excused myself from the girls and went outside.

"This needs to stop!" I said into the mic.

"Well, hello to you too, Detective Jackson," the voice gushed. "Are you enjoying your Easter egg hunt? How's business?"

"I'm in the business of putting people like you behind bars or in the ground," I snapped.

"Careful detective, you don't want me to take my anger out on the ones you're sworn to serve and protect."

"I can't wait to see the look on your face when I take out the trash."

"My murder game is tight," she said in a sultry, sadistic voice.

"I know you're not acting alone, and I'm going to find you and your puppets. It's just a matter of time.

"Temper, temper, detective, you're reaching now."

"Am I?" I questioned. "You might think you're tight work, but your people have been leaving breadcrumbs all over Central Florida."

There was laughing on the line.

"The Menthol butts found at crimes scenes tell another story, which means your pets have been going out without a leash."

The line got deathly quiet.

"They say imitation is a form of flattery. Be sure to check your rear-view for copycats," and then the line went dead.

Chapter 48

I tossed and turned, and it was hard to breathe. Gripping my sheets along with rapid movement beneath my eyelids.

A delivery man in a black suit appeared with a package in hand.

"P. Phantom, confirm for assignment," he said with one hand on his pistol and the other readying a scanner.

"Operative 214610, P. Phantom security code FUQ2," I confirmed, and in acceptance of delivery, activation of Pamela Phantom, professional killer. He scanned my left eye and handed me an envelope.

Three other code names were also activated. Stephanie Slaughter, Harmony Hatchet, and Yolanda Youngblood.

Objective, the elimination of four up-and-coming power brokers and lobbyist, Martin Abis, Janet Stills, Stephen Ward, and Timothy Smithers. The powers that be, felt they'd cause far more harm than good. Granting us authorization to be dispatched.

They were due in Miami Beach, for a ten thousand dollar per plate charity.

Stephanie Slaughter donned a fitting white and lavender gown as she talked over the power of influence with Martin Abis.

Taken in by how mysterious and entertaining she was, he noticed their glasses were almost empty. "Can I get you another drink?" Martin requested.

"Of course!" She smiled and handed him her glass.

They were drinking from the Chateau Margaux collection. When he returned with their drinks, she promptly took a sip before squirting a dose of cyanide in her wineglass. She stepped closer to him with the posture of a friendly hug, purposely spilling his drink.

"I'm so sorry, take mine, I'll get another," She apologized, taking his empty glass and giving him her full one.

Martin Abis, stood, gazing at her as she walked to the bar before taking a casual fatal last sip and collapsing.

Janet Stills left her penthouse suite on the 16th floor donning a blue evening gown. The elevator took some time to arrive but when it did, she stepped into the company of Harmony Hatchet, dressed in housekeeping attire and wearing an auburn wig.

"That's a lovely gown," Harmony commented.

"Thanks," was the one-word response from Janet Stills, giving the pretend housekeeper a nasty look, clutching her four-thousand-dollar purse.

Before the doors closed Janet asked, "Can you take the next ride down or the service elevator?"

"I'm sorry if I've offended you, but I really need to reach the 10th floor, and the service elevator is having problems," to which there was a disgusting eye roll coupled with a sickening exhale.

Harmony went to work before the doors even closed, strangling the rude power broker with a wire. Getting robbed of her expensive purse was the least of her worries while she kicked and struggled.

"Maybe next time you'll be more polite to the help," was Harmony's comment as Stills body went limp. Upon stepping out of the elevator she looked down at Stills lifeless body and commented, "Oh, there won't be a next time."

She walked across the hall to the service elevator and upon reaching the first floor, she stepped out wearing ripped jeans, a tank top, and a blonde wig.

Stephen Ward strolled from the hotel lobby to his black Porsche, pressed the key fob, the car chirped, and the door locks popped up.

"Nice car," Yolanda Youngblood called out across the parking lot to which he looked at her clunker with a snobbish nod.

"Why two spaces?" She asked.

"So people like you don't park next to me," he called out.

He turned the key and roared the engine to life. Before putting the Porsche in gear, he pressed the brakes causing the detonation of the gas tank to a massive explosion. He hadn't noticed the hair-thin wire running from the rear brake light to his gas tank.

Timothy Smithers was on the resort driving range, working on his long game. I saw to it that one of the golf balls in his basket was filled with explosives. A ball with a black stripe. He hit ball after ball.

"I'll bet twenty dollars he can't get the 200-yard mark," one of his bodyguards said to another.

"I'll take that action," Smithers gloated. He squared his stance with his shoulders, slightly buckling his left knee. "Whack!" He connected, and the ball sailed to the 210-yard marker. "Which one of you is next?" He dug into his pocket and held up a fifty-dollar bill. "Mr. Grant doesn't think either of you can club it passed the 200-yard marker," he boasted.

Preparing for the challenge, Mathew, one of his bodyguards removed his blazer and shoulder hol-ster. He pulled the golf ball with my black stripe on it from the bucket and teed it up. Took a few prac-tice swings, stepped up and squared himself with the ball.

"You almost look like you know what you're doing," the other bodyguard, Joel said.

"My nickname used to be Mathew Woods," he joked.

"I think it's Mathew stalling." Smithers joked back, still holding his fifty.

"Now for the moment of truth," Mathew mur-mured. He eyed the distance on the fairway, grip-ping the club with his thumb and forefinger, making the perfect V. He drew back, slightly buckling his left knee and exhaling a concentrated breath.

"Daddy, daddy, I want to play," was the plea from Smithers four-year-old son, who he had for the weekend.

I scurried over to the group of men. "Wait!" I called out, trotting their way. "I'd like in on that action," I gasped to which they all stared, looking surprised. I caressed Matthews' arm, took the ball with the black stripe from the tee. "Use my lucky ball. I have money riding on you," I said, holding up my fifty-dollar bill and setting another ball on the tee.

Matthew again poised himself in front of the ball and let off a whacking shot that floated 230 yards.

"I also take checks gentlemen," I said, handing Matthew a crisp fifty-dollar bill.

Later it would come to light that Timothy Smithers was making good on his intentions as a lobbyist for the betterment of states legislature.

I woke up drenched in sweat, clenching my .380. This was one of the many dreams from the Dark Circle, that has haunted me since the death of Timothy Smithers.

Chapter 49

These victims had two or three things in common. SC&D, sliced throats and on a few, carvings on their left arms. Which were numbers coinciding with their accounts. I exhaled a fluttered breath when I realized I had something in common with this killer. And aside from repenting my sins for the millionth time, I wanted that portion of my life to remain buried, but I know in the pit of my soul, everything dark, eventually comes to light. Staying focused and keeping my wits in check was becoming more of a challenge.

I went to the Cyber-crimes department to have a word with Jason Morris, an undergrad at UCF, specializing in internet crimes. "I could use your help with spreading bait," I said.

"Bait, how so?"

"I'd like to know if there is a possibility of starting some type of buzz for a company."

"You mean like something a site for inner office talk or the latest scuttlebutt?"

"Yes, is it possible to set something up to where employees have access?"

"Sure, we can create a site and give people usernames with the impression of it coming from a said company or group of people."

"How long would something like that take to set up?"

"Assuming I have the information I need, it should take a matter of hours."

"What do you need to get the ball rolling?"

"Not much, just the company's web address."

"Okay, and Jason, this has to remain quiet." I handed him a slither of paper that said "SC&D."

Chapter 50

Natasha's black Honda crept to a low speed as she rounded the corner in a downtown parking garage. She looked at Yasmin Perez's profile picture. She paid close attention to her long dark hair, and a mold just above her left lip. "Looks like your number's up," she murmured to the image.

She backed into a parking space across from Yasmin's red Blazer, cracked her window, lit a Newport and studied the tracking application on her phone. Aside from having the straight razor in the center console, she readied Joshua's .38 revolver. It was a big parking garage, and she was sure Yasmin wouldn't volunteer to have her throat sliced.

Seven cigarettes later and at 1:30 am, Yasmin walked through the entrance of the garage, looking like a perfect match to her profile picture. She was even wearing the same fuchsia blouse, but she wasn't alone. Either she had come with a date or was leaving with. Natasha's guess was the latter since Yasmin drove her own vehicle.

She watched as the two made their way to the SUV, walking hand in hand. Now or never, she thought, exiting the Honda, she took a last puff of the Newport and strolled towards Yasmin and her date. She played the SC&D recording while Yasmin eyed her, receiving a familiar glance and a smirk in return.

"Hi, do I know you?" Yasmin asked, studying Natasha's face.

"No. But I know you. Don't you remember me?" Natasha replied, holding up the phone and giving a glimpse of the gun.

"You're the murderer that's been on the news," Natasha's date said in an excited voice and pointing at her. "RUN!" He told Yasmin, stepping in front and pushing her behind a car. He ran the opposite direction to draw Natasha's fire.

She fired the gun, hitting him in the back.

Yasmin screamed and ran. But her run would be short-lived. Her high heels caused her ankle to buckle.

"Don't go any further!" Natasha commanded, training the pistol at her. "Do you have any idea how long I've been waiting to catch you alone? I thought I had you last week, but you left the movies with a group of people. Three days before that you talked up a storm with a co-worker in the parking lot, and last night you slept over a blonde guys' house. This must be my lucky day."

Yasmin's date groaned and called out for help before a .38 slug hit the back of his head. Silencing him forever.

"You won't be having a sleepover with him tonight. He was kind of fine too, Spanish poppy. It's funny, they say when you kill someone you feel instant remorse or sadness." She eyed and stepped closer to a hysterical Yasmin.

"Why are you doing this?"

"My shrink said I needed therapy."

Aside from the building that was going on, a lite tapping echoed in the distance but dismissed as construction.

Natasha held up the phone playing Yasmin's call. Until then, the only thing Yasmin paid attention to was the gun. Her face contorted into a look of horror when she noticed, it was her voice.

She spoke something in Spanish and cried out. Natasha eased the phone into her back pocket and slid the straight razor out. She hadn't noticed it, but the tapping was getting louder.

"It's time for you to go night-night," she crooned.

A gunshot rang out, hitting the load-bearing beam behind them, to which Natasha took cover, dragging Yasmin with her.

"Ayudame por favor! (Help me, please!)" Yasmine cried out.

Natasha steadied herself and returned fire, to which there were two more rounds exchanged, also taking notice that the tapping had stopped.

"Let her go," a female voice yelled out.

Natasha held the gun to Yasmin's head and the razor to her throat. "Show yourself or she dies!"

"You're going to kill her anyway. But I promise, she won't die alone," the voice said as an ebony lady partially stepped from behind a Saturn minivan.

Natasha sliced the side of Yasmin's neck, just enough to draw blood. Causing her to cry out again. "You have three seconds to come from behind that van. One, two–"

—The lady stepped away from the van to a sight Natasha nor Yasmin expected to see. A beautiful plus sized ebony, wearing shorts, high heels and had a prosthetic leg.

"I promise you she won't die alone," the lady reiterated. She continued to train her gun in Natasha's direction. "Manten la Calma mi amiga," she told Yasmin to stay calm.

Natasha maneuvered Yasmin towards her Honda, with the .38 to her head and the razor still to her neck. "Lower your aim and back off, or I'll see how much blood she really has."

The lady slightly lowered her aim, drawing her predominant arm in, in case she had to return fire quickly.

Yasmin's eyes were flooding with tears.

"On second thought, drop your gun," Natasha commanded.

The lady raised her aim again, this time training at Natasha's face. "I didn't get my leg blown off overseas, so I could come back home and be pushed around by a coward."

"Coward?"

"Yes! I know a little something about cowards. I can look at you and tell something's off. You're not even a real coward. The real ones aren't afraid to die. They're afraid of living. Looks like you're trying to tap dance your way to that black Honda." She aimed and shot out a rear tire.

Natasha sliced the side of Yasmin's neck before shooting at the Samaritan, hitting her, causing her to stumble to the ground.

Natasha ran to her Honda while still shooting. The military veteran took aim from a side prone position, firing her remaining rounds at the gas tank as Natasha escaped the garage.

The veteran sprung to her feet and over to Yasmin, putting pressure on her neck. Two minutes later another Samaritan entered the garage and called for help.

Natasha's rim imbedded streaks in the pavement surrounding Lake Eola. She exited the car and changed the rear tire, leaving the damaged one behind.

Driving around the outskirts of town, she was unable to calm herself down, replaying the earlier events in her mind. Worst of all she left the straight razor in the parking garage.

Chapter 51

Natasha arrived unannounced at Carol's house just after 4 a.m. She backed into the driveway and sat, smoking a Newport, trying to steady her nerves and regain composure. She wondered how many on-lookers saw her or got a description of her car as she sped off, sparking up the asphalt. A minute later she was standing at Carol's front door, on what may have been her sixteenth cigarette. She pressed the doorbell but didn't recall hearing it ring through to the other side.

In a daze and not knowing where to turn, as far as she was concerned two people were dead, and she was the cause. This gave taking it to another level a whole new perspective. She stood in the shadows of the patio light in deep thought. The clicking of the locking mechanism on the door roused her from her daze.

"It's after 4 a.m., somebody better be dead," was Carol's greeting. She creaked open the door and motioned Natasha inside.

She hurriedly stepped inside with her arms crossed and still smoking. Carol fingered the ciga-rette from her grasp, took a puff, and flicked it towards the planter by the drive-way before closing the door.

"Somebody is dead, maybe two people."

"What the hell are you talking about?" Carol griped.

"Something didn't go as planned."

Natasha explained what happened in the hours leading up to her standing at Carol's doorstep.

"Relax, it's under control. I have a plan," Carol said. "Give me a few minutes to put something on."

She got dressed, and by way of text, told Joshua to meet her by the wooded area near Lake Monroe in Sanford.

"Let's do breakfast. Put this on," Carol handed Natasha a green armband.

"What's this for?"

"It's called an alibi," Carol slipped the used Tyvek wristband onto Natasha's wrist. "I save these from time to time when I go out. Sort of a memento from different clubs and bars."

Unbeknownst to Natasha, it was the wristband from the night Carol met Shirley Murdock.

Carol cracked open a bottle of tequila. "Take a few swigs of this, and then we're going to breakfast," she said, taking the first drink and passing it to Natasha.

They rode in Natasha's Honda on the way to breakfast, while she explained what happened in more detail. With the tequila bottle in hand, they continued to take drinks.

"Do you think the lady with the gun was a cop or some nosey gun owner?"

"Hard to tell, she had a gun, and she was good with it. Besides, I haven't seen many cops with prosthetic legs."

"The important thing is that you made it out of there without getting tangled up."

She guided Natasha to a wooded area near the backside of the lake.

"I have a friend that lives out here. We'll report your car stolen after breakfast."

"Stolen?"

"Yes, stolen. You caught a ride out with me and Joshua last night, and your car was gone when you got home. Kapeesh?"

"Kapeesh."

"Go straight ahead, into the woods."

"But I'll scratch up my car."

"That's the point, it's supposed to be stolen. When the cops find it, they'll call you and insurance will handle the rest. But right now, scratches on your car are the least of your worries," Carol said, motioning to the wooded area.

They pulled deep into the woods before exiting the car. As they walked they had a smoke and talked more specifics. Until Natasha's cigarette fell to the ground. Struggling for air, she was being choked from behind with a cord. Unable to get a grip on the cord, Natasha wildly swung her elbows landing blows to Carol's stomach and chest. She cranked down harder, tripping Natasha to the floor. With a twist of her hips, Natasha landed on top, driving her knee into Carol's mid-section, which was more than enough for Natasha to free herself.

Gasping for air, Natasha pulled the cord from her neck. A slap and a punch to the temple put her at an advantage. With two fists full of hair, Natasha tried to drag Carol across the ground, only to encounter her wicked strength. She stood and slowly muscled Natasha's grip from her hair. Natasha's knee to the stomach and a chop to the esophagus had Carol slumped over and clutching her throat. Natasha's hands were then throttled around Carol's windpipe and squeezing tight. Carols attempts at reaching Natasha's neck were feeble at best. Unable to breathe and struggling to free herself produced a growing vein on the left side of her forehead. She strained and peed full blast before getting extremely weak. Seeing spots and on the verge of blacking out, her arms turned to spaghetti. She resorted from scratching Natasha's shoulders to barely nudging her forearms. She gasped and convulsed as their gazes met.

Unexpectedly, Carol stood erect, studying Natasha's face. She blinked her eyes from deep brown to light hazel and with a burst of strength, removed Natasha's hands from her throat.

"What the hell," Natasha wide-eyed Carol's eyes in horror.

Natasha was abruptly pulled away by strong hands holding onto the reins of something twisted tight around her neck. Hands belonging to Joshua. She was dragged back, and in a new scuffle to free herself, her shoe came off. The strength was too much to bear, nor could she wiggle her way out. Carol eased a knife from her waistband and lunged it deep into Natasha's navel, causing her body to jerk as she spasmed, making guttural sounds. Once again, their gazes met as Carol twisted the knife, making the rupture larger. Natasha involuntarily yelped as she grabbed for the knife.

"This isn't personal, but you can't lead them to us."

Natasha's effort to remove the twisting knife from her mid-section was a painful attempt. Her body jerked and convulsed.

Carol stood, body to body, closely observing Natasha's agony. "This is where you get off," she said, dislodging the knife from her navel and slashing her throat.

Aside from her observation, Carol embraced Joshua from the opposite side of Natasha's weakening body. The last thought Natasha would have would be of disgust. Her torso jerked hard one last time, and her left leg began to tremble before her body completely gave out.

"I won't ask what I missed," Joshua whispered as he and Carol continued to embrace each other. "For a second it looked like you had hazel eyes."

"Don't be silly, my eyes are brown. We have to wipe the evidence," Carol muttered as she wiped the knife on her sleeve.

Chapter 52

Another murder had me downtown. And I was still riding Davis's Suzuki. The slugs from the Thomas Huggins firefight hit more than my control box. They punctured the radiator and damaged the engine control computer.

I entered the parking garage and ducked under the tape to the sight of two ladies consoling each other. They sat in the back of the ambulance, on the far side by the exit.

CSI's took pictures of Manuel Santiago as he laid lifeless. *Another pointless killing.* I knelt and studied the body, one round in the back and one to the head. But this wasn't our killer's style. Her thing was somewhat of finesse. This was either a copycat or something botched.

A straight razor, shell casings, and deep grooves from the parking garage to the road told a near complete story of what happened.

I walked up to the two ladies sitting under a blanket on the back edge of the ambulance. One with a bandage on the side of her neck, and the other with a sling around her left shoulder. Her right arm draped around the other lady, who was still crying.

"Why aren't you at the hospital?" I questioned.

"I told her I would stay here until her mother arrived. She didn't want to go to the hospital," the younger ebony lady said.

"I'm Detective Jackson. Can I get you something?"

"I'm Monica and this is Yasmin," the younger lady said. "A policeman got us some coffee and bagels a while ago."

"Can you tell me what happened here?" I asked Monica, who seemed stable enough to talk.

"A lady with a straight razor and a gun killed her friend and then tried to kill her. I saw what was happening, I pulled my gun and we had an exchange. I wasn't able to hit her, but I managed to shoot out the back drivers side tire."

"Do you make a habit of carrying a firearm downtown?"

"Yes, I feel naked without my Glock," she said as she moved the blanket, stood and dug her conceal carry permit from her purse.

I briefly stared at her prosthetic leg, instantly admiring her. I didn't want to make the situation awkward by asking about it.

"Can you tell me what the assailant looked like?"

"She was two or three shades lighter than me, about five feet three, and maybe 140 pounds."

"Do you remember what she was wearing?"

"She had on bleached blue jeans and a long sleeve gray shirt."

"Any sunglasses or a hat?"

"No sunglasses but she had a ponytail sticking out of the back of a black hat and a bean-shaped face. She drove off in a black Honda Accord."

"Good job on shooting out the tire. "That will make it easier to track through traffic cameras," I said to which she nodded. "If you don't mind me asking, how do you come to shoot so well?"

"I was Marine ground combat, first division. I made sharp shooter on my last qualifier before I got hurt."

I did a double take. Although she was a big boned girl, she could have easily been a model or and actress. They were both yawning, and I didn't want to keep them with too many questions. I noticed talking beyond the perimeter tape. Hodges was going back and forth with an older Spanish lady, pointing in our direction.

"Is that your mother?" I asked Yasmin, to which she nodded.

I called out to Hodges, "she's okay," to which he escorted her over.

"I need a word with you," Hodges commented.

I gave Monica and Yasmin my card and made my way to Hodges.

"She played a recording," Yasmin said in a very strong Spanish accent.

I gave Hodges the "wait a minute gesture" and turn back towards the two ladies.

"A recording?"

"Yes, a recording on her phone from the SC&D."

"You mean the Snook, Cellular and Data Company?"

"Si," she said. "I was mean to her, and she had my call on her phone. She play it to me, she shoot Manuel." She sobbed onto Monica's shoulder.

I rubbed her shoulder, and she looked up. "From what I've seen, Manuel was a good man. I know he moved you from the path of that bullet, and I promise you she will pay for what she did here."

Yasmin continued to sob as she spoke to her mother in Spanish, motioning to Monica. Her mother gave Monica a teary hug.

I directed my attention back to Hodges. "What can I help you with, sir?"

"Looks like we have a description of our killer," he said.

I wasn't so sure of that. In the footage I saw at Altitudes Shirley Murdock and our mystery woman were the same height, granted they both wore heels that night. Murdock was five feet nine, and I seriously doubt our mystery lady was wearing six-inch heels.

"We're still missing a piece of the puzzle," I said.

And then my phone rang. It was Jason.

"Hey what do you have?" I questioned, trying to keep it brief and above board with Hodges staring at my mouth.

"Remember that thing you wanted me to do?"

"Yes."

"A few employees already have something like that in place."

Again, I gave Hodges "the hold on gesture."

"Okay, so why do I get the feeling this is where the rubber meets the road?"

"To be a member of this site, you have to have worked for them for at least six months but get this. That doesn't mean they're going to take you. They have 32 members. Whoever the admin person is doesn't grant access to employees with stellar records."

"That's odd."

"In their chats, they refer to customers by account numbers."

I walked off to give the impression that I was thinking; to keep Hodges out of my investigation and for sure, jumping the gun.

"That's the ticket right there," I said as I readied a pen and pad from my back pocket. "I need you to cross reference the victims' account numbers with their chats. And make sure you get plenty of screenshots. I'll check on it later," I whispered.

"What was that about?" Hodges boomed.

"Parent stuff, you wouldn't understand," I said as I walked over and revved the Suzuki to life, drowning out his voice.

Chapter 53

Joshua and Carol drove down her street, slowing to a snail's pace near her house. Both covered in Natasha's blood, wanting to shower and get rid of the evidence. Perhaps even burn their clothes. As they rolled by Carol's house they noticed her neighbor, Joanna, sitting out front, drinking coffee.

"Shit, there's that nosey bitch! Keep going," Carol whispered as if the neighbor could hear her.

"We can head to my house and change," Joshua commented, "My roommates at work."

"That would be a good idea," Carol motioned at the neighbor. "She's always out to see what she can see."

Twenty minutes later they were pulling up to Joshua's house. A press on the visor button opened the garage door.

There was an exhale of relief by Carol when the garage door closed. "Thank you, Jesus."

"Don't you think that's kind of a morbid thing to say? Considering what we just did," Joshua questioned.

"Yeah, well." Carol gave Joshua a stern look.

She was wearing a black bra and had her shirt balled up in a knot to prevent blood from getting in the car. Upon getting out, they cleaned the remaining specks of blood from the interior. They stripped down to their underwear in the garage and put their clothes in a black hefty bag.

"What do you have in a size eight?" Carol asked.

Joshua couldn't control his eyes, looking at Carol. She had the body of a fitness model. Toned stout legs, a slim waist with ripples in her stomach and defined arms. He stood, just staring at her. He eventually made his way to his roommate's closet.

He got dark jeans, a navy hoodie and an FSU hat from his roommate's closet.

"We have one more visit to make," Carol said as she slipped on the jeans, hoodie and FSU hat.

Chapter 54

I went over account numbers with Jason trying to fill in the gaps. Not only were all the victims discussed in the SC&D chat rooms, but they called them by account number. They said certain things about victims to let the ones involved know their numbers were up. Screen names IchiBomb, Acid-Rain and GothicSteele had to have been in cahoots. With exception of one account number, everyone they had an issue with turned up dead.

"Look," Jason pointed at the screen.

It was another account number.

"I need to know everything about customer 8386," I said.

My phone rang, and it was Captain Beckham. "I think you're going to want to see this," he said. "How soon can you get to the wooded area by Lake Monroe and the I-4 overpass?"

It seemed like I was there within a few minutes, to the sight of another gruesome murder. The real killer was covering her footsteps.

"This was one of the killers," I told Beckham.

"ONE?" He questioned.

Looking at her license, I said "Natasha Jones was involved in one murder and two attempted murders early this morning. She fits the description given by two eyewitnesses. Chances are her fingerprints will match the straight razor found at a crime scene from last night."

"Well, if she was going to Jacksonville, she didn't get very far," Beckham said.

I continued to study the deceased. There were ligature marks on her neck from being strangled, a knife puncture in her stomach and a sliced throat.

"Did they have to kill her three times?" Beckham asked.

"This is what you call twisted and sadistic."

And then my phone rang again. It was Jason. He got a warrant to hack into Cindy Radcliff's phone and her vehicle's GPS.

"I thought you would like to know Cindy Radcliff is on the move. I'm linking her GPS to your phone."

Chapter 55

Every Thursday between four and five o'clock, Cindy Radcliff went to the Oak Ridge Gun Range on Orange Blossom Trail. Through traffic cameras and cell towers, Joshua's Charger was spotted heading in the same direction.

Jason sent a photo of Cindy Radcliff to my phone. She was an older tanned brunette with a round face and freckles under her left eye.

The tracker showed Cindy was eight miles away and Joshua was 14 miles out and closing in her direction. I was on the other side of town, running every light I could. It was no better time to be on a bike. Their cars were in the parking lot when I pulled up. I'm not sure if Joshua knew Cindy was going to a gun range. The vehicle fitting his cars description and tag was occupied with two people, but hard to make out through his tint. I casually rode to the east side of the parking lot turning right, with the flow of traffic. I hid out in the parking lot of a neighboring sports bar, maintaining my visual. I asked dispatch to send a complete docea of Joshua Smitz and known accomplices to my phone, which came back with no hits.

They were on the move after an hour or so. Cindy was headed back toward her residence, on the outskirts of Wekiva and Apopka. She lived on ten acres of land. When I rode up, I saw the dark blue Hellcat parked alongside some hedges a hundred yards north of Cindy's house. Assuming that they were both armed I readied my Sig and grabbed an extra clip from beneath the Suzuki seat. I saw the same size elevens and another set of footprints as I approached the house. Trying to call Cindy's cell phone failed. I heard light murmurs as I got closer but couldn't make out what was being said.

"This is Jackson requesting backup at 830 Rosebud Lane," I whispered into my earbud.

"Stand down detective," An all too familiar voice boomed.

"There is a possible 187 in progress. I don't have time for your rank pulling bullshit."

Hodges was in the process of saying something when I turned my radio down and muted my cell phone. There was a loud crash, and a voice cried out. I crawled to the side window behind an extended wall to get a view.

"Where's all that mouth at now? You were real cocky on the phone!" A male voice I suspected was Joshua, barked.

I held the camera side of my cell to the window and snapped a picture. I counted four people. Joshua holding a straight razor to Cindy Radcliff's neck and the lady in the Altitudes bar footage, pointing a gun at a teenage girl.

I hid my back-up Sig around the rear of the house. I ripped a hole in the screen and placed it in

277

an old flower pot near the back porch. I was hoping it didn't come to that, but these perps had a rising body count.

I turned my radio back up. "This is Jackson, 6062, I need you to patch me through to Joshua Smitz's cell phone," I whispered into the mic.

Thirty seconds later his phone rang. He looked at it and ignored the call.

"Hit him again," I whispered.

A few seconds later he looked down, staring at his phone. I couldn't make out what he was saying but he looked puzzled.

"Hello."

"Hello, Joshua, I'm Detective Jackson."

He covered the phone and whispered, "It's the police! The fucking police! A Detective Jackson."

"How," Carol shouted!

"Bitch, you better not be a cop!" Joshua said, motioning in Cindy's direction with razor in hand.

"She's not a cop, she's a retired CEO," Carol said.

"Who is the lady acting as your accomplice?" I asked Joshua.

"She's asking about you," he murmured.

Carol fingered the phone from his grasp. "Well hello, Detective Jackson, long time no see."

"I need you to let those people go," I said into the phone in a firm voice.

"Now what fun would that be? They have to meet their destiny."

"You have a destiny as well!"

"And what destiny would that be?"

"The one where I slap the cuffs on you."

"Temper, temper detective. I have to say I'm impressed. How did you find me?"

"I followed all the breadcrumbs you sprinkled around my city. The cavalry will be here in a matter of minutes. Why prolong the inevitable?"

She laughed as if I told a joke.

"I never got your name," I said.

"I never gave it. But you can call me CC."

"No one else has to die today?"

"Isn't it a pity, it's not up to you? You have about five minutes to clear out or else it's going to be a table for three on the Grim Reaper express. Do you like surprises?"

"In five minutes, the cavalry will be here," I said.

"In that case, the more the merrier," she laughed a light chuckle.

"Tell me, detective, what do you hate more than anything?"

"For starters, I hate it when people are held against their will and unjustly murdered," I said as police sirens serenaded the background from a distance.

"Excellent. But how would you define being held? You of all people should know about being held. Law enforcement does it all the time."

"Enlighten me."

"Judges, cops, and bailiffs hold people hostage all the time. You use the word detaining and custody as an excuse. Both of you play judge, jury, and executioner. So, save your righteous babble."

At a glance, Cindy Ratcliff and a teenage girl were sitting on the floor, back to back. I could see their reactions to the approaching sirens.

"What's it going to take to have a peaceful resolution?"

"The fact that you're here means there will be no peaceful resolution, detective."

"You can still make it out of here alive."

"You're talking as if you have some sort of control in this matter. But let me assure you, that reality doesn't exist.

I looked over to speeding squad cars and a Maybach pulling up to the scene. My guess is it was Duron Smitz wanting to exert influence on behalf of his son, which meant someone had him in the loop. And that someone would be Kirkland Hodges. There was a black Yukon and the same black Escalade that had slowly pulled up before Hodges got out with a bullhorn. Duron exited the Maybach with two other men, one of them being Abram. But no one exited the Escalade, nor did it move.

What in the hell was going on?

"You are surrounded, there is no chance of escape," Hodges blared.

"Looks like your shift is over detective," CC said.

I heard a light shriek in the background. I popped my head above the window just enough to see that Cindy got sliced on the arm with the razor. I didn't like it, but it was better than the alternative.

"What was that?" I questioned, to see if CC would tell the truth.

"That's the sound of disobedience."

"The same disobedience Natasha Jones displayed? I saw what you did to her."

In the background, I could hear Joshua talking in a low voice. I couldn't make out what he was saying with all the commotion Hodges was causing. Luckily, he couldn't see me.

"Natasha was sloppy and lacked the skills to execute. Looks like your friends are here," CC said. "Ciao."

"Wait, how can I help you get out of this?"

"You can't. Worry about yourself and the boys in blue out there," She grumbled, and then the line went dead.

What did it mean to worry about myself and the boys in blue? I peered through the window again and they were all gone. I hadn't noticed it before, but there was a faint gas smell.

The SWAT captain, Walrick, took position behind an enclosure and ordered me to the barricade where Hodges was.

"What the hell are you doing, Hodges? They have two hostages!"

"That's no longer your problem! you're done here!"

"Who approved this?"

"Worry about your own ass!"

"I smelled gas, pull SWAT back!"

I turned up my radio and hurriedly warned SWAT about the gas smell.

"Madison, Stokes, relieve Jackson of her radio," Hodges ordered.

"There's a gas smell, they said to worry about ourselves! That house could go up at any moment!" I roared. "And what the hell is he doing here?" I motioned to Duron Smitz as Madison and Stokes gave my radio to Hodges.

"That's not your concern detective. Your information is way off. Joshua Smitz is a hostage. That crazy lady in there is not going to blow herself up or knock off her bargaining chips. Like it or not, this is my show now, I have command, so get a grip or leave my scene!"

Just hearing those words sent me into a rage. But something Hodges said made sense. They weren't going to blow themselves up.

"Who said anything about a crazy lady?" I questioned, squinting at Hodges and studying Duron Smitz. "Your son is a murderer!" I shouted.

"Watch yourself, detective!" Hodges said.

I gave them both an icy stare.

"I have evidence that links your son to at least three murders, actually four, as of this morning. So, believe me when I tell you that your money and influence will be well wasted."

"Abram," Duron called out to which he approached in my direction. "Get her out of here."

I unholstered my ankle weapon, shot at their feet and trained my gun at Abram who was going for his gun. "Maybe it's that time of the month, but for some reason, killing you really works for me," I said.

Arnofo caught the corner of my eye. He was barking at a lady plodding down the dirt road using a walker. As far as I knew he was a friendly dog and probably trying to get her out of harm's way. But his barks and growls gave me a different impression. She was a few feet away from the black Yukon.

I focused my attention back to Hodges and company.

"Have it your way," I said, continuing to back away, still training my weapon at them.

Once beyond the house, I pulled out my phone to call Payne, but I noticed two missed messages. One was Payne, and the other was Jason warning me about Hodges arriving at The Radcliff's ranch. More importantly, Jason's message was about the basement having multiple underground exits. It was built as a fallout shelter in the early sixties.

I still smelled gas. I had a feeling CC and Joshua were planning on igniting it once they got to the basement. Nothing like the confusion of an explosion and smoke to disappear in.

I yelled out to Walrick, "Pull SWAT back, it's going to blow!"

I ran towards the house when an unearthly explosion ignited, transforming the front section of the sturdy house into rubble.

Chapter 56

We were trapped in the aftermath of the explosion. I was able to finagle myself free. But Walrick's left leg was trapped under what used to be a support beam. I could see his lips moving but couldn't make out what he was saying. I don't think he could even hear himself because his ears were bleeding. It was the calm before the storm. Despite a slight humming in my ears, I saw Hodges yelling into his megaphone, but couldn't make out any of his words. I turned my attention back to Walrick and tried to lift the partial beam off of his leg. I pulled his AR-15 from the rubble and motioned for him to hold steady. I fired a single shot, splitting the cement slab into fragments.

Something in the distance caught his attention, but what?

He handed me his tac vest, radio and thermal camera. All other SWAT team members were accounted for. A couple came to assist with getting him back on his feet and away from the debris. I moved in towards the rubble in search of an underground entrance. I slid debris out of the way looking for stairs, a trapdoor or anything that led underground. Before the explosion, Walrick was in the process of putting eyes on the situation. He smelled the gas seconds before the explosion.

As soon as the ringing in my ears subsided I had dispatch connect me to Joshua's phone again. It rang and then went to voice mail.

Did they make it downstairs in time? Or was the blast too much for the old basement to handle?

I didn't rule out the fact they could also have ear damage from the blast. I heard a slight beeping that had probably been going on all the while. It was coming from Walrick's thermal camera. I looked down to see four figures on the screen that were all moving. I radioed dispatch and asked for Cindy Radcliff's next to kin, and anyone else that was listed at the address. Another glance at the camera had the figures not moving or at a checkmated position. Then I called Jason and asked if he could dig up anything extra about the Radcliff's ranch.

"I'm writing you up on this one Jackson. This was it for you! Suspension, review board and if I can't bring you up on charges! Demotion! And anything else I can add by tomorrow morning." Hodges roared, his voice loud and clear now. "You chased two maniacs into a structure and not only put yourself at risk but put the entire SWAT team in jeopardy. As far as I know, everyone in that dwelling is dead! And why are you wearing a tac vest with another radio?"

"I gave it to her Sergeant. There's movement below," Walrick said in a withered voice. "Show him." He motioned me to pass the thermal camera to Hodges.

"What the hell am I looking at? There's no action on this thing." Hodges howled, slapping the side of the camera to restore the screen.

It was black. No display or power. Probably the aftermath of the explosion.

I glanced over and noticed the old rusty flower pot I stashed my Sig in was still intact. It hadn't been touched.

"Cuff her!" Hodges barked to which no one moved in my direction.

We were all standing in the rubble of an explosion. The only thing the tac vest had was a radio and two magazines for an AR-15, which I no longer had. I darted to the flowerpot and grabbed my Sig.

"GET BACK! GET BACK!" A voice yelled.

The ground beneath me collapsed, and I fell into a world of darkness. I fell flat, but I crawled on trying to escape the falling gravel. I was in a tunnel. I took out my cell phone for light. It displayed another voice message from Jason.

"I got a hold of Elaine Stiner, Cindy Radcliff's daughter and the mother of the teenage girl, Bridgett. She says there are two underground tunnels that start in the basement and end in different parts of the surrounding woods. Her grandfather had it built in the late sixties. It was easier to get–"

The message was over.

I steadied myself and check to see how many rounds I had. I took a Maglite from the corner of the tac vest to manage my way through the tunnels while trying to listen for sounds that could lead me to Cindy and Bridgett. The tunnels were stuffy and had a soil-filled stench of what little air there was to breathe.

Is this something that CC and Joshua knew about? Or something they stumbled onto?

"What's your location?" Was a text from Payne.

"Underground tunnel that leads to surrounding woods," I replied.

I ventured down the first tunnel I came to. I could still hear Hodges's voice above ground, but unable to make out what he was saying. My gut told me he was too much of a coward to come down.

There was a faint light up ahead. I unholstered and began a light pace towards it, which was an exit from the tunnel. I slowly climbed up the withered latter. I lifted the old wooden lid to have a look around. The tunnel led to the nearby woods. I couldn't make out the figures from off in the distance and I could only hear light murmurs of voices. I inched out of the crawl space trying to make as little noise as possible. I belly crawled, trying to get a better look of the area.

Chapter 57

I was just in time to catch a glimpse of the back of someone's head. They were walking deeper into the woods. I could see Joshua, holding Cindy and Bridgett at gunpoint.

But Where was CC?

I moved in their direction, careful not to make a noise. Cindy and Bridgett's hands were bound with something attached to a guide rope. Maybe they were walking behind CC, because there was no trace of her anywhere, granted there were lots of trees and shrubs in the woods. They all stopped walking and Joshua appeared to be talking and walking around the two in a circle. He hopped up and down at one point. I wasn't far from him but still couldn't hear what he was saying, but he seemed to be yelling or singing. I took cover behind a tree with prickles on it. His behavior was odd like he was trying to draw attention to himself. Either that, or he was crazier than I thought. He talked and marched in a circle just like kids do when playing cops and robbers. I heard a twig snap behind me and felt the pressure of a gun barrel nudging at my left side.

"Aww detective, I need your gun. I recommend handing it over real slow if you want to prevent acute kidney failure," a sultry voice commanded.

"CC, I presume," I said, slowly extending my gun hand, with trigger guard resting on my index finger.

"For now, yes," she said.

I recognized her voice from the phone but couldn't get a good look at her face with the big sunglasses and FSU football hat she was wearing. I was surprised that Joshua wasn't more disguised, which implied that he favored killing anyone who saw his face.

"What's the purpose of doing this?" I asked.

"It's no fun when the rabbit's got the gun."

"This bitch ran her mouth to the wrong person this time," Joshua snapped.

"So, you guys are the ones that have been killing SC&D customers?"

"We've been helping them with their security issues."

"But why?"

"Because I hate people with a false sense of security," CC said.

"A false sense of security?"

"Yes, a false sense of security. Being a cop, I'm sure you've witnessed it in one form or another from time to time. Maybe some rich, arrogant prick or someone claiming they know somebody that can make your job and life a living hell."

The downside to what she was saying was that I agreed with her. But that's life sometimes. Even

289

though Hodges was trying to micromanage me, and this Doran Smitz character was undoubtedly everything she described, I didn't think they deserved to die. If anything, maybe a flesh wound.

"I sympathize with what you're saying, but why is killing the answer?"

"You ever have someone try to get you fired from your job, or try to make you look incompetent?"

"Yes, I deal with vindictive people all the time. It goes with just about every job there is. But killing people is not the answer."

"That's mighty hypocritical of you," CC said as she nodded in Joshua's direction, who had Cindy and Bridgett to kneel. "The truth be told, being a killer fits my character."

She tugged my cuffs from my belt loop and cuffed my hands. Joshua took a switchblade and ran it across Cindy's abdominal. She moaned out, violently jerking her mid-section, doubling over in pain, rolling onto the ground. The only thing that kept her from outright screaming was the duct tape over her mouth. Bridgett cried and went into hysterics.

"THAT'S NOT NECESSARY!" I shouted.

I knelt beside Cindy and told her to keep calm and focus on breathing. Since my hands were cuffed behind me I had Bridgett put pressure on her grandmother's wound. The front of her shirt was soaked in crimson.

"Just breathe steady," I said.

Joshua held the business end of the blade to the side of my temple, enough for me to feel the pressure.

"Stay put!" He growled.

Cindy squirmed in pain while CC stood over her. She pulled a small stun gun from a nap sack.

"Did you two have anything to do with that murder in Sanford?" I called out.

They laughed and snickered but didn't answer.

I was willing to try anything to get their attention away from Cindy.

I made it a habit to look towards the middle of CC's face every time we spoke. But still, I couldn't get a good look at her. She casually pushed Bridgett away and put the stunner into Cindy's wound.

"I could fry you from the inside out," she said. Cindy and Bridgett continued to whimper.

I tried to reason with them as I finagled the cuff key from my back-belt loop. Getting out of cuffs from the front was hard enough, let alone getting out from the back.

"SWATS combing the area right now. If you leave now, you stand a good chance of prolonging getting captured or the alternative, you can give yourselves up."

"We ain't doing shit! Be thankful we haven't sliced you up yet!" Joshua declared.

"I understand how you both feel. I have a sergeant that can't wait to nail my ass to the wall. He's the same guy that's sending SWAT into the woods right now. He doesn't care about bringing you in dead or alive."

"So why are you here?" CC said.

291

"He was in the process of having me arrested. Do you know a Thomas Johnson?" I asked CC.

She did a double take. Taken by surprise by my question. "Doesn't sound familiar."

"He was pulled over yesterday by Altamonte PD."

"So, what's that got to do with us?" Joshua barked.

"He had a straight razor and .38 caliber shell casings in his possession."

Joshua held the business end of the switchblade to my temple again. "We don't know a Thomas Johnson. So, who cares what he had with him."

"CC, knows him as Tommy. The odd thing is we couldn't match his prints to the straight razor or shell casings."

To my surprise, CC didn't say anything.

"What's that got to do with us?" Joshua asked.

"It depends. CC has been playing you both. He says she's his friend with benefits."

"THUD," Was the sound of the butt of a revolver hitting the side of my head.

"Now would be a good time to remain silent," CC said, her voice sounding less sultry.

"What the hell is she talking about!" Joshua barked.

"She's just talking out of the side of her neck."

"Is that why you hit her?"

"That's exactly why I hit her."

I don't know how I managed to hold on to the cuff key or even slide it into the lock. I twisted the key and held on to the left cuff as it came undone.

"THIS IS SERGEANT HODGES, WE HAVE YOU SURROUNDED." Was the sound from a blaring megaphone.

CC and Joshua took cover behind Cindy and Bridgett.

"Tell your man we have three hostages and on the verge of having two. It's all up to him." CC said as she directed me to yell out to Hodges.

"Do you think they're going to let you waltz out of here?" I said.

"No, but they will let Detective Jackson waltz out," Joshua said.

"Maybe, but before I do that. I need to confirm the owner of the straight razor and shell casings found in Tommy's Mustang," I said, *to divide and conquer*. "Which one of you is AcidRain and Goth-icSteele? AKA Carol Roach AKA CC and Joshua Smitz. I'm assuming Natasha Jones was IchiBomb."

Joshua questioned CC about Tommy which gave me enough time to dive towards my Sig. Once I had it in hand, I rolled and took cover behind a tree. They both shot at me, barely missing.

"Shots fired! Shots fired!" Was the sound echoing in the woods.

"That was a slick trick Jackson, you have to let me know how you did that before I kill you," CC said between shots. "That must be some new cop trick," she added.

"GIVE YOURSELVES UP!"

"I have a better idea, throw your gun out or I'll fry this bitch from the inside out!" She boasted.

"What's that going to solve? You're surrounded by Central Florida's finest. Former military bad asses who probably have you in the crosshairs right now."

There was an electric chattering coupled with a muffled scream that would have made God cry. I had no choice but to believe CC had the stunner in Cindy's wound. I became light headed and had a shortness of breath. I reached for my Tic Tac bottle with trembling hands.

"STAND DOWN JACKSON!" Was the echo from Hodges's megaphone. "DO NOT HARM JOSHUA SMITZ!"

"Joshua this is your father, it's safe to come out. I have everything taken care of." Doran Smitz yelled.

What the hell was happening? Hodges knew better than to give a pass to a killer. Who knows what he may have told SWAT. AR-15 shots splintered the tree I took cover behind.

"Jackson, throw your guns down and come out with your hands up," Hodges yelled from a distance.

There was no way I was going to chance getting shot by any of these characters. I was sweating and could feel my heart pounding. I dry swallowed what seemed like a few Xanax. The threats, shooting and shouting from both sides had my anxiety getting the better of me. In the distance, out of the corner of my eye, there was an older man in a black suit getting into position. He had an M16, with a silencer.

"You're going to be responsible for these bitches dying," Joshua howled.

"Officer Jackson, please throw out your gun. Don't let them kill my grandmother!" Bridgett sobbed.

"THUNK! THUNK! THUNK!" were the splintering rounds of an M16 hitting the tree, followed by the splinters of an AR-15. I rolled to my left to take inventory and met Warlick's gaze.

His weapon was low and positioned towards the man in the black suit. He gave me a nod, shifting his eyes to the left, where two SWAT members were getting into position. Next, a sniper signal, looking through a hole in his fist and nodding to the trees behind me. I lowered my head before more shots rang out.

There was a pounding in my head, the Xanax wasn't working, and my anxiety was getting the better of me. Shots from the black suit whizzed over my head. The blistering sound of a flash bomb struck panic into two SWAT guys to my far left. Then another to my far right. It was happening in slow motion. I crawled for cover behind a downed oak tree 30 yards away. The sniper in the tree was preoccupied training his scope near the flash bombs, searching for a target.

Hodges backed off, taking cover behind a cruiser. I crawled to the tree underneath the sniper and climbed.

"Lost visual, I repeat, lost visual," was the snipers chant as he slowly trained his scope over the thick brush of the woods.

I eased into position just underneath his left rib cage. His name tag said Jeffries, but he wasn't Jeffries, in fact, I hadn't seen him before.

"I need flesh wounds," I said as I cocked back the hammer on my Sig. "And hand over the 5.7," I added.

"Or what? Let me guess, you're going to shoot me, make noise and give our position away," he said.

"Worse," I said as I placed the barrel of my gun to his privates.

"One of two things are going to happen, and I'm fine with it either way. One, you're going to hand over the 5.7 by the barrel nice and slow or two, you're going to test me and meet your maker without a set of family jewels. I'm sure I'll be doing some poor girl a favor. Either way, my frustration will be satisfied."

He gave me an incredulous look and unstrapped his sidearm. *I was thinking someone must have gotten a two for one deal at Hit Men-R-Us.* This guy was sloppy and careless, but he had good position. He may have been one of Doran Smitz's guys and Just maybe Hodges was along for the ride.

"Your first target is Hodges," I said. "And remember, only flesh wounds."

He patiently waited for Hodges who was still behind the cruiser. *I wasn't surprised that he knew who Hodges was.* A minute later Hodges crept from behind the squad car. Sniper boy positioned his eye into the scope, took in a deep breath, slowly exhaled, and squeezed off a whispering shot, hitting Hodges's upper thigh. He went down like a deflated balloon and scrambled back behind the cruiser.

"Now lay down random fire," I said, motioning to the rest of his team.

"That'll give this position away," he said.

I nudged my barrel against his privates again.

"Your options are still on the table."

On second thought, I didn't trust him. Walrick and company had eyes on his entire team. I grabbed his earbud and tossed it along with his remaining ammo and backup weapon. I tossed my cuffs up to him.

"Interlace your hands around that branch and cuff yourself," I told him. "And if I were you, I'd be very still and very quiet."

Chapter 58

Joshua, CC, Cindy, and Bridgett were no longer in sight. I scurried around trees and bushes in the area where I last saw them. I heard coughing and crying up ahead, which were more than likely coming from Cindy and Bridgett. I wasn't sure what to think as far as Joshua and CC knowing their way around the woods. I spotted the tops of their heads in the tall shrubs and headed them off through a path around a bend.

"That's as far as you go," I readied my weapon. I trained it back and forth between them both. "Throw down your guns and step away," I said.

"Or what?" An accented voice behind me said?

The man in the black suit held a small caliber weapon at my head. Even though I was being held at gunpoint, I found his choice of weaponry interesting. It was an old .32 caliber. I dropped my Sig, but by the time I could raise my hands I heard a hammer cock back behind his head. It was Payne. I don't know how he found me, but it was good to be discovered.

"Two fingers, and real slow," Payne said. He stood using the black suit as a shield.

"I recommend you two tossing your guns," He told Joshua and CC.

"Or what? We still have these two," Joshua said, pointing at Cindy and Bridgett.

"THUNK! THUNK!" rounds hit a nearby tree. The older man in the black suit spun around and put a move on Payne. It was some sort of hand-to-hand. He had Payne in a wristlock and adding pressure on his right shoulder, maneuvering his gun arm towards the ground. The gun fell to the ground before Payne lowered his base, stepped back, and rolled through the wrist and shoulder lock. The results were Payne having the man in a reverse cradle.

Joshua planted his left foot as he swung at me. *He might have hit me had he not telegraphed his action.* I sidestepped him and connected with an open palm to the center of his nose.

He teared up and began blindly swinging with one hand and the other over his nose.

"THUD!" was the next sound I heard and felt. I was knocked to the ground. I looked up to CC standing over me in an offensive posture. A kick to my ribs made it hard for me to get to my feet, but it was like a breathing tube for my anger. I assumed Warlick had us covered and wouldn't risk hitting a hostile when engaged with friendlies.

I rolled towards CC, running my shoulder into her knee, hyper-extending it. I pulled her legs in towards me, and when she fell, I began the ground pound. After a few good punches,

I was tackled by Joshua. In the midst of my struggle, the corner of my eye captivated my attention, as it did Joshua and CC's. The older man in the black suit had real deal hand to hand moves. But the shocker was Payne's fight game. He used his elbows and knees in a way I hadn't seen; to block, strike and back up his aggressor.

A chop to the throat released me from Joshua's grip.

"It's just me and you," I told CC.

She landed a jab, and I returned a left hook to her chin, my long overdue therapy. With hat and shades gone, the only thing covering her face were my combos. She was wiry, strong and with good form. I could tell she trained. We went at it until I cracked her with an elbow to the temple. She stumbled back towards a tree when Joshua grabbed me from behind. I crashed the same elbow to his right solar plexus, I smashed his nose with a reverse head butt and spun around. I faced him and gave him an old school, uncle Elton style combo. A two-piece to his jaw, a hard jab to his nose and finishing him with a left uppercut. He went down like Glass Joe.

"Joshua Smitz, you have the right to shut the hell up and remained cuffed," I said as I put my last set of cuffs on him.

"My father will have your ass!" he murmured.

"Somebody needs to have his ass for not teaching you how to box. All those mob boys on the payroll, and you ain't got no hands. But Daddy Warbucks has his own problems right now."

I didn't hear it at first, but Cindy wailed out in pain again. After cutting her and Bridgett loose, I had Bridgett put pressure on her grandmother's mid-section. It wasn't a deep cut, but it was wide.

A few feet away, Payne and black suit were still at it.

I pulled the 5.7 from my back and trained it at black suit. "All right boys, play time is over," I said.

"I'm afraid play time is just beginning," Abram pointed a gun at me. "Drop your weapon, Jackson."

Payne and black suit stopped when Abram cocked the hammer. Abram eyed Payne, stepping towards him. "You look familiar."

Payne unholstered a .357 and fired shots, making Abram take cover. "I should look familiar, I gave you that beauty mark across your eye," Payne said. He emptied his remaining rounds at the tree Abram took cover behind, before pulling another backup.

"The detective from New Orleans?" Abram asked with an even heavier accent and sounding amazed?

Abram and black suit fired back at Payne, causing him to take cover.

Rounds splintered the trees they took cover behind. The splintering rounds came from Walrick and Stokes, causing a cease-fire as they trained the crosshairs of their scopes.

"What was that about?" I asked Payne as he readied another backup weapon, another .357. "And how many guns do you have?"

"That was about my family, and the only way he's leaving here is in a black bag."

"Don't do anything that will land you in hot water," I said. I tossed him the 5.7 and snagged my Sig from the ground.

But where was Carol? I went on the hunt for her.

"She went that way," Warlick motioned. Him and Stokes closed in with hardware training at Abram and black suit.

"There's one in the tree," I said. I ran deep into the woods searching to no avail.

We conducted a search for Carol after Cindy and Bridgett were safe with the Paramedics. There were no signs of her anywhere.

Guns were dropped, and bad guys were rounded up.

"Do you know who that is?" Hodges barked, gesturing to Joshua, the older man in the black suit and Abram.

"Yes, he's a killer and those two are aiders and abettors," I said as I motioned for two uniforms to take them into custody. "And this guy is wearing Jefferies SWAT gear. Any idea who he is, and where he got it?" I asked.

"My lawyers going to have you for lunch detective," Doran Smitz howled!

"Well then, that's a shame, I hear breakfast is the most important meal of the day," I replied and walked off.

"Do you have any idea who you just arrested?" Hodges yelped as he hobbled towards me with a bandaged leg.

"Yes, a serial killer. And we still have one on the loose. So, it might be a good idea to start a manhunt, a ten-mile radius." I leaned into Hodges and whispered. "If you jerk with me on this. I'll make sure you live to regret it."

"Are you threatening me, detective?"

"I'm giving you good advice."

As the uniforms loaded Joshua, the man in the black suit and Abram into the back of separate squad cars, a whispering shot exploded hitting Abram in the chest.

"SHOOTER! Take cover!" Hodges roared.

We all crouched behind cruisers, training our weapons towards the unknown. But there was only one shot fired.

Abram rolled behind a cruiser but not before being hit a second time. He grunted in pain as the second round hit him in the left butt cheek.

Warlick and Stokes trained their scopes across the wooded area and found nothing.

"If there is a shooter, he's long gone," Walrick said as he stood. "That shot didn't come from a sniper rifle, it came from a handgun."

"How do you know it's a handgun?" Hodges snapped.

"Because of the echo, genius," Walrick said, matter-of-factly. He trained the scope from left to right again, looking at the rubble of the house and the surrounding wooded area.

"Whoever fired those rounds knew what they were doing," Stokes bellowed, still training his scope in search of the unknown.

Payne came to mind. He wasn't anywhere to be found, he disappeared as stealthily as he appeared.

"Maybe we're not the target," I called out as I stood, holstering my Sig.

"Get down Jackson, that's an order!" Hodges boomed.

I walked over to Duron Smitz and eyed him. He crouched behind the cruiser like a coward about to shit his self.

"Get up, it's safe," I said.

"No, it's not. Get my son out of here!" He cried.

I leaned in towards him and whispered. "Tell me what everyone seems to know."

"I don't know what you're talking about."

"If I'm correct, you're from New Orleans."

"What does that have to do with anything?"

I leaned in again, "Checkmate. If I were you I'd watch my six."

Duron Smitz rode off in one of the cruisers out of fear of the unknown. EMT's stabilized Abram's wounds before taking him to ORMC. Paramedics laid him on his right side because of his wounds.

We combed the woods and surrounding area and even expanded it to a 20-mile radius to no avail. CC disappeared from the molecules of air.

It was nearing nightfall when we regrouped in front of the Radcliff ranch. I hadn't paid much attention, but the black Escalade was still in the same spot with the engine idling.

I saw the same lady on a walker, making her way down the street. She stopped and eyed me for a moment. Curiosity got the better of me, so I approached her, offering help, maybe she was lost. "Do you live nearby?" I questioned.

"There," she said in a withered voice and pointed down the street.

"It's not safe to be out here, Ma'am, can I get an officer to take you home?"

"I think I can manage, Pamela."

Thinking she may have dementia I went along with her calling me Pamela. I motioned for a uniform to walk her back home.

"Thank you, Pamela," she said. "Pamela Phantom."

I unholstered and moved in, training my weapon at her. "Don't move!" I ordered. I directed the uniform to back away from her. "What did you just call me?"

"Pamela Phantom," she said, looking me in my eyes with the look of an older lady that was anything but handicapped or had dementia.

"Holster your sidearm detective!" Hodges yelled. He hobbled behind me, working the action on his hammer to the back of my head. "I think you've lost your Goddamn mind. For the last time, holster your weapon and put your hands up."

I complied as ordered.

"Hands up," he reached over and relieved me of my Sig, stuffing it in his waistband. "What the fuck was that about? So now you kill kids, fathers and old ladies? You want to explain that shit?"

"It would be useless."

"I kind of thought you'd say something like that. You know the drill, left hand behind your back," he said with enjoyment. He motioned for Madison, and whispered, "Get a statement."

"Ma'am, would you like to make a statement?" He called out.

But the lady had vanished, leaving the walker behind. The black Escalade was also gone.

"What the hell?" Hodges murmured.

I pulled my hands away and fingered my gun from his waist, training it to what we couldn't see. "Like I said, I could tell you, but it would be useless."

Chapter 59

I had a conference with Principal Connor and Dean Williams the next day. I was eager to see what progress they made about Andre being bullied. But to my surprise, it wasn't what I expected.

"It appears that Andre is no longer the bullied. His recent interactions with Rodney is cause for concern," Dean Williams said in a croaky voice.

"Concern, how so?" I questioned.

"They had an altercation yesterday which led to two black eyes and a bloody lip." Principal Connor said.

"That's impossible; Andre doesn't have any bruises on him," I said, thinking back to something I might have missed.

"Rodney and another student athlete were on the receiving end of a black eye and a bloody lip and their parents want something done about it," Dean Williams boasted.

"And what might that be?" I asked, staring him in his eyes.

"They want Andre suspended," Principal Connor said.

"So, what do you plan to do?" I asked.

"I was hoping you could give us some suggestions, Mrs. Jackson. That's really what this meeting is about," Dean Williams chirped.

"I'm not sure you'll like my suggestion. But here's how I look at it. When Andre was getting bullied by this same kid, every day, no one did anything, and for one reason or another it wasn't a problem. Now that the bully got his ass handed to him, all of a sudden, it's a problem. But let me help you out. And speak up if I'm not clear. Andre and I have reached out to you both on several occasions about him being harassed and bullied around your school, and for one reason or another, you saw fit to overlook it. 'Rodney was just blowing off steam,' is what I believe you said. And the more I think about it, aren't you one of the freshmen football coaches Dean Williams?" I said.

"What does that have to do with anything?" He barked.

"You're Rodney's coach and you're more confused than you look if you think you're suspending my child." Was the statement that came out as I laughed out loud. "My child will continue to come to school. So, if you have to, you put the word out. And start with Rodney's parents. People need to keep their hands to themselves where my son is concerned. Or take boxing lessons. This wouldn't be an issue if the Miller's son had kept his hands to himself. Or even if you had done the right thing, to begin with. So maybe you're evaluating the wrong child, and for sure the wrong parent. I'm not going to say that I don't condone violence, because honestly, I do. If you don't know how to box, keep your hands to yourself. Dean Williams and Principal Connor, will there be anything else?" I asked as I shook their hands.

"You didn't speak up, so, I'll assume that we're on the same page about keeping our hands to ourselves."

After leaving Andre's school I noticed a missed call from Doctor Morrell. Davis was showing signs of improvement. I revved the Suzuki to life and made a beeline to Orlando Regional. Riding Davis's bike made me feel closer to him. I missed that over-sized kid.

Doctor Morrell and a nurse were taking his temperature and checking his blood pressure when I walked in. When they moved away from him, he was holding his head up and looking around. A young lady sat in the chair next to him, waiting for Dr. Morrell to finish up.

"You must be Kimberly, I'm Traycee," I said as I shook her hand.

"I've heard a lot about you, Mrs. Jackson," she said with a smile.

"Hey, what's going on over there," Davis said in a faint voice.

"Just a little girl talk," I said. "By the way, your Suzuki is a little stiff on curves. You might want to put a damper bar on it."

"You've been riding my bike?"

"Right now, it's my only transportation."

"I didn't know you could ride," He said. "Cap says you have a new partner."

"Just until your back on your feet!"

Dr. Morrell said Davis's recovery should take a few months now that he was out of his coma.

"I'm going to let you two have your time. I'll check up on you in days to come," I told Davis and Kimberly as I left.

"Where are you going partner?" Davis called out into the hallway!

"Bad guys ain't gonna catch themselves!" My voice echoed, to which he laughed and yelled out.

"Tell Uncle Elton to come see me and bring food."

When I arrived at my desk, there was an envelope staring me in the face. At first, I thought it was something from the Miller's but to my surprise, it wasn't.

Detective Jackson,

you may think you've accomplished something by taking Joshua in, but you haven't. I am the revelation for those that have no voice. The wolf sporting Sheep's skin. A seeker of tyrants who treat service people as slaves and second-hand objects. They are forever hiding behind a false sense of security embedded in cowardly scapegoating. In this new world of technology, cowards are just right for the picking. I'll be close, waiting, and watching.

CC.

Chapter 60

The Smitz's team of lawyers saw fit to cooperate and gave us the name Carol Roach AKA CC, which didn't add up. They suddenly wanted to be of service which would make Joshua's docket look a lot less crappy. We got a warrant for Carol Roach's residence. A CSI team and myself went through the entire house and didn't find so much as a fingerprint or a strand of hair.

Carol Roach lived in a four-bedroom, three-bathroom, two-story house. But, the picture on the file was not the lady I dealt with in the woods. Nor were the pictures in her house.

She was an older thin blond that owned several businesses and traveled frequently. It was my guess and hope that she went on a trip. But that wasn't the case. Jason confirmed there hasn't been any activity on any of her credit cards over the last five months. Before that, there was a transfer of almost two hundred thousand dollars to the Cayman Islands. I got light-headed when I saw the name of the company, Nephews and Sons. I reached for Xanax but there weren't any. I staggered outside for a dose of fresh air, walked passed the perimeter of the house to one neighbor smoking a cigarette and bummed one.

He was a heavyset bearded guy. "What's going on over there?" He asked.

"Just a routine check," I answered, not giving any details.

"Is everything okay with Carol and her roommate?"

"Roommate?"

"Yes, she moved a roommate in about six months ago. I believe her name was CC from St. Louis. She was Carol's VP."

"How many times did you see her? And what did she look like?" I asked.

"After Carol went out of town to start another company, we spoke on occasion. A simple hello or a wave. She was a nice-looking black lady, with your same complexion. She took care of herself, she ran every morning."

Out of the corner of my eye, I saw Callahan duck under the tape and make a beeline to me. "Detective, you need to see this," he insisted.

"Is there anything else you can tell me about CC? Did she have any strange habits or company?"

"That's about it. She struck me as a quiet, private person."

I gave him my card so if he thought of anything else, he could get in contact with me, and then I rushed back inside.

Callahan walked me to the garage. "We couldn't figure out where the humming was coming from."

They tore a hole in the drywall to get to the source. It was a large Kenmore freezer, and inside was the body of the real Carol Roach.

"We estimate she's been in here for the last four months," Callahan said.

"I want everything on Carol Roach for the last two years! Every email, snail mail, phone call, chat room, all social media friends, and every comment. And I want a docea on all her relatives, employees and business partners! Along with bank statements!" I barked.

My chest was getting tight, I was on the verge of hyperventilating.

"There's no sign of a struggle and still no prints or hair follicles. It's like she volunteered to jump into the freezer. We're not sure how long it will take for her body to thaw," Callahan said.

After wrapping up, just outside the crime scene, a light rain began to fall. I leaned on a cruiser going through the names on Roach's payroll until I came across a Calynn Catalyst. I was hoping it was a coincidence and not what I was thinking. First and last name beginning with the same letter. First name harmless and last name, anything potentially dangerous. *No Xanax, damn*.

A black Audi pulled to the curb. From the driver's seat, a man wearing a black suit, holding a yellow envelope exited the car. He readied a scanner as he approached me.

"Operative 214610?"

I hadn't heard that number in years.

"What's this about?" I questioned. "That number is inactive, has been for years."

"Operative 214610," he said again in more of a statement as opposed to a question, caressing the sidearm on his belt holster.

I answered him. "Operative 214610, security code FUQ2, status inactive."

He held the scanner to my left eye, pressed a button, and a green light flashed, scanned and beeped. "Operative 214610, Pamela Phantom, you've been activated." He handed me the envelope before returning to the Audi.

A phone inside began to ring.

"This life is behind me," I said into the receiver.

"Nephews and Sons have been activated, with a new can of worms that have gone rogue. Each of them is a nightmare in their own right," an older female's voice murmured. "I believe you've already met Calynn Catalyst. The Dark Circle's newest recruit."

"Glenda, what happened to erasing my file? I'm not that person anymore."

"Things have gotten complicated. After a failed attempt to contact you in person, I had to send a messenger. And with that comes activation."

"Contact me in person, how?"

"Rosebud Lane, the old lady with the walker."

"Most people meet over coffee."

"I couldn't risk coffee. This can of worms has a new team of watchers. Each with a specific skill set."

"I need you to deactivate and erase Pamela Phantom from your records!"

"I'll be in touch."

(The end of volume 1)

A letter to my readers

I hope you've enjoyed reading "The Call Center" as much as I've enjoyed writing it. If so, I would appreciate you leaving a review or telling your friends and families. Leaving reviews and word of mouth helps independent authors like me get discovered by new readers. I always welcome comments about my books. Please feel free to give feedback at (WriterEWade@gmail.com). You can also request to be on my advance reader copy or street team.

P.S. Follow me on Twitter, Facebook, Instagram or Linkedin.

See you soon...

E Wade

ACKNOWLEDGMENTS

Betsy Bolden, "Auntie Happy" *(Matriarch)* *You're a force of God's nature.*

In memory of:
Rosa Tillman (Big Momma), Annie Thompson (Grandma Dear), Mary Simmons (Auntie Tudy), James Bolden (Uncle Lightning), Carl Westerbeke (Pop Pop)
Annie Ray (Auntie Mae Mae), Mary King (Auntie Noona), Robert Thompson I (Reb), Hazel Edwards, Eddie Bolden (Eddie Jr.) and Big Justin Elmasian. *You are missed with every passing day.*

In honor of:
Rosalie Pitts, *(I thank you for your unyielding love, guidance and the Lord's word)*, Verla Westerbeke, Roy Ray, Genell Thompson, Gary and Kay McNutt, Joseph and Gail Morrell, Paul Morrell, Betty Brown, Major King, John and Blanch Bolden, Gloria Simmons, Regina Bolden, Betty Anderson, Diana Morrell Greene, Terry and Mary Beth Westerbeke, Sally Westerbeke, and Edwin and Deborah Wright. *There are no words to describe what you've done for my soul, spirit and life. Thank you for all the love and advice.*

A special thanks to:
Kellie Wade, Earl and Meisha Wade, Glenda Allen, Lee and Gwen Allen, Traycee Jackson, Maurice and Jani French, Robert and Carla Thompson

III, Terry Porter, Kim Morrell, Marty Brown, Edward and Andrea Bradley, Desmond and Paula Morrell, Joey Morrell, Garrett Bolden, Tremain Tillman, Kimberly McNutt, Millard Livatt, Alex and Tamara Ray, James Carter III, Stacy Boden, Michelle Back, Bernard Bryant, Marcus Bolden, Brian Bolden and Ellen McElwain. *Love you guys!*

Kailey Wade, Kamille Wade, Dominique (DP) Peterson, Ruben Jackson, Sierra McNaughton, EJ Wade, Sophia Elmasian, Kennedy Wade, Justin Elmasian, Justin Thompson, Jordan Thompson, Aaron Wade, and Jaren Thompson. *Keep an eye on the hour glass and you'll do just fine.*

About the Author

 E Wade is an American author. Born in Winter Park, Florida, he's worked as a public speaker and in the field of telecommunications. When he isn't writing he enjoys traveling and hosting shindigs with family and friends.

His hobbies include reading, chess, poker, a good game of spades and playing paintball with his three sons.

He also moonlights as a part-time dog wrangler when his kids leave the front door open.

For more information on E Wade; upcoming books and events. Follow him at:

Facebook:
https://www.facebook.com/E-WADE-Author-Page/
Twitter:
https://twitter.com/egwade01
Instagram:
https://www.instagram.com/egwade1
Linkedin:

https:// www.linkedin.com/ in/ e-wade-

Teaser site:

http://www.genre6.com/